Also by Patricia Traxler

Poetry:

Blood Calendar
The Glass Woman
Forbidden Words
Naming the Fires

Fiction:

Blood, a novel

In the Skin

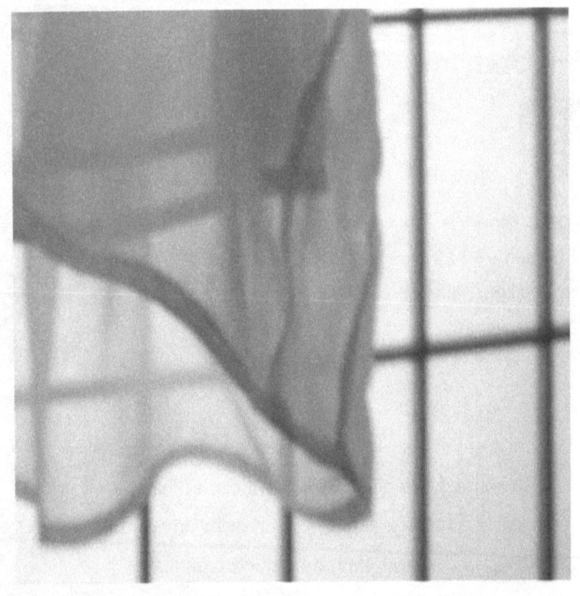

stories by

Patricia Traxler

Spartan Press
Kansas City, Missouri
spartanpresskc.com

Spartan
Press

Copyright ©Patricia Traxler, 2020
First Edition 1 3 5 7 9 10 8 6 4 2
ISBN: 978-1-950380-98-5
LCCN: 2020938084

Cover art: Lily Pine
Author photos: Fergus McCarthy, Stephen Hebert, Newsweek

Acknowledgments:

"Adultery" originally appeared in The Boston Review

"A First-Name Basis" was the winner of both
the Cecil Hackney National Literary Award for Short Fiction
and the Georgia State University Award for Short Fiction;
it was originally published in The Georgia State University Review

"Earthly Luck" was originally published in Glimmer Train

"The Mushrooms of Maisie Zupnik" won the Writers Voice
of New York City Open Voice Award for Short Fiction;
it was originally published in Hanging Loose Quarterly

"The Egg" was a winner of The Moth 2019
International Short Story Prize (Ireland)
and originally appeared in The Moth Magazine

"Obbligato" originally appeared
in Vignette, Los Angeles

"Sincerely" originally appeared in Other Voices,
(University of Illinois Press)

Many thanks to all of the friends and family who read these stories
in various incarnations and offered critical advice and steady
encouragement. I'll always be especially grateful to my late mother,
Eileen, who read all of my stories, and even when some aspects
of them shocked or appalled her, she somehow managed to love
them--and me--all the same. And finally, I feel enduring gratitude
to the late novelist William Cotter Murray of the University of
Iowa for his faith in my stories and for his endearingly stubborn
insistence that I needed to get them out into the light. Here they
are, Bill--I'm sad you aren't here to see that I did finally let them go.

Table of Contents:

Dedicated to all who can still hope for love after the first disappointment, who treasure its intimate knowledge and accept its absurdity, its truth and its lies, its hope and its despair, its impotence and its fearsome power to transform-- and who understand that no matter who we are or whomever we may desire, love is love.

Listen baby
I'd even sigh for you, I'm 'bout ready to cry for you
I'd tear the stars down from the skies for you
If that isn't love, it'll have to do, baby, yes
Until the real thing comes along

-Fats Waller, "Ain't Misbehavin'"

A First-Name Basis

I guess I should have known better than to get involved with a man who had no first name, but I was living in Harvard Square at the time and had lost sight of reality. Also, I was lonely, and even a poet who went by the initial "C" and refused to divulge his given name was an improvement over my previous relationship, which was with the palm of a blind panhandler at the corner of Brattle and Church who could be counted on to say, God BLESS you, Ma'am each time I crossed that palm with paper money.

I'd never been so lonely as I was during those first months after I arrived in Cambridge from Wichita, rambling around the square alone, pushing past handbill hawkers, evangelists, street musicians, portrait artists, magicians, tightrope walkers, tourists, skinheads, bag ladies on doorsteps, street kids in on the T from Dorchester and Revere to stir things up in the square, and Harvard students with asymmetrical hair and endless wardrobes of black, queuing up for cash by the automatic tellers at BayBank on Mass Ave.

I had a one-year appointment as a literature fellow at Radcliffe's Bunting Institute, a post-doctoral research and study center, though I didn't have a doctorate, nor had I ever even completed my master's. The Bunting made exceptions for writers and artists if their publications or exhibits compensated for the lack of advanced degrees. The project they'd funded was my second novel, which was about half finished when I arrived in Cambridge, though it didn't have a title yet. I received a paycheck from Harvard each month just for staying in my dingy little Harvard Housing apartment in the square and writing my heart out in a flannel nightgown and athletic socks. They'd given me an office at the institute, but I was under no obligation to go there, and since it was nearly a mile's walk from my apartment, I found it easier just to slide out of bed and over to the laptop I'd installed in a corner of my bedroom.

During the two-day orientation for our Bunting class, I felt a bit shy of exchanging histories with my colleagues. It wasn't that I doubted my own qualifications--I'd won the fellowship, hadn't I?--but my c.v. looked distinctly modest beside many of the other fellows' lists of accomplishments. There was a former governor; a National Book Critics' Circle Award Winner in Poetry; a delegate to the U.N.; an actress-cum-playwright whose one-woman Broadway theater piece was up for a Tony; and an agronomist from India who was rumored to be in line for a Nobel Prize.

I had no impressive answers for the getting-acquainted questions that seemed to be routine: Where did I teach? Actually, I wasn't permanently attached to any university. Yes, one published novel—but it had been remaindered a year ago. Who was my mentor? (Really? Who was my mentor?) Mine was my late Italian grandmother, who had schooled me in the art of storytelling while teaching me to knit, crochet, and make gnocchi. Where had I studied? Wichita State. I'd had some great professors there, by the way.

Frankly, I wasn't entirely sure what I was doing in the Harvard community, and more and more I found myself hunkering in. It was very easy not to have a social life under the circumstances, and I've never been gregarious anyway.

I did walk over to the Institute each Wednesday for the weekly colloquium presentation by one of this year's fellows--I'd scheduled my own colloquium for late spring, when I figured it would be too late for them to take back my fellowship--but I wasn't on a first-name basis with anyone, since I hadn't as yet let any conversation get beyond *Fine, and you?* And it was more, really, than professional and academic diffidence that kept me apart from my colleagues--it was also jealousy of my time. I'd been working as a freelance manuscript editor and typist for years, but now I was actually being paid to work on nothing but my own book for a year. I knew that when this year was over, I'd be back to typing other people's work again. I had to finish the novel this year. Had to.

I was on cordial passing-in-the-hall terms with Stacy, my next door neighbor who was in her second year at Harvard Law, and I'd actually had tea a few times with Soledad, my neighbor on the other side, who was from Peru and had a fellowship at the School of Medicine. But I was older than either of these women, who were both in their twenties and energized by the optimism of unspent experience. I was in my mid-thirties, divorced, filled with free-floating pervasive anxiety, worried that there might be an afterlife, and in serious need of a sex life though too unworldly, cautious, and formerly married to have the slightest idea of how to get one.

Not to mention too formerly Catholic. The nuns of my childhood at Mary Mother of God School in Wichita, Kansas had taught us many things, nearly all of them having to do with sin. Not that I was still a practicing Catholic (I still felt a sort of familial connection to the Church, but I'd long since figured out that no amount of practice would help me to get it right), yet even when you cease to recognize a particular system of theology as the guiding ethos in your life, often its darker and more ominous admonitions stay with you after the fact. And the Church of my youth was rife with dark and ominous admonitions. The truth is, Catholicism sort of sticks to your soul the way gum sticks to the sole of your shoe, and no matter how far afield you go, you can feel it impeding your stride, reminding you with each sticking step that you are more than likely headed for hell.

Even after I fell away from the Church somewhere in my twenties, I'd continued to pray...out of habit or fear of hell, or maybe out of simple courtesy. And the thing about prayer is, it really helps you to sleep. Nothing in the world can shut down the human mind the way a rosary can, bead after bead between finger and thumb in the dark, the repetitions of Our-Father-Hail Mary-Glory-Be until you've drifted off on sleep's black sea in the fragile bark of rote devotion. When I stopped praying--which happened soon after my arrival in Cambridge from Wichita, I became insomniac. I'd found I couldn't pray in Cambridge because, well, because...

...I felt no answering presence in the void?

...I'd forgotten the words?

...God seemed more like a man every day?

I don't know. All I know is that I couldn't sleep to save my life. And then each day I found myself too fatigued to write. I had one year to finish this novel, and sleep deprivation was about to do me in. I was so depleted of creative energy that I couldn't even come up with a title for my novel, and that was a problem: the book wouldn't seem quite real to me until it had a name.

Finally, I bought some Sominex at Sage's in the square, but then Soledad told me that I shouldn't take sleeping pills indefinitely or they'd interfere with various internal organs, such as my liver and kidneys, so I flushed the pills down the toilet. I am not now, nor have I ever been, on intimate terms with my internal organs. To call them innards would be pretentious, an effort to ingratiate myself with the netherworld of my own body by nicknaming it. And when Soledad said indefinitely, I had to admit that was probably as precise as I could be in reference to my projected need for sleeping pills, so if I didn't like having to think about my insides, I figured I'd better keep them happy. Soledad brought over a little baggie of loose tea--some sort of herbal decoction guaranteed to help me sleep. Sleep wasn't actually what it brought me, though. What it did was give me a case of the trots you wouldn't believe.

It was as I sat on the wobbly toilet seat in my crumbly little bathroom one morning at 4:00 AM, thinking of my internal organs and feeling morose and quite literally drained, that I decided I needed a lover. I hadn't slept--or written--all week. Anything was better than this. And after all, I'd slept fine when I was married, hadn't I? I'd been divorced for eighteen months now, and hadn't really dated much in that time. Not at all, to be exact. I decided to find a man. One way or another.

The next day I picked up a copy of the Boston Phoenix and turned to the personals. I couldn't believe I was doing this. But the idea seemed worth considering, at first. Then when I finally found an ad in which a man was hoping to meet a woman, I got as far as, "Man looking for lactating female..." and decided that there must be a better way. I began going to more and more movies by myself, mostly foreign films, imagining that I might meet some man who was as nuts about cinema as I was. As I fantasized it, after a few weeks of running into each other again and again in the ticket line or buying treats in the lobby, we'd laugh and say, We've got to stop meeting like this! But sitting alone in a blackened auditorium--which is roughly 99% of one's time at the movies--didn't turn out to be a great way to meet a guy.

The closest I came, in fact, was one Saturday in the balcony at the Harvard Square Cinema on Church Street, on my third visit to see "Goya's Ghosts" (it was Javier Bardem's face that kept bringing me back), when a large guy in an Eat Me sweatshirt staggered in during the middle of the movie, mumbling loudly to himself, and fell up the balcony stairs, raised himself halfway up, and then, with what seemed a pleasant enough expression on his face from what I could make out, fell onto me and my large cup of Cherry Garcia ice cream. It wasn't really any big deal--I moved out from under him somehow and watched the rest of the movie from three seats away while he snored in my former seat--well, his face was in my former seat and the rest of him was on the floor with my Cherry Garcia. The movies weren't working out as a way of meeting first-string guys.

Which brings us back to the man with no first name.

That evening as I walked home, I found I couldn't stand the idea of going back into the building, riding the elevator to the fifth floor, opening the door to my empty apartment, and preparing for still another bout of insomnia. Then I remembered that the Brattle Cinema was having a Preston Sturges film festival, and on a whim I went straight there from Javier. As I stood in a long line on Brattle Street waiting for my ticket to the 7:00 PM movie, I noticed a very tall, bearded guy walking in my direction, and I saw several people in the line greeting him as he passed them. I realized then that I'd seen him around the square before--once or twice at the corner newsstand, and a number of times, now that I thought of it, just wandering around the square, like me. His hair was a little thin on top--pretty much gone, actually--and the rest was sort of longish, very pale blond, and pulled back into a tiny ponytail. He was nice looking, had great bones, and the way I saw it, he couldn't be an axe murderer if he knew so many people--axe murderers are loners from the word go. So, I watched as this man came closer to my part of the line and that was when I made my decision--I would smile at him.

Go ahead and laugh, if you're thinking Big deal, so she's going to smile at the guy. But I was raised by a mother who warned me so often not to look at, talk to, or smile at strangers that in my memory her words came through like a liturgical chant, and if it's hard to depart from the Church's teachings, a mother's dogma is even harder to shake because unlike the Church, a mother can be on the phone night and day, jogging your conscience with aphorisms and news of the bad ends to which women come when they play fast and loose with romance. This was, for me, a big decision. I waited till the man was a couple of feet away from me, and then I directed a significant smile at him. He nodded down at me--way down--

this guy must've been nearly seven feet tall—and then he said hello. He had a great voice--baritone, naturally. Imagining his testosterone levels made my head swim.

"Oh, hello," I answered demurely, as if this whole exchange were his idea.

And then he just kept walking.

My first-ever attempt to pick up a man, and he just kept walking. I sneaked a look around at his retreating form and saw how he dwarfed everyone he passed. Maybe it was just as well he'd kept going--I could imagine the size of his penis--the words cudgel and baton came to mind. I'm not a very large person, and I remembered reading somewhere that back in the early days of film, Fatty Arbuckle had actually killed a woman by having sex with her, because he was so big. Or was it that he used a wine bottle? At the moment I couldn't remember, but I was breathing a sigh of relief.

Not that I'd have slept with the guy—anyway, not right off the bat (so to speak), but if I was ever going to have sex again I had to learn how to take the first step, which was obviously getting acquainted. I could hear my mother admonishing me in her most ominous tone, *That is not the way to get acquainted. Not for nice young women.*

But I wasn't feeling all that young these days--or all that that nice. I was feeling sleep-deprived, lonely, displaced, horny, thirty-five, and agnostic at the very least.

I sat through two movies that night without really absorbing either one, even though I'm a real Sturges fan--I can't even remember now which of his movies they were. I was seated behind a couple who kept whispering into each other's ears and giggling, and I started wondering what it felt like to have someone you would want to whisper to right in the middle of a movie. As it was, I found this couple annoying and cloying. I'd have given anything to be them.

When I got home that night it was midnight, and instead of showering and changing into my nightgown, I just sat right down at the computer in my street clothes. Why pretend I was going to sleep? I forced myself through a chapter revision until six in the morning, when a car alarm and a trash truck's back-up beep signaled the approach of a new day in Cambridge and I pulled down the shades to block the incipient light and fell onto my bed. I woke up a couple of hours later and ran off the reworked chapter, then watched a rerun of an old interview with Oprah while I ate macaroni and cheese I'd prepared from a box mix.

It was a couple of thrill-packed weeks later when I ran into the tall guy again. I'd given in and decided to buy some more Sominex--the jingle from their old commercials had been ringing through my head all week...*Take Sominex tonight and sleep...safe and restful sleep...sleep...sleeeep....* So I was at Sage's trying to grab the Sominex and put it into my basket in a way that concealed the name of the product. Not that I was likely to run into anyone I knew--I only knew two people in Cambridge--Stacy and Soledad--but I've always been alarmed at the thought that strangers might think ill of me. You can imagine how I worry about the people I actually know.

After I had my Sominex safely in the basket, I decided to strike a blow for healthy living--sort of a counterbalance to the sleeping medicine--by buying some fresh fish and veggies for tonight's dinner. No more boxed mac and cheese for me if I was going to be using a sleeping aid. A person had to have some standards.

As I stood at the fish counter trying to decide between a sort of shiny tan fish and a whitish one, I heard a voice say, "Don't get your fish here--it's much better at the little seafood place over on Huron."

I knew who it was before I looked up and saw his face.

"I beg your pardon?" I said, sounding even to myself like an uptight schoolmarm.

"The fish is much better at Flynn's, over on Huron," he said, and then just sort of smiled down at me. God, he was tall. "It's odd," he added, "the way I seem to run into you all the time."

"Yeah," I said wittily.

"I'm C Benton," he said, though I hadn't asked.

"Steve Benton?"

"No--C. Just the letter C. What's your name?"

"Elizabeth. But my friends call me Bee. Not the letter, more the...well, the insect."

He laughed. "I just wanted to direct you to Flynn's. Hope I didn't startle you."

"No, not at all. I appreciate the help--I don't really know that much about fresh seafood, because where I'm from, there's no, well, no sea. How far is Huron from here?"

"Actually it's a fair walk, but not bad if you like walking... Would you like to get a cup of coffee at a little place I know on Huron? It's right by the seafood place."

I hesitated. Was it okay to go for a coffee date that had originated in a chance meeting with a stranger--almost a pick-up? Was this a pick-up? My mother's mouth hissed the word Yessss! in my mind, but I shut it out and repeated her word aloud to him, without the hiss.

"But could we go someplace closer?" I asked, thinking that if we didn't walk so far, it wasn't so big a deal to be doing what I was doing.

"Sure--how about the Cafe Paradiso--it's just a couple of blocks from here."

Suddenly I remembered the Sominex in the basket I was carrying on my arm. I wondered if he'd noticed it. It didn't seem like something that would make a great first impression. No way I was walking through check-out with this. I set the basket down on a pile of potatoes in produce and walked out of the store with him. He never noticed.

And the next thing I knew, we were strolling toward Cafe Paradiso together, swapping details of our lives. He lived in a three-story Victorian in Watertown, he said. Rented out the bottom floor to another writer. Yes, he was himself a writer. A poet. Well, no, I couldn't actually buy his book just now, because it wasn't on the shelves. Knowing the world of remainders only too well from my own experience with one well-reviewed but wildly uncommercial novel, I didn't see anything to sneer at in this information. C said he'd just returned from Buenos Aires three months ago after a two-year stay during which he'd taught English to the Argentinians ("Not all of the Argentinians," he amended modestly, cocking an eyebrow and grinning), and was now busy undoing all the damage a pair of student tenants had done to his own quarters while he was gone.

"I should never have rented it out," he told me. "But they had references and I felt I needed the money." As we walked, he took a little pearl-inlaid wooden box from his pocket and extracted a long thin brown cigarette which he lit, careful to keep his smoke from blowing in my direction. "And now the repairs to the house may cost more than I actually made in rent while I was away." He tossed the cigarette onto the sidewalk, stopped, and ground it with his toe until it had nearly disappeared.

There's one thing I haven't mentioned, because I know you'll form an instant judgment of C--and of me by association--if I do. I don't know exactly how to say it. It's like this. He was wearing a beret. There, I feel better now that I've just come out with it.

Wearing a beret and smoking little brown cigarettes out of a pearl-inlaid case.

But he was very nice, really. He was. He asked me about myself, too. Lots of men don't. When I told him about my writing fellowship at Harvard, he said, "Well. That's impressive." And he said it in a way that made me check his face quickly to see what he meant. Apparently he meant that it was impressive. He asked if I was a poet or a fiction writer, and it seemed to me that he was happy to find that I wasn't a poet. I wondered if he was the competitive type--or maybe insecure about his own work. Then he asked where I was from that "didn't have a sea." When I told him Wichita, he seemed to like the idea that I was from Kansas. I've noticed that people on the eastern seaboard tend to find the prairie a romantic image, as long as they don't have to live on it.

"You have a little bit of a Kansas drawl," he said. I hated hearing that and I don't believe it. "But you don't have the look of a typical Kansas farm girl at all," he added. "You look more east coast, actually."

I knew he meant my coloring. Lots of Kansans are of Scandinavian, Czech, or German descent, and there are blondes everywhere you look, but my maternal grandmother is from Italy--Rapallo--and I look pretty much like her--black hair, fair skin, very dark eyes. I explained this to him, but I didn't bother explaining that not everyone in Kansas lives on a farm.

"Rapallo," he said, "that's where Pound lived."

"I know," I said, "but my grandmother was gone by then." Why did I say that?

"I love Italy," he said. "Especially Firenze."

Of course I knew that Firenze was Florence, but just the

same, it seemed a little pretentious for him to call it that. I'd
never been to Italy and I told him so.

"Oh, you'd love it," he said.

I noticed that he had beautiful hands, which he waved
around a lot when he talked. Beautiful manly-looking hands.
And a long, lean body. I could see the contour of his calves
pushing at the legs of his jeans as he walked just ahead of me to
open the door of the Cafe Paradiso.

"I'll have to take you there one day," he added, and flashed
me a grin.

What a line, I thought. But then I decided to give him a
break. Most men wait years before even joking about anything
that smacks of commitment, and this was a first date. I looked at
his backside as he walked us to a table at the rear of the Paradiso.
As we walked, the waitress and some people at a couple of tables
greeted him by name--if you could call C a name. There was
something arresting about him--an aura he had that made him
seem special, made his presence seem a sort of occasion, an
appearance.

I ordered a cup of Earl Grey tea and a pastry.

"You have wonderful eyes," he told me in front of the
waitress and then, looking a little abashed at having blurted
such a thing in public, he ordered an espresso with a "dollop" of
cream.

Dollop. I found his pretensions kind of goofy and
endearing. It seemed as if, underneath, he was actually a little
unsure of himself, and though I'm not usually attracted to men
who are unsure of themselves, I was definitely attracted to C.
He had a quick wit, a great smile, lovely eyes, an aquiline nose,
and lips that gave me ideas. And I had the sense that whatever
insecurities he might have, they didn't involve his manhood.
This was a guy who definitely knew his way around a bed, I was
sure of that. And it was time I allowed myself to take the tour. I'd
been celibate for nearly two years.

I watched C as he sipped his espresso. I guess I'd have
preferred that he was a dentist or a plumber--someone with
what my mother would call "a normal life"--but I should have
known he was a writer. Everyone you see in Cambridge is a
writer in some sense of the word. One day in this very cafe,
I'd seen one of the panhandlers to whom I'd been giving $5 or

$6 a week (not the current God-BLESS-you-Ma'am guy--this was a skinny white guy with a wispy mustache), only now, he wasn't lugging big green trash bags that ostensibly held all of his earthly possessions--he was writing intently in a blue spiral notebook and occasionally snapping his fingers to get the waiter's attention for a coffee warm-up. A few days later I saw him putting his trash bags into the trunk of a late model Nissan on Church Street and driving away--no doubt to his home in the 'burbs. I was certain the trash bags were stuffed with fiberfill from Walmart.

I told C about my divorce, careful not to sound embittered, though honestly, I guessed I was, a little. I couldn't bring myself to say that Mark had seen my acceptance of a year-long fellowship 2,000 miles away as a sort of betrayal of our life together because he couldn't leave his new teaching post in Wichita, so I would be going to Cambridge without him. My mother had taken Mark's side, saying, "What in the world has gotten into you, my own daughter, that you would put Harvard before your husband?"

I'd tried to explain to her—and to Mark—that this wasn't about Harvard so much as about my writing: It would be a year during which I would actually be paid to write my next novel! The day I accepted the fellowship, Mark told me he was through. I couldn't really blame him for his frustration, though I felt he was wrong not to understand what he was asking of me.

I guess the truth was that we'd both felt abandoned. He just seemed to find it less painful to end the marriage than I did. It would have been more comfortable not to think of him anymore, but I still did. Sometimes I dreamed that I was out somewhere with him, some crowded place--a movie, maybe, or a grocery store, a street bazaar somewhere--and in my dream, I would turn around to say something to him and find him gone. The chill of abandonment was still real in me, could still make me cry if I let it. I chose not to let it.

"We just grew apart," I told C.

C told me he'd been "deeply in love" with a woman he'd met in Buenos Aires.

"But it was all too impossible," he said, and seemed not to want to go into detail.

I didn't press him, but I thought it had probably been that she couldn't bear to leave Buenos Aires when he did, couldn't bring herself to go off and live in a strange country.

When we finished, C asked if he could call me, and I gave him my phone number. What was the harm in having someone to talk to on the phone?

After I got home, I realized I hadn't bought anything for dinner, having aborted my veggie-and-fish buying at Sage's. Not to mention my Sominex purchase. That night I made another round of mac and cheese and turned on the evening news while I ate it. So what if it wasn't the greatest dinner? My coffee date had been worth it.

At 9:00 PM I sat down at the computer to work--this hour was getting to be the start of each work session for me, and I wondered if I would have permanently set my internal clock to these nocturnal habits by the time I returned to Kansas where people get up at six a.m., eat dinner at six p.m., and go to bed just when my day was now beginning in earnest. As I worked, I found myself calmer than I'd been in a while. I got into my work more quickly than usual, actually revising one chapter and writing half of the next one by the time the phone rang at eleven thirty.

"Good night," I heard him say, and his voice curled into my ear.

How sweet he is, I thought. How romantic. Never mind that I wouldn't be turning in for at least another six hours.

"Good night," I answered, not wanting to spoil his illusions, or the moment.

It was about five in the morning when I turned off the computer and the phone and rolled into bed. I had seven chapters finished, though as yet I still hadn't found a title for the book. I slept very well then, for me--about five hours.

The first thought I had when I woke was that one of these days I'd have to ask what the "C" stood for.

Over the next two weeks I saw C three times--twice more for coffee and a ramble around the bookstores in Harvard Square, and then on the third date (if these were dates--I still wasn't sure) we met for lunch. He gave me a copy of his book of poems--more of a chapbook, really, just twenty-six pages. It seemed to have been self-published, but the poems weren't bad at all, if I can be any judge of poetry, not being a poet myself. Many of the poems made mention of his Argentinian lover,

Beata, including one long, erotic poem about a bath they took together. I was surprised to feel a twist of jealousy, which I knew wasn't at all rational. I wondered if he'd told her his first name. After all, he'd shared his body with her. Once you've let a person see you naked, why hide your first name? I convinced myself that this woman knew his first name, and I was surprised to feel more jealous over that possibility than over the mental picture of him in a bath with a beautiful Argentinian woman.

Finally, on our third coffee date at the Paradiso--fourth date in all--I asked him about the C. What it stood for.

"It stands for C," he said with a smile.

"You know what I mean--what's your given name?"

"I've given myself the name of C," he laughed. "Doesn't a man have a right to do that if he's so inclined?"

"Sure," I told him, "it just feels kind of odd not knowing your actual name."

"You do know my actual name," he said. "I've used C for the past ten years or so. I don't think anyone but my family has any idea what my first name is...was."

I could see that he was bent on not telling me, and I didn't want to pry, in case it was a terrible name. Besides, obviously if only his family knew it, he hadn't told her. Beata. I let the subject drop, though once in a while I teased him after that, calling him Clarence, Claude, Chester, Clark, Clement, whatever C-name popped into my head.

"Do you know," he teased me one night on the phone after I'd called him Crispin, "not one man I know has ever pressed the issue with me, but every woman I meet can't bear not knowing."

I resolved right then not to be like every woman.

Talking with him was getting to be the thing I looked forward to most in my day. He phoned me every night now to say good night.

"He must be married," my mother told me over the phone. "Why else would he only see you in the daytime? That's what married men do when they cheat. I've seen it on Oprah and Dr. Phil a jillion times."

"He's not married, Mother--he lives alone in Watertown, rents out the bottom floor of his house. We're writers, remember? And we both happen to write at night."

Which had actually turned out to be the case: when C had found out that I was staying up every night writing, he'd laughed and confessed that all the nights he'd phoned to say good night, he'd actually gone back to his computer, too, imagining me sleeping "like an angel."

"Have you ever seen his place?" my mother asked, and I couldn't tell if her suspicion was more directed at his marital status or my possible sexual activity.

"Of course not," I told her truthfully. "I've only known him for a couple of weeks." Three and a half, I amended mentally, but who's counting? Then, to torment her, I added, "He's awfully attractive. Once I go over there, I'm going to mean business."

And I knew that was true.

"Oof," she huffed.

One day when C and I were walking around the square, we ran into my neighbor Soledad, her arms full of books and her glasses propped on her head. I introduced her to C, feeling a little funny that I didn't have any first name to offer for him except C, which must have sounded to her like "yes." As we chatted on the sidewalk, it struck me that Soledad and I hadn't talked in a while, and I realized I'd been turning down most of her invitations lately because I was afraid I'd miss C's phone calls if I went to her apartment. I'd also stopped going to the institute on Wednesday afternoons for the weekly colloquium presentation, which had been the only time I ever went. I'd stopped going because on Wednesdays C had been asking me to coffee, which had been taking up the same time period a colloquium ran. I hated that I was doing such a stereotypical woman-thing. All through my marriage I'd sneered at various single women I knew who allowed a man to become so much of a focus that their women friends ceased to exist. I promised myself that I would stop shoving Soledad aside just because I had a man in my life again.

That evening I stayed for three hours at Soledad's, drinking wine from Sage's and talking about climate change, a Picasso biography she was reading, and a man she'd loved in Lima. It was the first time Soledad had said anything about her love life, and I guessed that seeing me with C had made her feel freer to bring up the subject. Still, I noticed that she didn't even hint at sexual matters, the way U.S. women might do over a bottle of wine. When she asked me about C, I found that I wanted to talk about him, wanted any excuse to say his name--I mean, his initial--and I guess I did go on about his charm and his intellect for a while.

"It sounds like you are falling in love," Soledad said with a wide, knowing smile that made me laugh out loud. I realized I'd been having a great time with my neighbor, and was only slightly antsy about the possibility of missing a phone call.

When I got back to my apartment, the phone machine was blinking and I found that C had indeed called, to say he was driving out "for a midnight ice cream cone" and wanted to know if I'd like him to bring me one. His first nighttime invitation, and I'd missed it. I was a little tipsy from the wine, and very disappointed. I was afraid Soledad was right. I wasn't sure if I was in love yet, but I knew without a doubt that love was possible with C. Did that make it okay to sleep with him, a man I'd met on the street? I knew my mother would say no, but that didn't count. My mother would also say that no two people should have "relations" unless they were married. Even being in love wasn't enough to make her dismiss that act outside of marriage, so I knew that having the potential to fall in love was definitely not a situation that would merit her green light. And besides, any man you'd met on the street was always, irrevocably, a stranger.

I ran a hot bath, put some generic baby oil in it, along with a free sample of Diva perfume, and settled into the tub to feel sorry for myself. All my life I've associated baths with comfort and security. I sank into the oily, decadent water and closed my eyes. I'd only been there for a little while when I heard the downstairs buzzer ringing in my hall. Of course I knew it had to be C. I threw on my robe, buzzed him up, and answered the door warm, oily, wet, and flushed beneath white terrycloth. And that was how it happened that the first time we made love it was in my apartment--not at his house, as I'd pictured.

And he was good. He brought new meaning to the word *good.* To say he was a sensual kisser is not nearly adequate--he was able to make kissing more exciting than most men are able to make sex. Not that I've been in bed with most men, but I've slept with a few and I've never been kissed the way C kissed me.

"If this part is good," he whispered after we'd been kissing awhile, "then I know the rest will feel right."

And then he slipped my robe off my shoulders and let it fall to the hallway floor. I should have mentioned that at this point we still hadn't made it out of my apartment's entry hall.

There was a really bright ceiling light shining on us both, and beneath C's gaze I found myself experiencing keenly the shyness I always feel the first time a man sees me naked--I guess you could say that's what has kept me relatively "moral" (my mother's word), though I have to admit, it's always been more a matter of privacy than morals. It just feels like such a big deal to take your clothes off in front of someone the first time and stand there without benefit of style to give you context, camouflage, and courage. I don't like to give up that much privacy without a very good reason.

I have to say, I'm pretty sure I've never met even one man who was the least bit shy about removing his own clothes.

I led him to my bedroom, and C kept his eyes on me the whole time he undressed--I don't think he blinked once. As he walked toward me then, fully erect, I couldn't pull my eyes away from it--his dick. It was not just your run-of-the-mill, garden variety one. It was--how can I say it?--pretty. Really pretty. Gorgeous. I guess there wasn't anything unusual about the size or the shape of it... maybe it was simply the way C carried himself with an easy, long legged grace as he brought it to me like a candle through the midnight air of my bedroom. I couldn't take my eyes away. I guess I may have seemed like one of those women who haven't had sex in nineteen months.

C was a quiet, self-assured lover, and I have to say--my feminism aside--that I like a man who has that command. Especially in bed. A man who feels he needs to narrate us through sex is just getting in the way of himself. (I think it was Bessie Smith who once said to a talkative lover, *I don't need the words, honey, 'cause I can only dance to the music.*) My shyness evaporated pretty quickly in the heat and pleasure of our mingling on my bed.

All I have to say beyond that is, I slept that night. I slept from the time he left at 1:00 AM until about eleven the next morning. Say it was the wine if you want, say it was the bath, but I know better.

Yes, I did ask him once, when our two heads were on the same pillow, what the C stood for, but he changed the subject most engagingly with his fingertips, and anyway I didn't much care by then. Yes, it did occur to me the next morning when I woke that I'd had sex with a man whose first name I didn't know. But by that time I was so twitterpated that the idea had an erotic ring to it. Everything had an erotic ring to it.

I was almost embarrassed to see Soledad in the hall that day, because I was sure that it showed on my face. I couldn't stop beaming. I actually walked the mile to the institute and aired out my office. Then I went down to the common room and got to know a few of the women I should have been getting to know for the past three months. I happened to get there at the tail-end of a brownbag luncheon, and so quite a few of them were there. I especially hit it off with Mary Cane, a lawyer from Australia specializing in women's causes. She was very earthy and had a great, contagious laugh. And there was a poet there from Arizona who was friendly, said she'd read my novel and was very interested in the one in progress. She asked me the title of the new book, and I had to tell her that it didn't yet have a title. I felt the sudden urgent need to name it. I also felt guilty that I wasn't familiar with her work; hadn't made any effort to get to know about my colleagues before the fact, as she obviously had.

There were about forty-five fellows there from all over the world and representing many disciplines--law, science, medicine, political science, painting, sculpture, filmmaking, dance...I felt ashamed to have wasted so many weeks of this Bunting year burrowing into my own head. Of course, I reminded myself, I was here to write my novel. But I mustn't forget that I was *here.* I resolved to make it over to the common room at least once a week, no matter what.

It was on Thursday afternoon a couple of days later that I discovered the truth about C. He'd called to ask if I'd like to drive to Provincetown with him for the weekend, and I'd said yes without hesitating long enough to even hint at a mystique. We were discussing times and what to pack when I heard a sound in the background. First I thought it was an animal. Then I realized it must be a child.

"Is--is that a child?" I asked him.

"Yes. Yes, it is," he said rather brusquely.

"Does someone live with you there?" I asked in surprise. He'd never mentioned having a housemate.

"Yes," he said, and his terseness made the hairs on my neck prickle.

"Is the child...is the child yours?"

"Yes."

"Do you—" (I could hardly say the words, and he wasn't helping me out here) "--do you live with someone?" (I'd already asked that, but this time we both knew I meant something else.)

"Yes," he said. "Yes, I do."

"Is it...a woman?" I asked, just to be sure we were both talking about the same thing. This was starting to sound like Twenty Questions.

"Yes. It is."

"Are you...C, are you married?" I didn't know where the roaring in my ears came from right then, but it was there and it stayed there until his voice finally cut through.

"Yes, I am," he said, "I am." I heard a mobilization of sorts going on inside him, evident in his voice. "And I will never hurt my wife," he said with a kind of--well, I can hardly be objective, but it sounded to me like ostentation. "I will never do anything to hurt her," he repeated in a staunch and starchy voice that sounded for all the world as if he had his shoulders back and his chest thrust out to receive some sort of medal.

My immediate response may have been selfish, but *What about me?* is what I was thinking--*If you have a wife and you're never going to 'hurt' her, what were you planning to do with me?*

Instead I said, "Well, Provincetown's out of the question. I can't go away with you now."

"Bee, wait--we need to talk about all this—"

"What difference would that make? You'd still be married." And then I hung up.

I walked around my apartment, my computer on but idle, its bright gray eye following as I paced the outline of the Kilim rug on my bedroom floor. The same Kilim rug he'd walked over, bringing that beautiful candle to me through the darkened air of my room. I kept lacing my fingers together and pressing them against my mouth--it felt like self-control. I sat down at the desk, then stood up again. Once I typed a title page, *The Chameleon as the Letter C,* then erased it, since it had nothing to do with my book.

He called me at around midnight.

"I miss you already," he said, "It's horrible. I can't stand it."

"Don't," I said, "Please don't do this."

"I'm not 'doing this'," he said, "I'm trying to talk to you."

"I don't even know you," I told him. "I have no idea who you are."

"This hasn't been some sort of game for me," he said. "I have real feelings for you."

"How do you talk on the phone like this without her hearing?" I asked, and I heard the remoteness in my own voice.

"I, we have separate phone numbers--she's in real estate and she's on the phone all the time, so...." He seemed a little stunned by the coldness of my question. I felt stunned by the sound of his "we," in spite of myself. I'd never before heard him use the first person plural about anyone but us. I guess I forgot to answer him.

"You're treating me like I'm some sort of a criminal or a creep," he said.

I didn't answer.

"Thanks a lot," he said.

"You never even hinted that you might be married," I told him.

"Right from the start, you and I had so much to talk about," he said. "Then, too much time had passed and I didn't know how to tell you, I couldn't think how to bring it up. Would it have made a difference?" he asked, in what sounded like honest curiosity.

"Obviously it would have made a difference. It is making a difference. I might've still been attracted to you, but I hope I wouldn't have allowed myself to entertain the idea of you at all. At the very least, I'd have been forewarned. Then I could have made my own decision. Instead you made it for both of us. And what about your Argentinian lover?" I threw the words at him, realizing that my question was a bit of a non sequitur.

"That was two years ago," he said. "When, when Lauren found out, I promised her it would never happen again, and I've kept that promise. I didn't know I would meet you. But I will never hurt my wife again. Never."

It made me mad when he said this, because it completely disregarded my humanity, my feelings, but I couldn't find a way of saying so without seeming to be saying that this was all about me--and that would disregard her.

"You know what I think?" he said then, and I heard an edge of anger in his voice for the first time, "I think you're just angry at yourself because you didn't care enough to ask me if I was married."

I couldn't believe my ears.

"What?" I said hotly, "The whole narrative of your life was told in the first person singular! 'I live in a three-story Victorian,' 'I just got back from Buenos Aires,' 'I rent the bottom floor out.' Come on, C, I told you I'd been through a divorce, and in turn you told me about falling in love with Beata. I thought we were exchanging life stories. I had no reason to think you were married!"

"You could've asked. I think it says a lot that you didn't."

"When someone offers you a gift, you don't ask if it's stolen! You just assume that you can believe it's not." Before he could respond to that, I added, "I don't even know your name."

The next Wednesday I made a point of going over to the institute for the colloquium. This week it was by a geologist from London, and she talked about tectonic plates, accreted terrain. I thought of how people are like that--when they come together they seem to be one, even though they're not, really. All they've actually done in growing together is to create the illusion of oneness, and inevitably they change each other in the process. I thought of Mark, how I'd felt when he left me because of the yearlong fellowship I had accepted--how impossible it had seemed to me that anyone, even one of us, had the power to end our marriage forever when we'd seemed so irrevocably committed to each other.

And I thought of C, of all his phone calls that I hadn't answered this past week, and of the note I'd received in the mail that very day, and which was still in my jacket pocket. "My name is Charles," it said. "I just wanted you to know." And for just that moment I'd been able to love him again.

What we remember of people and events in our past is what we choose to remember. I'd like to choose to remember that scrap of paper with his name on it. But I'm afraid of remembering only that. It seems important to remember everything, how it was, to stay safe.

I went to a lot of movies during my Radcliffe year, sometimes alone, but once in a while with the geology fellow, Angela, or with Mary from Sydney. Mostly I spent time with Soledad, talking about books and world events. I tried to stay away from the subject of men. She asked me once about C, and I told her he'd gone to Argentina. It wasn't a lie exactly, since he had once gone to Argentina. Catholicism inadvertently trains the faithful to be expert in the loopholes of sin, makes us lawyers of the eternal. We can thank the Jesuits for that, I guess. Soledad looked at me strangely, as if she didn't believe C was in Argentina, but she never brought up his name again.

I gave my novel a working title, *Naming the Invisible,* but my editor hated that and retitled the book *Evidently.* It would go on to get good reviews, though it would be remaindered after twelve months. My modest advance would take me through another six months at home in Wichita before I had to go back to typing manuscripts--time for which I was grateful.

I never did get to the point where I was sleeping regularly during my year in Cambridge, nor could I pray in the old way I'd been taught. But as I worked at the computer each night, I did find myself talking out loud a lot, saying things into the air like, "Will you--will you look at that!"

And, "Help!"

And, "No way. Get outta here."

I took that to be a kind of prayer.

In the Skin

I watched them again last night. They were making love standing up, him behind her. She was bent over a table or desk. They'd been out somewhere together and he was still in his suit, a dark suit. I've always loved the way a man looks in a dark suit with a white shirt and tie. She was dolled up, too--her dress a deep teal, of some shiny fabric like taffeta or satin. He pushed it up around her ass, leaving her buttocks bare, then unzipped himself and entered her.

I kept my lamp off so they wouldn't look out and see me watching. Not that I felt guilty about what I was doing. After all, they were having sex in front of an open window that faced the back of an entire apartment building. And anyway, I've often enough been the one being watched by strangers while I made love with a man. Maybe it's my turn now to do the watching. It's true that I was only acting, playing a role when people watched me, while for the couple across the way it's real. I wouldn't have wanted them to know I was looking, because then they might have stopped.

Not that they were likely to look up from what they were doing--they were completely lost in the rhythm of it. I remember how that felt.

I'm not a kid anymore, that's for sure, but I remember passion.

When I was young I never realized that people can feel sexual when they get old, that they don't necessarily stop having those desires. It's just that eventually people's bodies lose their attractiveness, and then sometimes they--we--become ashamed to be seen. To have our deterioration exposed. Of course, sex makes people vulnerable even when we're still young and beautiful, and that's why it's so affecting...but when we get old and the body loses much of its beauty, that kind of intimacy can seem a terrible invasion of privacy. And then the irony is that the corruption of the flesh is what prevents you from seeking its satisfaction.

Skin is its own worst enemy.

It's not that I've ever stopped desiring men—I just stopped being able to take off my clothes in front of strangers. And every man's a stranger, really, before you've slept with him. So.

A thought of Joe comes rushing through my mind now and I feel it briefly in my skin at first, like a shock, then it settles like a stubborn blush in my skin. I saw him yesterday in the hallway. He was replacing some ceiling light bulbs. Up on a ladder as if he were a much younger man. I'm sure when he looks at women—and somehow I don't doubt he still does, even at our age—it's most likely at women who are younger than most of my shoes! I guess I'd never let a man see me naked now.

Conditioning, maybe. A film actress is conditioned to live in the skin—the skin of a made-up character. And in her own skin as a marketable commodity striving to hold onto some measure of big-screen appeal. Your skin is your living. Then it forsakes you.

I'm not some maudlin malcontent full of self-pity about aging. It'd be ludicrous to feel sorry for myself—aging's normal, after all. But if I'm going to be completely honest, I have to say I don't like the process. All my skin--face, torso, hands, limbs--gave up the fight at once, it seemed, in a surrender that to me felt as sudden as a body dropping dead on the street. There's a definite dividing line between aging and old, and sometime I must have crossed it unawares. Then I was there. Here.

What can be keeping Wilma, I wonder. She's getting so undependable. I keep looking toward my front door, as if watching it will conjure her presence. I remember watching my door for this man or that man when I was younger...but I never imagined I'd end up waiting for a sulky personal assistant with that same impatience. While the men were my connection with the world of the flesh—and sometimes the world of the heart— I've had to face the fact that Wilma is now my connection with the world, period--like it or not. Getting old--it sucks, as kids nowadays say about whatever they don't like.

It's not the state of being old that's hard to bear--it's the awareness of having once been young and then having lost it. That's what I think--it's about loss. Seeing your physical failure in the eyes of those who knew you before. It's interesting how we say that when someone is visibly aging--he's failing, or she's failing. As if they could have done better.

Maybe I think too much. But there's everything to think of now.

How soon doth man decay, George Herbert wrote. Sometimes I read his poems from a book I keep beside the bed. Who'd have ever thought I'd take to the poetry of a 17th century English cleric? I've changed since I left L.A.--I know that. I'm not saying I'm an intellectual by any stretch--I never even went to college--but lately I read all the time, three or four books a week. And the more I read, the more I see how long I lived in the top layer of life's skin, one cell deep. It all comes down to this: I haven't the energy anymore to play by the rules of my old life. There's so little time left to be real.

I'll admit I'm probably still vain, but at least I know it now and try not to indulge it. It's a bit of a burden being "an aging beauty," especially when you've had some notoriety. But I find that if I keep to myself it doesn't much matter how I look—I can decay in peace and no one's going to write about it for publication! I can concentrate on more substantive things here, after a lifetime of getting by on my looks.

It's amazing how interesting the world seems since I left Hollywood. Maybe it always was, but honestly, nothing felt so real in those days as the make-believe that sustained us there, both on and off the job. It's very different to look at the world when it's not looking at you. I'm determined to keep it that way.

I had that in mind when I left Los Angeles nine years ago and came here to Boston, where I grew up. I still had a dear, close friend here--a pal from high school, Sunny Brodsky. Oh, Sunny and I got into so much mischief in our younger days, and over the decades we never lost touch. To Sunny I was always just Anne Sullivan, so when I came home again to stay, it was oddly just a matter of picking up where we left off, even after so many years away and all the Hollywood business in between.

Since Sunny died unexpectedly two years ago of an aneurysm, I'll admit I've become a bit reclusive, but that's certainly not how I planned to live when I came back to Boston. It's just hard to meet new people and not feel paranoid that they might recognize me. My life seems to depend on not allowing all that craziness in again.

Hard as it may be for some to comprehend this, I just prefer to age outside the presence of people who knew me as Aja Sullivan. Witnesses. It's too much pressure, too much to keep trying to be. I see my name in the showbiz rags from time to time--they call me a recluse, but that's stupid. I'm not avoiding all humanity, I'm just avoiding them! I no longer like to be seen through the lens of public expectation. It's that simple.

No one in my old life would understand that, I know. In Hollywood everyone jockeys to be seen. For a time, I was caught up in it myself. Being "someone."

It all began to seem a futile exercise--putting on the make-up, dyeing my hair--trying to keep it that dark auburn I was known for in an era of blondes. Finally I just stopped—the chemicals were making my hair dry and porous, and anyway, there's something about a dark dye-job that ages the face, defeating the whole purpose. It's a known fact that blond hair is easier on an aging face, and of course that's why Hollywood women of a certain age go blond. They also get their faces lifted and their lip-cracks filled with ass-fat, all their life's evidence Botoxed away. I guess I'd rather live with my evidence. It reassures me in some odd way.

My God, in So Cal they hit fifty or fifty-five, and they all begin to look the same! There's such an eerie feeling about it when you lunch with friends, all those identical blondes sitting around a table in their Chanel and Armani, shriveled fingers tipped with acrylic claws, the skin of their faces pulled so tight they can barely smile.

Worse, I hated the way they'd begun looking at me. As if *I* were the crazy one. A wrinkled face in Southern California is looked upon the way one might look at dirty hair: poor hygiene. Plastic surgery is simply considered routine maintenance, good grooming. They call it *having a little work done.*

The final straw was when Marty Kline called me self-destructive because I wouldn't have a facelift. The man was my agent and friend for thirty-one years!

--Aja, he said, how can I get work for you if you won't help me out here? It's just a tuck at each ear, for Chrissakes.

That was easy for him to say, with his face like a scrotum and no one minding that because he's a man! Dating a nineteen-year-old at the time.

That was the day I decided to come back to Boston. I've not once regretted the decision.

Oh, sure, I miss the lunchtime chitchat sometimes. Maybe it's the Irish in me, but I love gossip, a good story. I take Variety in order to keep up with the industry, and a couple of tabloids to keep up with the dish. Not that the tabs are always factual, but then neither was the lunch gossip.

It may be hypocritical to say this after admitting I like to read them, but I hate it whenever one of the tabloids revives talk about me. Why can't they concentrate on people who still have a public life? I'll admit we're all fair game while we're in the public eye--but once we've retired, haven't we the right to choose obscurity if we wish?

Where is Aja Hiding? That was the lead on the cover of the *Enquirer* two or three weeks ago, right above a photo of some crone in a bandana ambling along a beach in Cabo. They actually thought she was me! And, my God, the article inside! It was headlined The Mystery of Aja Sullivan, and it read as if I were a fugitive on the lam. It included several middle-aged photos of me, taken before I got smart and stopped going out in public as myself.

I understand the art of disguise better than most people. I've learned that less showy is always more effective. That poor Michael Jackson creature just never understood disguise, with his silly fright wigs and surgical masks, his poor face melting away. I always suspected he didn't really want to be anonymous—if he did, he'd have done a better job of it.

Now, Garbo--she was truly good at camouflage--she knew how to be invisible on the street with no real disguise at all. She once told a friend of mine that it was all in the attitude. She said you can become invisible if you learn to walk as if you were. I never liked Garbo much--she was actually a very cold person, and selfish as hell in my humble opinion, but she did have style, real style. And I admired the way she disappeared once she'd decided it was her time to live outside the public eye.

Sometimes, though, nothing will hide you.

That tabloid story made me feel so exposed. I guess I'd begun to believe I had put Hollywood behind me once and for all, even to think they might've forgotten me—and far from hurting my pride or my ego, the idea seemed a blessed relief. I was even researching some Boston and Cambridge political groups and book clubs I thought I might join.

Now in the last couple of weeks, thanks to the bloody *Enquirer* and all the gossip websites that picked up the story, I feel awkward even going down to the laundry room in case someone in our building has seen the article and might recognize me. One incident could be all it took to turn my life upside down. I guess I may have to have Wilma start doing my laundry for me, at least until this Enquirer nonsense blows over. But I would hate that. It isn't that I would mind paying her the extra wages--it's that to stop my weekly trip downstairs would be just another loss of liberty. I like doing for myself after all those years of excess, and anyway, I need to get out of this damned apartment sometimes.

And of course there's Joe. I'd miss out on our occasional visits if I did that. Joe's our building's super and sometimes he and I chat when I'm in the basement laundry facility and he's down there puttering around. He's an interesting man. Played in an army dance band during the Viet Nam War--lied about his age and joined up at fifteen. Later played saxophone in a jazz combo in New York and sat in as a session man for a few doo-wop groups in the early '70s. Says his mother was a great beauty who married six times. Joe himself was married twice, like me. He lives alone now in an apartment in Allston.

An attractive man, that Joe--always cheeerful, and a great conversationalist. Doesn't know Aja Sullivan from Adam, thank God. He's not particularly handsome, but I like his face, the blue-black of his skin, and the way he carries himself, the innate grace of the man. I love his voice, too—there's a quiet confidence in it.

Sometimes I think he gets a bit of a glow on, too, when we're talking.

Oh, please, what a silly train of thought.

Where in the hell is that ditzy Wilma? Should've been here hours ago.

Everything gets on my nerves lately, since the renewed press interest. I don't know why a few vultures out there have become hell-bent on finding me--I haven't made a film in twenty-one years unless you count my unbilled cameo in that airport movie all those years ago. I only took the part because I hadn't had any other offers in a long time--everyone knows how hard it is for a woman over fifty in Hollywood, and I was eager to work. So where did it get me?

I'll tell you where: one of the critics wrote--and this seemed unnecessarily mean, since I'm only onscreen for three minutes and did rather nicely in the limited role--he wrote that it was so sad to see Aja Sullivan in a schlock movie, and sadder still to have to see her legendary face showing the ravages of time. As if by growing older and showing my face I'd committed some kind of crime. And I was just in my late fifties then! It's not easy aging in a place like L.A. when in your better days you were known in all the columns as The Face. I'd rather let them remember me as I was in my prime.

I remember once soon after Daddy died—I was nine at the time—I saw my mother in front of her bedroom mirror... she must have been in her early forties then, and she was still a beautiful woman. She wasn't aware that I was in the hallway watching her as she put an index finger to each cheekbone and laid a thumb-tip along each side of her jaw, pushing up and back until the skin of her face was taut and smooth, transforming her mother-face into more of a girl-face like my own. It scared the hell out of me at the time, as if beneath her own face she'd been harboring a stranger. For a long time after that, I couldn't look at my mother without seeing that other face.

I thought of this yesterday because it occurred to me that for years now I've been doing the same thing--those finger facelifts--to find my real face again beneath this saggy mask it seems I woke with one day without warning. Mother would never have had a real facelift, of course, and neither would I. I guess I inherited my sense of propriety from her, and there's no doubt that a Boston upbringing sticks, even after one is transplanted to California

Whenever I read interviews of young starlets who swear they don't think they're beautiful, I know they sound false but I have to believe them, because I always thought I was fooling everyone with make-up, that I was really a plain Jane underneath. Now when I see my old photos I realize that even without all the make-up I was quite a beauty. I'd have to have been, because I was just an adequate actor and my modest talent would never by itself have earned me such fame. Oh yes, I'll admit it, I was bloody famous--good old Wilma likes to remind me of that whenever she gets a chance.

Where is she, anyway? I really should dock her wages when she does this.

I had a lot of lovers in my youth, but not many relationships. And I was usually the one to leave. For all my early life love disappointed me, and each time things began to go wrong in a romance I wanted to quit so that I could try again. Like reshooting a flawed scene over and over until it's right. I guess that mentality got into me--the movies.

Each time I met a man who was going to be my next lover, I would know it immediately in my skin before we'd ever touched. Feel it in my bones, people always say, but I felt it in my skin. All my life I've known things in my skin

I sometimes wonder if it would even be possible for a man to want me now. I'm not bad looking for my age--I'm slender and straight, though I have to admit I sag a bit and all the skin of my body has lost its firmness and tone. But it's mostly my face that's let me down. Though I have good bones and nice eyes and lips, my face sags at the jaw line, and unless I'm smiling I look a little dour all the time now, even when I'm perfectly happy, because of the furrows on my brow and the lines that run along each side of my mouth like parentheses. My hair has a lot of gray in it, too--or maybe it's more accurate just to say it has a little auburn left. But I'm a woman of seventy, after all. I suppose anyone would find the very idea that I might have sexual desires ridiculous--even disgusting.

After my divorce there were so many men. I don't know why I wanted it so, but I did. Looking back now, I think it could be called a kind of sexual hysteria. Whatever it was, it went on for several years, and it wasn't till I met Stephen that I learned a woman can be fulfilled by one man.

My God, he was a wonderful lover. I'll tell you, the man was not afraid of a woman's body, her parts, the way so many men are. He would do absolutely anything for pleasure--and my pleasure was as important to him as his own. And oh he was beautiful--Jewish and Italian, black-haired with dark olive skin. With my auburn hair and pale complexion, I suppose we made a striking couple. The two of us did every sexual thing a man and a woman can do. I never wanted anyone else while I had him. It never once crossed my mind, and that's God's truth. Well, maybe not God's...God never seemed to have much to do with that part of things. But it's true. I only wanted Stephen.

Those damned race cars took him away from me, and I'll never forgive him the loss of our life together. It's been thirty-five years since he was killed driving at Riverside, and I've never fallen in love again. No one since that time has made me feel the way he did--in bed or out.

I haven't had sex in fifteen years, unless you count the couple across the way.

That was supposed to be funny, but it suddenly seems true. Our twin buildings are set around a courtyard, and the back of their apartment faces the back of mine. I have a clear view of their bedroom. What would they think if they knew an old crone like me was watching them? I've an idea they don't mind who is watching them, since they never draw their drapes. They may even be inviting it, though I imagine I'm not quite the sort of viewer they had in mind.

Where could that damned Wilma be! We're going to have to have a little talk, get to the bottom of things. She's been so surly these past few weeks--surly and remote, late a lot--and I could almost trace it back to the *Enquirer* piece, except that would make no sense. Why should that change her attitude toward me when she already knew perfectly well who I was? In fact, she's always brought up my past too much to suit me. Since the article appeared, though, I shush her if she brings it up. Now she's acting strange. I guess the whole thing has affected me so adversely that I'm attributing some of my attitudes to her--projecting, as they say.

To think I bought this apartment because I thought the Back Bay an ideal neighborhood for my walks. I've always been a walker. During the first few years after I moved here to Dartmouth Street, Sunny and I used to go on long, long walks around the neighborhood—she lived just two blocks away—and we laughed constantly as we walked, remembering silly things from our teen years. After she died so unexpectedly I didn't know if I'd ever have the courage to just go out there alone and risk being recognized. Somehow when she was with me it didn't often enter my mind.

After a time I got stir-crazy though, and began walking to the Boston Public Library over on Boylston. I started spending a lot of my time doing what I realized was really just catch-up reading...making up for all the years when I didn't open a book, catching up on the education I know I've missed. History, biography, art, religion, poetry, philosophy. I'd sit with my books on a stone bench in the library courtyard, pigeons swooping around in the shady enclosure. It was nice. I began to feel more...I don't know...*viable,* if that makes any sense. More viable as the person I actually am.

Then one day inside the library near the card catalogue, a woman asked me if I was Aja Sullivan. Our eyes met and held for a moment in a silence that felt like paralysis. Her eyes were fervid as she waited for my response.

I managed to mobilize my internal forces and, without even attempting to answer, I walked right out the door. I never went back to the library after that. Now I have Wilma order all my books on Amazon. And though for a while after that I tried to keep up my walks around the neighborhood in the evenings, too often I'd find someone staring and I'd get jumpy. Eventually I just preferred staying here at home, high above the street, with my own things around me. Here, there's no worry about being recognized, photographed for the tabloids. Taken out of context.

I do miss the world, though. Sometimes when I stand at my window and look out onto Dartmouth Street or up toward Copley Square, seeing the Hancock building with Trinity Church reflected in its smooth glass surface I feel a kind of grief, a longing for the world out there.

I haven't gone out beyond the courtyard in ages except in Wilma's car, and then only to visit the doctor. The last time I went to see my doctor was six months ago and it's getting time to go again. I'm in fairly good health though I'm diabetic--just mildly, so I'm able take pills rather than shots. Dr. Nachman likes to see me every six months. I'll have to talk to Wilma and make an appointment for a time when she'll be available. Also, I'm running out of my insulin prescription. She can go and get that refilled when she gets my groceries on Saturday.

Where is she? It's not that I'm thirsting for her company-- but she's the only one I have to do things out in the world for me. I guess you could say I trust her well enough, though I'm not much of a one for trusting and she mightn't ordinarily be much of a one to be trusted.

You could say it's a kind of symbiosis we have. We get along because we need each other: She needs the money I've paid her for the last seven years, and I need her to run interference for me out in the world, to preserve my privacy. She knows better than to talk about me in public. She'd be out of a job, and her salary frees her to do her art, she says.

A year ago Wilma quit her part-time job clerking at Filene's and went full-time with me. That was about the time she changed her name from Wilma Brownlee to Willow Skye. I still call her Wilma, though. About that time, she traded her normal street clothes for her idea of a poet's garb--a cobalt blue velvet dress and scuffed black cowgirl boots from AmVets, though mind you I pay her plenty and she could dress nicely if she wanted. She chooses to wear that same outfit nearly all the time. Smokes those little all-color cigarettes and writes things down in a notebook about her sex life. Lately her poems affect her skewed idea of a Black patois. Which is just goddamned silly. My God. It makes no sense! If I were Black and heard her poetry I'd want to smack her. I almost wanted to anyway.

Well, hell. It's past midnight and Wilma never did show up today. I can't believe it. She didn't even bother to call. Between fits of anger I worry that she might be sick or something. I tried ringing her but got no answer. Very strange. Maybe I should phone the police, to check on her. I imagine her lying in her apartment with a garrote around her neck. But who would kill Wilma? Annoying though she is.

I keep thinking that maybe she told me she had to go somewhere today and I just forgot. It's awful to think I may be forgetting things! I'd have no way of knowing how much I was forgetting, or which specific things. It happens to old people sometimes. Am I losing my marbles? How would I know?

At ten tonight I realized I'd had no dinner and was getting a bit out of focus--I have to watch that because of insulin reaction. I heated up some leftover Chinese food Wilma picked up for yesterday's dinner. While it was heating, it occurred to me that she forgot to give me my change again when she bought the food back, and this time it was change of a fifty. If anyone kills Wilma, let it be me!

I sat in my chair then and watched them--the couple across the way--while I ate moo-shoo pork and Szechwan broccoli. It felt like being at a movie--sitting in the dark with a snack, watching two beautiful bare bodies writhing and turning, wrapping together, making love. In a way those two seem almost a cliché of glamorized movie-sex: he's olive-skinned and black-haired the way Stephen was, muscular and athletic looking. She's blonde and stunningly white-skinned, slender with full breasts and a round bottom. Except for her hair color they could be Stephen and me in our heyday. Suddenly I realize I've been seeing them that way. As us.

This time they did it on the bed, and she ended up on top of him, sitting astride him in what Stephen used to call the equestrienne position. At one point he lifted her forward, pulled her toward him, and held her over his face, put his mouth between her thighs and kept at it for quite a while as she straddled his face, kneeling, his hands holding her hips. I could feel their heat in my own skin as I watched them.

At one point the girl turned off the lamp beside the bed and slid down on his body so he could enter her, and I wouldn't have been able to see them anymore except that their large-screen television was on behind them in the room, and it made everything so strange, lunar almost, colors flickering behind their bodies and against their skin so that they became moving silhouettes illuminated at the edges. First she rode him in a hypnotic motion, almost slow motion at first but gradually gaining in speed and intensity, and then she reared back suddenly and even in the semi-dark I could tell when she came.

I realized then I'd been rocking too and had stopped when she did, holding my breath while she came, the moo-shoo pork forgotten in my lap. What a silly and pathetic old woman I've turned into.

I guess I'll go to bed. No point waiting up any longer. If I don't hear from Wilma tomorrow I'll have to call someone to check on her. I'm not wild about the woman but I don't like to think of anything happening to her--she's a pretty hapless creature, really.

A few weeks ago she asked me for the money to get a face-lift! I couldn't believe the irony--that she would ask such a thing of me when my whole life has changed because of my resistance to such things. I told her that if she wanted it done, she'd have to save up the money herself, from the generous salary I already give her, or from her annual Christmas bonus, which would be more than enough in itself. I will not contribute directly to such foolishness. Wilma would fit in only too well in Los Angeles!

I do hope she's all right. God knows Boston has its street crime these days.

Aside from my concern for her safety, it doesn't escape me that it would be very bad for me if anything should happen to her. What would I do? I don't know a soul in this city now, except for Wilma, Joe, and Dr. Nachman. Wilma may still be angry with me about the face-lift issue. I guess I could offer her a little raise in pay. Of course I'd have to argue with Sam Firebaugh about that--he already thinks I pay Wilma twice what I should. He's my lawyer in Los Angeles, and he handles all my money...electronically deposits a sum in my checking account at BayBank once a month, as I've asked him to do. After my pampered years, I find I like living on a specific amount each month--unlimited means are part of a past I'd just as soon put behind me.

Wilma seems quite fond of money. The last time I gave her a raise she was downright solicitous for a month. Or was that after I bought her the Lexus? Well, it's been nearly a year since she's had a raise, so I guess I'll have a talk with Sam. He mails her the check at the first of each month, and that way money never need change hands between Wilma and me. I like it that way, almost as if she were a relative or friend who was simply doing for me out of kindness or affection. Sort of a laugh, when you think of Wilma. As if she would do anything for me out of affection, I mean.

The bedroom has a chill tonight, but maybe it's just me. I refuse to go into my hall and raise the thermostat...I will not be one of those old biddies who lives in an overheated house no one can bear to sit down in.

I see the two of them in bed asleep across the way, blankets thrown off, their limbs in a glorious tangle. Ah, God.

I undress quickly, avoiding the mirror, and slip into my nightgown. I don't want my bath tonight. I take my insulin tablet and realize I've just got three pills left--I'll need a refill before Saturday's grocery shopping...I'll need it by the day after tomorrow.

I'm all the way to the bed when I turn and go back to the dresser, dab a bit of Patou's Joi at my throat, breast, and wrist. Invisible in the dark room and wrapped in this scent, I remember how it felt when men desired me.

*

Oh, God, what time is it? Must be five a.m. and I haven't slept a wink. What's the use? No matter how I try, I can't get to sleep. Something is definitely wrong, I feel it. The Globe will be here by now, I guess...and yesterday's is waiting as well, since Wilma wasn't here to bring it up and I never went down to retrieve it. I may as well go down to get both of them.

As I pull on my old green silk kimono, it occurs to me that I didn't go down to collect yesterday's mail, either, so I fetch the key to my box. Not that there's likely to be much there. I hope no one sees me. Quickly I brush my hair, twist it into a French roll, put on a touch of lipstick in case one of the neighbors might be around. I take my morning insulin pill. Two left.

The elevator has never seemed so noisy and clanking as now when I wish not to attract the attention of any neighbors while I stand in the hall waiting for it to ascend to this floor. When it arrives and the door sighs open I get in quickly, and when I get out at the lobby I keep my eyes down at first, just in case.

I find the lobby empty and still lit from the night, the sky dark through the glass front doors, and I hurry over to the bench that holds our newspapers, collect the two marked #753, and then make my way quickly to the mailbox marked Martin, #753. Not for the first time I note the irony of using my late stepfather's name to protect my identity. I've been using his last name since I arrived back in Boston, along with the first name my mother gave me at birth: Anne. No one would ever think to look for me under the name of my long-dead stepfather. So I'm Anne Martin now, even though decades ago I changed my name legally to Aja for the screen. I was Aja Sullivan for nearly fifty years. Funny, really: Sullivan was my real name--my father's name--and Aja just a name made up by Freddie when he cast me in my first movie role--Aja, pronounced like Asia because, Freddie said, it sounded exotic. Now I've got back my real first name and have lost my real last name. It seems I'm doomed to always be half real, half made up, thanks to Hollywood.

Hurriedly I unlock the box, find *Variety*, the *Enquirer*, and two envelopes. One is just my monthly NYNEX bill, but right away I notice that the other is hand-addressed to Aja Martin.

No one who knows that first name would ever use it with that last name! Those few who know where I am address my mail to Anne Martin. There's no return address on the envelope, but I'm pretty sure I know the handwriting. I recognize it from the poetry notebook.

I feel short of breath, a worm of panic curling in my stomach. Where is she? And why would she write to me instead of phoning? I'm filled with foreboding and have to sit down on an upholstered bench near the mailboxes. Something is very wrong. I feel it, my whole surface prickles.

I am not a bad person, the note begins, and as I read, my world collapses. *I know you won't understand what I've done, and I also know I can't keep it from you after Wednesday, when you'll read it in the Enquirer. But life is short,* Wilma writes, *and each of us have to think of themselves, irregardless. You certainly think of yourself alot. You refused to help me when I asked you, so I had no choice but to find my own way--you're the one that told me that, in case you've forgotten. I think it's poetic justice that at last I'm now a published writer.*

Each of us have to. Themselves, irregardless. Alot. The one that. And she calls that poetic justice.

My hands are shaking. Of course I know what she's done. It all begins to fit now.

The letter is signed Willow, and there's a postscript scrawled at the bottom: The Acorn Domestic Service can find someone to replace me. Their number is 617.755-8263.

Even in her treachery and betrayal, that plodding sense of duty--or self-righteousness, more likely. I can imagine her telling people, I helped her find a replacement before I left. Wilma always exaggerates things having to do with herself. She should have been an actress.

Over and over I read the letter, as if some deeper truth will emerge with many readings, but always it comes down to the same thing.

My hands shake and fumble as I open the Enquirer, and sure enough there's the headline, My Life in Hiding With Aja Sullivan. In the article, Wilma describes me as gaunt and ravaged, paranoid, desperately vain. I suppose I am desperately vain--why else would I hide myself away like this? But even allowing for vanity's delusions, I know I'm not gaunt and ravaged. It just makes a better story if she describes me that way. Makes me sound like Howard Hughes, who was a real nutcase, believe me. Wouldn't even bathe. My God, I wonder if people will think I don't bathe. Wilma tops the whole thing off with the statement that being in the same room with Aja Sullivan day after day felt like being locked in prison without the possibility of parole.

I suppose it's true she may have felt that way about my company—and God knows I wasn't crazy about hers--but in the article she never mentions all the times we played cards and Trivial Pursuit, or how we enjoyed watching the soaps together.

Nor does she mention the new car I bought her when her old one gave out. The Lexus. In the article she claims I refused to give her financial assistance when she needed surgery--but she doesn't mention that the surgery was a facelift, and she doesn't tell about the health insurance I've paid for since she went full-time with me.

She exaggerates, takes things out of context--like the way she describes that time last year when I asked her to drive me to church on the anniversary of Stephen's death. I'd always gone alone after moving here, but because I'd stopped going out by myself then, I asked her to drive me on the day I bring my yearly flowers to put by the statue of St. Stephen in the church. I've done it every year since leaving California because now I'm 3,000 miles from his grave. It's just a way of acknowledging him. But in the article she says, Aja worships a statue and believes it to be her dead husband.

Somehow she's gotten hold of some of my old photographs--she must have taken them from the albums in the den. There's one of me at eighteen with Freddie in Capistrano, and one of Stephen kissing me as we sit on the beach wall at La Jolla. And here's a shot of Wilma, looking soft and solemn, with a caption beneath it that reads, Boston poet Willow Skye seeks a publisher for her memoir about the claustrophobic life she shared with reclusive former screen star Aja Sullivan.

A memoir. Claustrophobic. Well.

∗

I have no idea how long I've sat on the bench in my robe, but the sky beyond the glass doors has bleached to morning. I feel dizzy and weak.

--Are you okay, ma'am?

I see him standing in front of me in his gray work clothes. I can't even think of his name at first. I swallow, stare at him. I'm dizzy, feel disoriented. My fingertips are numb.

--Joe, I finally say.

--You all right, Ms. Martin?

--I--I need to get back upstairs, Joe.

I try to stand then, but vertigo forces me back down and I see him reach for my arm and miss it.

--I'm not feeling very well, I say.

--Let me get you upstairs. He takes my elbow, helps me to my feet. All the way up in the elevator we say nothing, but he keeps his hand on my elbow; I feel it there.

Upstairs, when I find my own hand too shaky to open the lock, Joe takes the key from me gently. I'm ashamed of my infirmity, of the veins and age spots on the backs of my hands. As he turns the key in the lock I see the smooth backs of his hands--no discolorations, though I know he's around my age. Black skin seems not to suffer the ravages of time the way white skin does, as if nature meant to make up in some small way for the inequities a black skin would bring upon a person in our particular world.

He leads me into my living room and over to the sofa. I'm still holding the stack of mail but my fingers feel weak. I press it all against my chest in order not to drop it. I couldn't bear to have Joe see the Enquirer headline. I'm becoming more and more disoriented, my head is swimming. My mouth is dry and my lips are numb. I seem to land in a heap on the sofa, despite the care with which Joe handles me. The tabloid and the two envelopes slide out of my hand and onto the floor. Joe stoops to pick them up, puts them on the coffee table, takes Variety from my hand and sets it on top of the rest. I can barely focus enough to see him.

--Now, ma'am, you just try to relax, he says kindly. Ma'am?

I can't form the words to answer. I have never liked to be called ma'am.

He squats down before me so that our faces are level and he stares into my eyes.

--You gonna be all right? he asks.

--I think...I think I'm having an insulin reaction, I say as I suddenly realize it. I hear the slur of my words. Please, I tell him, could you get me some juice...some orange juice?

Without a word he turns and nearly runs to the kitchen. The refrigerator opens, closes, whoomp, then I hear him open a cupboard, set a glass on the counter. Then I seem to slip away.

He's spooning the juice into my mouth, rubbing my gums with it, crooning in a soft singsong voice, Okay, okay now, okay. Strangely, for a moment I feel certain he is Sam Cooke. He sounds exactly like Sam Cooke. I open my eyes and it's Joe again, but the voice is still Sam Cooke's.

--Now try to drink some right out of the glass, he says, and I do what he tells me.

In a while, I feel my head clearing a bit, my focus returning. I'm distracted by the thought of how startling it was when he rubbed my gums gently with the orange juice. It's the first time a man other than my doctor has touched me so intimately in years.

He brings in the juice carton, refills my glass.

--Another swig of juice, he says. After you were so bad off, you need it. My old friend Scooter, he had diabetes too, and sometimes he'd get to jamming with the boys in the band and forget to eat after taking his insulin shot. I had to bring him back more times from that than from his whiskey drinkin'. Joe shakes his head, smiling a little, looks down. Then he looks back at me.

--Shouldn't you be eating something now? He asks. Maybe some eggs or something? I know people are s'posed to eat when this happens. I came to work early today, so I got a little extra time right now. I could fix you something.

I smile at him, and before I can answer he's on his way to the kitchen. I hear him rummaging around, humming softly as he prepares the tea, the eggs. It's a song I remember vaguely from long ago, but I can't place it. Probably a song he used to play on his saxophone. More bustling, sound of the toaster popping up.

I think of the *Enquirer* and note gratefully that it's out of sight beneath *Variety*.

Joe and I eat breakfast at the little table in my kitchen nook. It's good--he has put out some hot sauce to go with the eggs, which he's scrambled with onion and cheddar cheese. I'm not talkative, but that seems to be all right with him. He tells me about USO trips he took when he played in the band--how he met some of the biggest movie stars of the day.

--I was just a kid then, he says, --fifteen, sixteen years old.

I start to comment on the coincidence, even start to mention the USO trip I made with Edgar Bergen when I was eighteen--but then I realize I can't tell him without revealing myself. I ask instead if sometime he might play his saxophone for me. He grins and says he'd be glad to but he doesn't drag his horn along to work. He chuckles, and I'm surprised to find myself smiling, too, despite everything.

*

When Joe came back late this afternoon after he'd finished his day's work, I'm ashamed to say I was still in my robe and nightgown, though I'd managed to wash my face and brush my hair and pin it up in a knot on my head. Anything more seemed like exertion, suddenly.

He brought my prescription refill, which he'd picked up at the pharmacy. He let me reimburse him for the prescription itself, but when I tried to pay him for his time, he said, No, ma'am. That's not necessary, not necessary. He wouldn't take a cent for himself.

Tonight I fixed a Lean Cuisine frozen veal dinner in the microwave and watched the Thursday night shows, such as they were. Then the late local news led with a Take Back the Night march in Cambridge and a fire in Mattapan. In the Cuff Stuff segment, there was mention of Aja Sullivan's presence somewhere in the Back Bay. I turned off the TV and went to bed.

*

I don't know what has wakened me, or why I find myself getting up automatically now and walking to the window. It must be three or four A.M. and the two of them are up. They seem to be arguing. Yes, they are definitely arguing. She's crying, he's waving his hands around and pacing the bedroom floor. They are both in robes; hers is white, his dark blue. I try to script the words from my imagination as he speaks and then she speaks, but I'm at a loss: it has never before occurred to me to wonder about their life beyond the fucking, since that's all I see, all I know of them. Suddenly it seems indecent to watch them fighting, her crying. I go back to my bed. The sheets have cooled since I left them and I feel the chill all along my skin, even through the cloth of my nightgown. Under blankets I hold myself in my own arms, wondering how I've become such an exile. I close my eyes and try to drift off, but the air is full of presences, shifting and feathery in the dark air. I really haven't a lot to be proud of, and I know it. How much trust it takes to fall asleep.

*

In the morning, Joe's at the door first thing, asking if I need anything. I say No thank you, but I know he sees the desperation in my face and it humiliates me. Before he can say anything else I thank him again and close the door.

Sam Firebaugh returns my call, telling me I have no grounds for a suit unless the article contains lies. He says exaggerations or a weird slant put on things, implications of my instability and infirmity--none of that really counts, since it isn't concrete.

--It's hard to sue over slants and implications, he says in that lawyerish, absolute tone of his.

--What about the photos? I ask. --She took my private photos for her own use!

He asks if she stole them from me, and I tell him how I'd found them back in my albums slightly askew. She must have taken them and had copies made, then put them back when my attention was elsewhere, I say.

--It would all be hard to prove, he tells me, and what would it gain you besides more unwanted publicity?

So it seems that for someone to steal my most vital and treasured possession--my privacy--is not a crime; it's simply a living.

41

All day I worry: I'm running low on bread, milk, juice, fresh produce, eggs. Since I've been so reclusive I've become like a Mormon about keeping a supply of stored food. When my stores go down, I become unsettled, insecure. I've got plenty of canned and frozen goods on hand, but you can't really hoard produce and dairy products in that same way. I have to face the fact that I'm going to have to make my way over to the little grocery store four blocks away.

In the mid-afternoon, I put on a hat and dark glasses, forgetting my theory about clear glasses being a better disguise. I'm not myself at all. My heart is beating too fast and my legs feel rubbery. It's the first time I've gone out to the street alone in quite a while.

At the outer door of the building I stop, look both ways. I can't see beyond the shrubs at the sidewalk entrance. The fresh air feels like a slap on my unaccustomed skin as I step gingerly down the steps and out to the sidewalk to await the cab I've called, praying the driver won't recognize me.

That's when I see the man standing across the street. He has a camera and he starts toward me, calling out, Miss Sullivan? I turn and rush back up the steps and through the doors into the building, cursing Wilma's tatty blue-velvet ass.

By the time I reach the elevator in the lobby and press the button, the nosy lummox is rapping on the glass lobby door. I can hear him calling Miss Sullivan? Miss Sullivan? As I step into the elevator, I suddenly fear that he might see the elevator lights as he peers through the glass and then he would discover which floor my apartment is on when it stops to let me off, so I press the Basement button instead of the seventh floor button.

I must look quite loony standing in the basement near the laundry room with my hat and sunglasses on when Joe comes around lugging some sort of toolbox on wheels. Quickly I remove the sunglasses and hat, try to set my face into a look of composure. I know it's hopeless.

--What happened? Joe asks me. What's wrong?

I take a deep breath--what's the use of hiding anymore?

--I have a problem, Joe. I need your help.

--Sure thing, ma'am. What kind of a problem?

A pair of women get off the elevator, walk into the laundry room with baskets full of towels and sheets.

--Could we talk where it's more private? I ask him. Do you have time to come upstairs for a cup of tea?

--In just about five minutes I could do that, he says, nodding his head vigorously, then walking ahead and calling back over his shoulder, Just give me five minutes, ma'am, and I'll be right up.

I go upstairs in the elevator, wishing he would stop calling me ma'am.

I wait inside my apartment, right next to the door. When Joe knocks I open it immediately and find my words spilling out while he's still in the hall. I tell him I'm Aja Sullivan and he looks at me blankly. I tell him a man is stalking me and I'm afraid to go outside. As I say this I fear I may cry, and at all costs I know I must not cry. The effort not to cry makes me tremble, makes my mouth quiver as I attempt to speak. I press my fingers to my mouth to hold my lips still, but my hand is shaking too. I look at Joe. He has an expression on his face I haven't seen before. I suppose it's pity. He reaches out toward my hand as if to remove it from my lips and then stops mid-air before his fingers touch mine, lets his hand fall to his side again.

--Ms. Martin...

--Sullivan.

He looks at me quizzically.

--Sullivan, he says, Ms. Sullivan, could we go sit down?

Before I can answer, he takes my elbow and leads me into the living room. I'm so tired. Let him be in charge.

--Where's that lady that helps you? he asks when we're settled on the sofa.

--She...she's gone. Wilma doesn't work for me anymore.

He looks surprised.

--Look, I tell him, I'm not who I seem to be. I changed my identity when I moved here, and then Wilma betrayed me. Sold my secrets to the National Enquirer.

Joe looks perplexed, pained. It takes him a full minute to formulate what he needs to say, and then he speaks with impeccable courtesy.

--Ma'am, I think maybe we need to call the doctor.

I realize that he thinks I'm delusional, gone round the bend. I really thought Joe would help me--he was my last chance.

I clam up, can't possibly talk to anyone who thinks I'm crazy. How has it come to this? We sit in silence on my pale-yellow sofa, and then he speaks again.

--Please, ma'am...tell me the name of your doctor? I just want to help you. Please.

I hear myself sigh. There's no choice now, though I hate for him to see the things Wilma said about me. I pull the Enquirer out from beneath a stack of magazines beside the couch. Unfold it, show him the headline, My Life in Hiding With Aja Sullivan. Show him the article inside, with Wilma's photo, the old photos of me.

He studies all of it for a few minutes. Then he looks up at me, back down to the article, up at me again.

--Sweet Jesus, he says softly, and there's something like fear in his voice. I lead him to the front window and show him the paparazzo camped across the street.

--I can't even leave to get groceries, I say. What am I going to do, Joe? How can I live?

That's when I begin to cry. For the first time in many years, I cry. It's a strange and foreign sensation, and I feel a kind of abandon as I give into it.

--I'm afraid, I tell him, weeping and at the same time utterly ashamed of myself for it. My mother always said that to be aboveboard one should only cry in private, and all my life I've tried to follow that principle.

--Sweet Jesus, Joe says again, my good Jesus. He pats my shoulder. --There now, he tells me, it's gonna be all right. Everything's gonna be all right, Ms.... His voice trails off at that point, unsure what last name to use, but his obvious sympathy makes me cry more wretchedly.

--Dammit, I sputter, and then I try to get hold of myself. My voice sounds hoarse, like Tallulah Bankhead's used to sound.

--Shhhhh, he croons, still patting me, it's okay. It's okay. We're gonna figure this thing out for sure.

--I was in a USO show, too, I tell him, apropos of nothing. I couldn't tell you before.

--Yeah? he says, Well, what do you know. Look, he says, I'm gonna go and get you some groceries. You just make me some kinda list, okay?

--Don't leave me yet, Joe--I feel so...uneasy.

--Well now, I can't help you if I don't leave, he says gently. How about if you come with? He looks at my ravaged face. You could go and wash up a little bit and you'll be just fine.

--I can't go out there, I tell him.

--We can go down the freight elevator, he says, out the back way. I do it all the time. In fact, that's where I got my car parked. I look at him doubtfully and he grins at me. You just go ahead and get yourself together and I'll wait right here, Ms. Martin. Sullivan.

--Aja, I tell him. If we're going to be friends, you should call me Aja.

He sighs, grins again, shakes his head.

--Well, okay, he says, I'll try. But I can't guarantee I'm gonna be able to remember that every time.

*

I guess it must have been the fourth or fifth time Joe came over for dinner. Since he wouldn't take any money for all the help he was giving me (I already got a job, he told me), I'd taken to cooking for him, though I hadn't cooked in years. He would bring over his favorite recordings, and after dinner we'd sit on the couch sipping a little bourbon and listening to the greats-- Coleman Hawkins, Art Tatum, John Coltrane, Charlie Parker, Ella Fitzgerald--in the darkened living room, and the light from outside was dim and gentle as street fog on our skin. Joe said listening in the dark was the only way to get the music all the way inside you.

This particular night we were listening to some Chet Baker and Ella Fitzgerald CDs. What I remember in particular is Chet singing My Funny Valentine and Ella doing I've Got You Under My Skin. Joe and I were laughing about something, I can't even remember what, and then we just turned and leaned into each other, still laughing. Then we held each other and everything went quiet.

After a time he stood and I had a fleeting thought he might leave, but instead he took my hand and pulled me to my feet, led me to the bedroom.

Everything moved slowly then as we undressed each other, back and forth. There was a small lamp on in a corner of the bedroom, and we left it on. I wanted him, but I was afraid I wouldn't remember how to please a man, afraid I wouldn't come, afraid I would come, afraid I was too old for this, and then he was inside me and my head cleared of thoughts and worries and I could still hear Ella's voice from the living room and then I was coming, and Joe pressed hard against me all of a sudden and shuddered O sweet Jesus.

--I always knew, I whispered close to his face afterwards. The first time we talked I knew it in my skin.

He never said a word in reply, just kissed my lips, and after a while we fell asleep holding each other, time in abeyance, and the world off somewhere else.

Making love at seventy is different, I've discovered, but not necessarily in the ways I'd imagined it would be. There isn't so much athleticism, such emphasis on how we look. It's quieter but more passionate. More passionate because it's deeper, flaming inward from the surface, and holding fast there.

Though I learned long ago that love isn't the answer to everything, I'd be a fool not to realize that it makes a person less vulnerable to the world. The proof is that Joe finally talked me into going out late at night to his favorite haunt--a club in Allston called the Blue Door. We've been back several times. Though mostly we just have a couple of whiskeys and listen, we always dance at least one slow dance. On our second night there, Joe sat in with the musicians, who are all friends of his. I can't explain how it excited me to watch him making music up there. I could feel the blue, blue notes of his saxophone all through me.

That was the night he introduced me to the others--Uwe, a ruddy young German who plays the saxophone; Fidel, a muscular middle-aged drummer from Puerto Rico; Thomas, the sweet-faced vocalist who grew up in Harlem; and Michael, a tall and angular blue-black Jamaican, soft-spoken and shy, who is the most wonderful jazz pianist...his long sensitive fingers like spiders rushing over the keys. Joe introduced me as Anne, and our eyes met for a moment in the dim light before I nodded and said, How do you do.

Even in private now Joe calls me Anne. No one ever called me that after I was eighteen, and I mean no one, not even my mother who'd given me that name at birth, because for so many years I'd insisted on Aja, and it stuck. Now I'm finding I like being Anne again. Joe says it's my natural name. That amused me at first, the idea that a name could be natural, as if it were in the genes or something, but then, come to find out, Anne is my natural name. What a surprise.

Not one person has recognized me at the Blue Door--and not only because of the dim lighting, either. I'm convinced it's because in a world shaped by music, people are living more fully in the moment and aren't so worried about what everyone else is doing or who they are.

Or, let's face it, maybe none of them would know who I am, anyway. Or maybe I should say, Who I'm not. Because Aja Sullivan isn't really me. Never was, of course.

I still won't go out in my own neighborhood in daylight--who needs the prying eyes? Most evenings we stay in and I cook for us. Joe enjoys a good meal. He and I do the grocery shopping at Star Market late at night, and he takes me to my doctor's appointments in Cambridge. He says I should either try to get over my feelings about being seen or I should move to his building in Allston where there's a vacancy and no one ever seems to notice me when I visit. I'm thinking about it. In fact, I'm planning on it, though I haven't told him yet.

We haven't talked about sharing just one apartment, and though I guess it could happen, I'm not sure it ever will. Both of us like our independence.

I saw Wilma out my front window a couple of days ago--she was standing across the street with some man who had a camera. She was gesturing up towards my apartment, her hands big and flat like pancakes. She almost looked like a mime. They didn't stay long out there, and he only took a couple of photographs. Maybe it was all in my mind, but I thought he looked a little bored. It was liberating to feel that perhaps the press had lost interest in my whereabouts.

Speaking of liberating, we're going to the Blue Door again tonight to be in the music, as Joe puts it. He's going to sit in for Uwe on both sets--Uwe's girlfriend Angela is in the hospital to have their baby.

Already I'm imagining the cry of Joe's sax, the flow of that indigo sound through my veins and the pounding in my blood, a beat of certainty that comes when you're in your real skin, I've learned.

The couple across the courtyard have moved away. I have a feeling they're not together anymore, wherever they are. The apartment is still vacant, and the bedroom window is bare of cover, just as it was when they lived there, only now there's no light inside the room and the glass is black at night, black and faintly gleaming, like the eye of a camera.

The Mushrooms of Maisie Zupnik

I have a slight fever today, which makes it easier than usual to be maudlin. This is not a good day to be sick or maudlin, because my heart is freshly broken. Flattened is a better word.

If my mother were here right now, which thank God she isn't, she'd say, "You must be coming down with something."

Coming down. As if in times of good health we rode out our lives somewhere just above the surface of the earth, descending only for trips to the doctor. If my mother were here she'd also say I'm a fool to care that he's gone. That is, in fact, what she said when she was here yesterday.

"He's not worth it," she told me, her lips gathered like the top of a drawstring bag. "Be glad you found out how he is now instead of later. Don't cry over spilt milk, Jamie. Better safe than sorry, you know."

"A stitch in time saves nine," I said sourly; "Good luck comes in threes, I could've danced all night, Through the lips, over the gums--look out, Stomach, here she comes."

"Sometimes I don't understand you," she said in her worried voice as she stood to go, smoothing her beige vinyl raincoat. "Remember, you have your whole life ahead of you. Or most of it. A few good years, anyway. About four."

Now I lie on my back atop the bed and stare at the plaster ceiling, tracing its map of fine cracks. I pick up the mirror from the table beside the bed and stare at my face in the magnifying side, to make it bigger. I think I have kind of a small head. That seems a public humiliation in a way, as if it announced the size of my brain.

I try looking dead. I stare at myself for a long time, expressionless, letting my mouth fall slack, my eyes go fishy. I look a little too alive in the magnifying side, so I flip to the normal side for distance, which allows me to appear somewhat deader. I decide to see how long I can stay this way.

If it didn't wear out my arm to hold the mirror above my face like this, I figure I could sustain the pose indefinitely, so

I roll to one side and set the mirror beside me on the bed, propped against my old college copy of Anna Karenina, which I'm rereading for the despair and depression in it. This side angle feels more comfortable, and the effect is more real, too, because now my mouth kind of hangs to one side. Verisimilitude. Vronsky. Voilà.

My cell phone rings and I jump. I'm definitely not answering it. I let it go to voicemail. The mirror falls over onto the quilt. It isn't him, I know that already. Still, my hand shakes a little as I reach for the phone to see who it was.

Maisie Zupnik.

I lie back without playing her message and resume the pose without righting the mirror to view myself.

I knew it wasn't him. All the time.

"What's so compelling about her?" I say out into the air. "She wrote a book of poems she titled *Deconstructing Desire*." I hear myself as if I were listening to someone else speaking; my voice sounds strange to me out in the air--small, attenuated. I get up and pace around the bedroom, following the border of my dhurrie rug. He told me that maybe he and I had just "gotten to know each other too well."

Well, if he didn't want to be with a woman he might get to know too well, he may have a point there—how well can you know a woman who wrote a book called *Deconstructing Desire?*

"Are you saying familiarity bred contempt?" I asked him.

His face brightened. "*Exactly,*" he said. "It's not you--it just happens after a while."

I love when they say *It's not you*. Makes me want to say, *Who is it, then?*

"Well, I guess for me familiarity bred *content,*" I said. "But then I don't live my life by aphorism." Immediately regretting my admission of having been content with him, I quickly added, "Not that I was actually still content. I've…really been feeling… kind of claustrophobic recently, to tell you the truth."

He believed me. He did. Because he wanted to, I guess. His face brightened as he said, "Yes! That's it exactly."

Oh, go deconstruct yourself, I thought but didn't say. Instead, I lied and told him I'd been seeing somebody else, too. For a moment, I thought he looked perplexed, even hurt.

"You have?" he said. "Why didn't you tell me?"

I go out into the hall and pace some more, feeling the uneven grain of the floor against the balls of my bare feet. Well, why should I care if he's left me for somebody else? And even if I do, it's not important in the big picture. Of my life. I push my hands into the pockets of the pants my mother criticized yesterday.

"Why do you persist in dressing like Charlie Chaplin?" she asked me, a look of earnest curiosity on her face.

I lie back down on the bed, reach over and play Maisie's message on my voicemail, put it on speaker. I hear her voice booming into the room, inviting me over for tea and fried crackers. Fried crackers are Maisie's specialty, her own invention, she claims.

When the message ends, I set the phone upright against the potted prickly pear cactus Jake gave me for my birthday last year, and then I watch the phone standing there beside it like a little soldier. Who gets their girlfriend a cactus? I should have known we were doomed.

"Should have known," I say again, and then I reach for the mirror.

I think this time I really do look dead. Even the hands. I lie perfectly still for a time, and then the phone rings. I regard it sidelong, wary of what it might not be; feel my breath catching in my chest as if something dangerous is lodged in there, maybe some object swallowed in childhood and lost for years in the caverns of my body, only now making its way to my heart on the dark mumbling rapids of my blood--something small and hard, pointed. A bottle opener or something. Church-key.

I pick up this time. Maisie again. She's already launching into a story about a mushroom she found at the park, before I've even said hello. Maisie is a robust eighty-year-old. For five years she's been taking my Painting in Oils After Sixty class at the Golden Age Center. She was a switchboard operator in the 1950s. Went out dancing to the sounds of the big bands every chance she got. Maisie has piano legs, a wasp waist, and the hugest, most pointed tits I've ever seen. Like rockets. Well, they were like rockets until she got cancer a year ago and had one removed. She sewed and stuffed her own prosthetic breast for the missing boob, and it doesn't nearly match the other in pointiness or even quite in size--it's more like a rocket and a sand dune now. Maisie's something. Sews all her own dresses from one pattern, in different fabrics. Always has food stains on her clothes. I love her.

"Hello? Maisie?" I say, cutting in on her mushroom story.

"Yeah honey. I got your crazy voicemail last time."

"Yeah I know. Sorry I didn't answer before…I was…in… the middle of--"

Before I can think of a lie less embarrassing than the truth, she starts talking.

"So, how's tricks, honey? I was thinking about you," she says.

"You were?"

"Yeah. How come you haven't been over to see me? I found another mushroom at the park the other day. Since you weren't there to snap it, I brought it back here with me. It's in the fridge. That makes seventy-three now."

Sometimes Maisie and I go to Golden Gate Park to look for mushrooms. She claims there are over 200 varieties to be found there, and her goal is to find and collect one of each. I tag along and photograph them for her, and she puts the photos in a big album labeled THE MUSHROOMS OF MAISIE ZUPNIK.

"So what're you doin', honey?" she asks.

I look at the magnifying mirror in my left hand. Not an easy question to answer.

"Oh, just thinking about life and death," I tell her.

"What a silly kid you are," she booms. "Now why'd anyone want to think about a crazy thing like that?"

Crazy is Maisie's all-purpose adjective--she uses it the way other people use words like terrible or interesting or nice or godawful. When she was coming out of anesthesia after having her breast removed, she looked up at me and said, "Now isn't this just the craziest thing!"

And after her beloved obese dachshund, Chummy, was hit by a car and killed, she said brusquely, "What a crazy morning!" Only her eyes, glistening wet, gave her away then.

"So why don't you just trot on over here for a visit," she says.

Oh, God. Not today.

"I think I have a little fever," I lie. What's with all the lies? "I might have something you could catch," I add.

"Oh fiddle-faddle," she snorts, "pish-tosh. I don't have room for new germs! I'm full up, like a germ hotel." She guffaws at her own corny humor. "The trouble with you, honey, is you never have any fun. You're too young to lead such a dull life. Come on over to my house for some fried crackers!"

The last time I had Maisie's fried crackers I was stricken with heartburn for two and a half days. They are just literally that, too: saltine crackers taken from a box and fried in butter with a vengeance while Maisie talks a mile a minute and shifts the old cast-iron pan around on her dirty stove to keep the crackers from sticking.

Somehow, somewhere along the line, Maisie got the idea that I liked her fried crackers and now they are a condition of our visits, in much the way I imagine scones or crumpets might be de rigueur for Queen Elizabeth and her lady-in-waiting, of an afternoon. The solid truth is, I'd rather eat bees than Maisie's fried crackers.

"Yeah, okay," I tell her. "I'll be right over."

I get a fresh roll of film and my Hasselblad from the little darkroom I've rigged up just off the bathroom in what used to be a laundry area. Everyone else seems to have gone digital, but I take pride in doing it the way my idols used to. I love the process of developing those images alone in a small and silent space, watching them materialize like apparitions. Those are the moments when I really know whether a photo is true. And, yeah, it has to be true.

At the bathroom basin, I brush my teeth and wash my face quickly, trying hard not to look dead, but somehow I keep seeing the dead face in the live one now. I wonder what Maisie and I will talk about today. Mushrooms, cancer, dirty minds, her husband Floyd's forgetfulness, the Kennedys, Oprah, Amelia Earhart, body hair and estrogen. Last time our subject was religion. Maisie's a Catholic. She was talking about sin, the Seven Deadly Sins in particular. Maybe when you get cancer it makes you more conscious of sin, of trying to do right, just in case there is an afterlife.

I try to recite the Seven Deadly Sins now, as I stand before the mirror, but I keep confusing them with the Six Warning Signs of Cancer: Pride, Envy, Lust, A Sudden Change in a Wart or Mole....

My mother's Jewish and my father was Protestant, a Welshman. They settled on a connubial compromise: Just forget the whole thing. They never took me to any kind of worship, not once. Maybe that makes me a heathen. All I know is the Ten Commandments, though I'm not even sure I can remember all of them. Ten Commandments, Seven Wonders of the World. Twelve Apostles, Seven Dwarfs. Peter, Matthew, John, Paul, Sneezy.

Now I run through the Ten Commandments while I pass a cold wet washcloth over my clean face, to close the pores. Which commandment makes lying a sin? I can never remember, but I've been breaking that commandment a lot lately, whichever one it is--like when I told Jake I was fine with breaking up, fine that he'd found someone else he didn't feel he "knew too well." That I'd been seeing someone else, too. Well, that wasn't a complete lie—I'd been seeing a lot of Maisie Zupnik, whether I felt like it or not. She was really calling me all the time, lately.

Back in the bedroom I change to a clean white shirt, one that Jake left here the night before he broke up with me, tuck it into my baggy pants, and head over to Maisie's, my broken heart concealed in the way a fugitive robber might conceal a bullet wound from the law-abiding public, and as I walk I feel that heavy bag of grief knocking against my rib cage from time to time, just to remind me it's there, and will be, even in the semi-polite society of Maisie Zupnik.

Maisie's Find No. 73--a small sticky mushroom she says is a Rosy Russula—has now been photographed from several angles. Blackberry tea is steeping in a brown teapot and the crackers are sizzling in butter. Maisie is cackling about something while I sit nearby at the little blue drop-leaf table, looking around her kitchen. She doesn't see so well anymore and every cupboard door is gummy and soiled around the edges. There's what looks like egg-yolk on the stove and the floor, but that is the least of the stove's problems, or the floor's. There's a thin layer of grease over everything. Dust-bunnies clog corners. Maisie has three different kinds of food stains on her lime green polyester dress. She's happy as a clam and I feel strangely at home.

Out the kitchen window next to where I sit, I see her laundry flapping on the line in the cool gray afternoon air. The Victorian across the way has been painted teal, plum, gray, and ivory. Maisie and Floyd bought their half of this Noe Valley duplex forty years ago, before the neighborhood went upscale. Theirs is the only place on the block that hasn't been renovated-- even the other side of this duplex has been scraped and painted, re-roofed and landscaped.

Maisie has a soft cloth stuck in the neck of her dress today, where yesterday's radiation therapy burned her flesh pink. Her homemade prosthesis has slipped askew, and seems to be pointing down and in, while her real breast points up and out.

"That Floyd," she laughs, "what a dope. He walked all over the house this morning looking for his hat, and it was on his head the whole time. Did you ever hear anything so crazy?"

"Where is he now, Maisie?"

"Oh he went to play that crazy shuffleboard. He's been going off to do that every day, lately--thank God, or I'd go nuts!"

Floyd had a minor stroke ten months ago and had to retire, under protest, from the car dealership where he worked part time. He'd started forgetting the makes and models of the cars. I watch Maisie draining the fried crackers on a white and blue paper towel, and I'm kind of horrified to see her starting a second batch.

She drops a glop of butter from a big spoon into the smoking pan, and we watch it sizzle and melt. She takes some saltines from a generic box and lays them carefully in the pan, where they begin to fry and darken. I see my foot wiggling, and I realize I'm thinking of Jake again, wondering if he could be stopping by my place now, while I'm away, having had the sudden realization that his new girlfriend is shallow and foolish. Or just to get his shirt.

Maisie sets a melamine plate in front of me with about a thousand fried crackers heaped on it, still draining into a fresh paper towel.

"Now eat 'em!" she barks, and I begin my work. As I munch and swallow, I think Why would I want to see him, anyway?

"Have a nice deconstructed life," I mutter, momentarily losing track of where I am.

"What?" Maisie says from the stove. She's lifting the second batch of crackers one by one with a spatula onto another white and blue paper towel. The cloth at her neckline has slipped, and I wince at the redness of her exposed skin.

"Does it hurt, Maisie?"

"What," she says, "this? Oh, not so much, but there's a terrible itch down deep inside here somewhere and I almost go crazy trying to get to it."

I notice suddenly how much less zaftig Maisie looks today, then I begin to wonder if she could be dying from this. It seems to be the first time I've truly considered the possibility, she's always so lively and vehement, sputtering and gesturing, talking non-stop.

"You know," she says, "it's just the luckiest thing the trouble has been on my left side, not my right. If it had been my right boob, it'd be more of a problem, with me being right-handed. Might make it harder to sew and knit. Or paint. I guess I could still do those crazy mushrooms with my left hand, though, since picking 'em is all I need to do, just one yank. Number 73...that's 127 to go, kiddo."

Maisie turns then, suddenly silent, spatula in hand, and looks at me full on. I wonder if it's fear I see in her eyes.

"How soon do you think you'll have today's pictures developed?" she asks me. "The newsletter at the Senior Center wants to run a piece about my mushrooms in their Hobbies After Sixty column. I want to give them pictures of my favorite ones, and this rosy rossula is my all-time favorite so far." For a minute our two gazes lock and fuse across the greasy kitchen.

Just then Floyd walks in, tall and skinny like a stork, a down jacket on and a green knit cap pulled way down over his ears. I remember when Maisie was knitting that cap. Floyd is still a nice looking man, even in his eighties. He hangs his coat on the door peg, moving with easy grace; leaves the hat on.

"Oh," he says mildly when he sees me, "now, what's your name again?"

"Jamie," I tell him. We go through this each time, and it's become a social ritual, like shaking hands.

"Yep, that's right," he says, as if he was just testing me and I've answered correctly. Then he leans to kiss Maisie. They kiss on the lips, and not just a peck, either. A full-on-the-mouth kiss that lingers a second or two. I feel that foreign object in my chest again, the church-key, moving dangerously close to my heart, getting in the way of things like breath and pleasure.

Maisie pats Floyd on the cheek and says gruffly, "Take that hat off."

"No," he says. "It keeps my whole body warm, not just my head." Then he does a double take at the plate on the blue table, and his face brightens like a kid's.

"Crackers!" he says, making a beeline for the plate.

I wonder how many hundreds of times Maisie has fried crackers for Floyd in the fifty-eight years they've been married, and how he has managed to sustain such joy. I watch his bony hands, their veins and spots, as he reaches delicately for one cracker at a time and chews with his eyes closed. I think of Jake, his sinewy hands, feel my eyes filling up. I look down, pop a cracker into my mouth as a diversion just in case someone might be looking. *I'm the one who knows you.* Familiarity, I reminded myself then. Breeds contempt.

I think I'm already starting to get fried cracker heartburn. I look up and see Maisie's eyes on me.

"I gotta go," I say, and grab my camera case, sling the strap over my shoulder. "See you in class on Tuesday, Maisie?"

"Don't you always, honey?" she says.

I walk up Chenery Street to the bus against the wind, past houses and yards, eucalyptus trees. In one otherwise decorous three-story house I spy a lone third floor window painted with a moon and stars, like those pictures of Haight Ashbury during the Summer of Love. I have never understood time very well.

I look back once at Floyd and Maisie's place, shabby and peeling amid the stylish transformations all around it. When Maisie walked me to the front door, Floyd stayed at the blue table in his green knit cap, snarfing fried crackers, a dreamy look on his face. As usual, each time I turned to leave, Maisie found something else to tell me. It always takes about a dozen goodbyes before I can pry myself free from Maisie Zupnik. The older people get, the longer it seems to take them to say good bye.

When I get back home, I take out my phone and check my voicemail. No message. I stare at it for a moment, and then Maisie pops into my mind, how our eyes caught and held for a second, unblinking, in her kitchen; the momentary panic I thought I saw there. The mirror is still lying on the quilt next to Anna Karenina. I sit on the edge of the bed for a minute, then stand and go into the darkroom to develop Maisie's film.

Earthly Luck

--It's not the World Out There, I said. It's something smaller, easier to disappear in, not heroic.

I was trying to describe my new life.

--Do you have many lovers? he asked. Things always get back to sex for Jonathan, I suddenly remembered, which may have been the quality I liked most and least in him when we were married.

We went for a walk by the ocean then, which did not help. But of course, it's never easy to become reacquainted with a person. Nor with an ocean. In the case of the person, so much has usually changed, so many presences have intruded with the passage of time, that you feel in some way crowded.

And in the case of an ocean, exactly nothing has changed, which allows you to feel as if you've never been gone from it, which only serves to remind you that you have indeed been gone from it. Which makes you feel keenly the loss of it from your life.

But after all, didn't I choose to leave the ocean five years ago when I fell in love with Will Shanley, brilliant playwright who once had a play produced for National Public Television, and who lives like a hermit in Blue Eye, Nebraska?

And didn't I, for that matter, leave a husband, as well? Whom I loved, but felt I couldn't trust? And with whom I was now strolling by the ocean?

And didn't I leave a life that allowed me luxuries like silk dresses, health insurance, and good wine? And my days free to pursue my writing?

--No, I don't have any lovers at all, I finally said. --Mostly I don't even think about sex these days. Really.

I could tell he didn't believe me.

--I've changed, I told him.

--No one could change that much, he answered.

I thought of Will then. Of how he literally took me that first time. I'd always thought the term *took,* as in he took her swiftly and without sentiment, was sexist and dumb. But the first time I went to bed with Will he undressed me, then undressed himself, looking me over all the while. I wondered if this was his idea of foreplay. And though I was to discover as time went on what a scholar of every sort of foreplay he was, this first time he simply pushed me back on the bed and took me. Never asked about me. Did not show the slightest concern for my pleasure.

And even though I didn't come that first time, it was in some way thrilling. Like being run over by a train in the dark.

That was before he fell in love with one of his students.

That was before my mother, Eileen Sweeney O'Toole, who's never gotten over being Irish, wrote me the first of several letters mentioning earthly luck. How we should never give up in our quest for it. No matter how badly we've screwed up our lives. Earthly luck, she wrote, is a horse of many colors. My Mother has a facility for malapropism.

That was, in fact, three months before I sold the house in San Diego and took the twins out of school, packed us up, shipped our furniture ahead, and moved to Blue Eye, Nebraska where Will told me in short order that although he realized he'd asked me to move there, seeing me with two thirteen-year-olds to raise and a house to run took the magic out of it somehow.

How can I help but see you differently now, is how I believe he put it.

And there I was, in Blue Eye, Nebraska.

--Why have you stayed there, Jonathan asks over dinner. I mean, *why?*

--I didn't want to come back to California with nothing to show for it.

--Wouldn't that have been better than staying in Blue Eye with nothing to show for it? he inquires, working intently on his sushi.

I watch him, never having understood how people can be logical and eat at the same time. I don't tell him what Alf Brandert, my editor, has said more than once. That I only stay in Blue Eye because I hold out hope that someday Will and I might get back together if I stay in the vicinity.

I wouldn't take Will Shanley back, not on a platter, but I find it too embarrassing somehow to tell Alf--or Jonathan--the real reason I can't leave Blue Eye: I'm broke...I haven't the money to leave, now that I'm here. There. A fine mess I've got myself into. It'd cost a fortune to ship everything home again, and once I scraped up that money, how would I afford San Diego's high dollar rent and still limit my work to half-time jobs to leave time for my writing?

I figure I've already disgraced myself as a romantic sap anyway, by moving to Blue Eye for Will. Why add economic ruin to my list of public embarrassments?

Involuntary exile is way more humiliating than the voluntary kind, no matter what the reason.

I fiddle with my sushi. No way I'm telling Jonathan I'm broke.

Instead I tell him that under no circumstances will I consider eating the raw quail egg before me though I will be happy to eat the salmon eggs that form a bed beneath it.

--You still haven't got used to sushi, he says.

--Remember, Jonathan, there isn't a sushi bar on every street corner in Blue Eye. Anyway, a lot of things about So Cal make me laugh, now that I'm away from it all.

--Sushi isn't California cuisine, it's *Japanese,* he says, as if he were talking to a wheat farmer who'd just stepped down off the combine to ask for dining information.

--Whatever, I say.

--And anyway, he says, what's this California attitude? You're a native Californian, remember? Could it be you've absorbed some of that provincial heartland attitude towards the Coast?

I bite my tongue to avoid saying how much I hate hearing people refer to it as the Coast, as if it were the only one. Coast. Instead I just grin at him and say, Well, at least you don't wear white shoes and a pinky ring. Yet.

--Don't insult me, he says.

We sit quietly for a while, chewing and thinking.

--I blame myself for our breakup, he tells me.

--It wasn't all your fault.

--You stopped loving me, he says.

We both know that isn't true. In the least. But we're both silent for a time.

--I lost faith, I finally tell him. Someone else touched me in a way that gave me new faith, so I left, but then he didn't meet my train. The kids and I got off the Amtrak in Obart, Nebraska at three in the morning and no one was there. We walked down the dusty main street of town, and no one was anywhere. Nothing was open. We saw a light flickering in the window of a storefront down the block. We walked to it with our suitcases bulging, the twins in front of me on the sidewalk. The Nebraska winter cold was sharp and unfamiliar against our faces. The sight of Andy's ears bent outward from his knit cap like pearlescent handles filled me with dumb grief. Inside the storefront with blue lights we found a fat couple: the man was wearing a sleeveless undershirt and some oil-stained green polyester slacks. The woman had on a gaping chenille robe. Her red hair had gray roots and was held back by black bobby pins. I hadn't seen bobby pins in anyone's hair since I was a kid. The light I'd seen flickering was their TV. They had a small cab service. Always waited up, they told us, for the three o'clock train. The wind-up clock on the man's TV tray said 3:11. His name was Mervil Shank.

Jonathan has paused over his sushi.

--That has an odd appeal, he says, the way you tell it. Walking down the sidewalk, I mean, of a one-street midwestern town at three a.m.

He says it as if what I'd described contained some sort of Real Life ambience. Southern Californians often pine for that.

--Sounds good to you, eh? I level my gaze at him and keep it there, to shame him. He pops a quail egg into his mouth.

--Well, it's easy for you to say, I mutter.

--Mwrrf, is all he says.

--Don't insult me, I reply.

--How's your writing coming along?

--I write nearly every day.

--But are you sending it out?

--No.

--What does your pal in New York say about that?

--What does any editor say about that? He says if I don't get the book to him soon, I can forget it. But I know he doesn't mean it.

--What about magazines? Are you sending your work out to magazines?

--No.

I sigh, look out at the ocean. Earthly Luck, my mother wrote in a recent letter, is there for every one of us on God's Green Earth. But sometimes we don't know Earthly Luck when we come face to face with it, so we squander it or turn away from it. When that happens, we have only ourselves to blame. My mother is fond of pointing out things like that.

I look at the Jonathan's hands, his long fingers like a carpenter's fingers. It's easy to remember why I loved him from the night I met him, though I mustn't let myself forget that Jonathan can be a difficult man. He has a volatile temper and can be impatient with such mundanities as fidelity.

He is also the only man I've ever known who cared about my work.

Let me revise that: he is the only man I've ever slept with who cared about my work.

Most men I've met are incapable of doing both with a woman at the same time.

Will's mother Myrtle told me once, The problem is that both you and Will are overflowing with devotion and concern--for Will.

She was right and I resented her for it

--How long will you be in California, Jonathan asks me.

--I can only stay a few days, I say. Just to get the kids set for college. I have to avoid his eyes because that is a lie. I could stay for two months if I wanted. But then I wouldn't be able to bear going back to Blue Eye. And I have a contract with the Nebraska State Arts Council. To teach poetry writing to the blind. Starting in October, which is two months away. In Blue Eye and surrounding counties.

--I wish you could stay longer, he says. I look at his hands.

--So do I.

He puts his arms around me and I can hear the ocean behind the pounding sound that is either in his chest or in my skull. It's easy to remember why I loved him. Beyond his hands and my work.

--I don't want to be someone you have to tell Clare about, I say. Clare is the woman he lives with now. When she isn't bobbing noses in San Francisco.

--I have no intention of talking to Clare about us. This thing with you and me--it was before her, before everything.

--Well, I don't want to be someone you don't tell her about, either.

He sighs.

Obart, Nebraska is about seventy miles away from Blue Eye, but it is the nearest Amtrak stop. We had Mervil Shank drive us to the Obartian Arms, which looked like a Holiday Inn gone bad. Gone worse. The twins slept fine, as kids often do, Andy on his stomach, his face crushed into the pillow, mouth open in an astonished sort of way, Bird snoozing on her back, arms up like a holdup victim, the front of her tee-shirt sporting the legend, Toto, where the hell are we? which inexplicably caused my eyes to well up a little.

I sat up and smoked till five thirty A.M., a half-full pack of Parliaments I found in the drawer of the bed stand with a red Bic lighter. I don't smoke, wasn't sure how to, had last smoked a cigarette when I was fourteen and trying to be cool, but I smoked every cigarette, as if changing one longstanding truth about myself might help me to accommodate other personal changes more difficult and of obscure, still undisclosed necessity.

Obartian, I thought. What have I done to my children.

He'd asked me, pleaded with me, to move to Nebraska so we could be together. Once a man has found a woman who understands his jokes, pleases his eye, replaces his muse, and satisfies fantasies he didn't even know he had, life stalls, Will had written me, and he can't go on unless he has her with him.

That was easy for him to say.

A lot of things are easy for people to say, I've noticed, and those are the things I try not to believe. These days.

After dinner we drove to the Del Mar beach house Jonathan took after our divorce, and which he still keeps, although he and Clare often stay at her La Jolla place when she's in town.

Clare is a plastic surgeon who divides her time between San Diego and San Francisco. Jonathan is a psychologist-turned-entrepreneur who divides his time between Los Angeles and San Diego. I teach poetry writing to the blind in Blue Eye, Nebraska. And surrounding counties.

But I still have the silk dresses, which I do not wear, having no place to wear them in Blue Eye.

I do not still have the good wine, having long since guzzled it.

I do not have the group health insurance, since I do not have a group.

Nor do I still have the free time to pursue my writing as I used to.

Nor do I still have my kids with me, having helped them to relocate to their father's place in Orange County because they can attend a good college more affordably in California than is possible in Nebraska. And they can reestablish connections with relatives and friends they haven't had a chance to spend time with in five years. That's always been our plan. And of course they are almost eighteen, an age when lots of kids move away to go to school.

And I will stay on in Blue Eye, Nebraska where I know I can afford to live without working so many hours that I haven't any time at all to write. I will teach poetry writing to the blind, half time.

And my second husband is walking beside me near the ocean. My ex-second husband. Sounds pretty Southern California I know, but it never seemed so in reality.

The kids' father, my first husband, is a fire chief who wears sweatpants at every possible moment of his life. And who once, in a restaurant of his choice--I believe it was called the Raging Bull--told me that I could not order the baked potato with my steak because it cost extra. And who then ordered himself a baked potato, saying that he was larger than I and needed it more.

Then I married Jonathan, who is now walking beside me near the ocean, which doesn't help at all, and whom I always loved although I suspected he was fooling around on me--well, okay, people told me he was--and I finally left him in a lapse of faith and ran off to Blue Eye, Nebraska to be with another man--a hermit who tired of me in seven months and fell in love with one of his students, a girl of nineteen who thought white bread was elegant and whole wheat ethnic. And who had once confided in me her philosophy of make-up.

Am I making all this sound as if I never really loved Will? Because if I am, it's not true. I loved him. My mother says I was addicted to him. I realize the two statements are not the same, but I imagine both were true. The thing is, it's never easy to explain love or addiction.

Her philosophy of make-up was that a woman should wear it at all times, including to bed at night, because otherwise she would have two different faces, one for daytime and one for night. And that would be phony, she told me, to have two different faces.

--I can't stand anything phony, she said.

--I think you should come into my bedroom, Jonathan tells me now, and I think to myself, Your bedroom--though she undoubtedly sleeps there with you fairly regularly and has two or three sheer nightgowns hanging in the closet.

But I say nothing except to ask if I can use the bathroom, and he says yes. I go past the one in the hall and toward the one that must be in the master bedroom, remembering that he has said there are two bathrooms in his townhouse at the beach.

--Wait, he says, there's a bathroom off the hall--you just walked past it.

--That's okay, I tell him. And I keep walking.

Sure enough, some black cotton Eileen Fisher stretch capris are there, same size I wear, hung to dry, and a terrific batiked linen shirt by Issey Miyake. Next to them, hanging over the towel bar, is a silk shirt--the roomy kind of shirt I love--in a sort of Mondrian-looking magenta, black, and yellow tiny geometric print. I look at the label: Armani. Suddenly I know I can't go to bed with Jonathan. Before I leave the bathroom, I spritz some of her Hermes Rouge perfume behind my ears, just to mess with his mind.

When the kids and I got to Blue Eye, which we accomplished early the next day by asking Mervil Shank to drive us the entire seventy miles in his taxi (and which cost just $47), we went straight to Will's house. (Wait till you meet him, I told them. We've talked to him on the phone a jillion times, Bridget answered; Yeah, we already know him, said Andrew. Yes, but he's much better in person, I told them as I rapped on his front door.)

He wasn't home. Wasn't home, though he'd told me that the day I was due in to Blue Eye would be so red-letter that he wouldn't think of leaving his house for even a minute. That was, in case he was unable to drive to Obart and pick us up at the depot. Which he apparently had been. Unable.

So we had Mervil Shank, the Obartian cabbie, drive us to the Blue Eye Hilton. Which I later learned was being enjoined by the Hilton Hotel chain to stop using their name. It seemed that Jimmie Dean Hilton, local Blue Eye hotelier, could not see where he was in the wrong for using his own name above the official Hilton Hotel logo. The Blue Eye Hilton became, in time, the Blue Eye Hillside inn, though there was not a hill for a hundred miles in any direction.

--I can't possibly sleep with you *now*, I tell him.

--Why? What do you mean now?

--I've seen her clothes. Somehow it makes a difference. Now I perceive her as real. A little hung up on designer labels, but real, in a way, all the same.

--I don't want to hurt you, he says. If it would hurt you, let's forget it.

I hate him for saying that. Even though it's true that I can't sleep with him now anyway. Having seen her clothes.

--I love you for that, I tell him. *Really.*

--How about some Chet Baker? he suggests. He remembers that Chet is my favorite.

--I'd prefer Mozart, I tell him. Or Willie Nelson.

I'm punishing him.

--Sure, he obliges, and puts on The Magic Flute.

What else, I think, feeling snide. I close my eyes; imagine Clare as Queen of the Night. Somehow it helps.

He takes me in his arms again.

--Let's just lie close together, he says. I understand about the rest.

I look at his hands and my eyes fill up. I look down so he won't see, and that causes some tears to fall onto his right hand. He kindly pretends not to notice. But I know him better than that.

I know him better than anything.

Which doesn't help.

If anyone had told me that Will would fall for Tiffani Lynn Snapper, I'd have laughed. I would never in my life have believed such a thing. She personified everything he claimed to despise in a female: artificiality (she wore eye shadow under her cheekbones!), superficiality, giddiness, vanity. (Okay, maybe he regularly made exceptions for female vanity, I can't be a complete hypocrite. And I have to admit that behind the gaudy make-up, her skin was like a Botticelli. A nineteen year old flame-haired Botticelli.)

When she had the lead in the spring play at the college, soon after I arrived in Blue Eye, I'd gotten to know her (as far as one can get to know someone like that) because Will had called on me to help design the sets. So she knew all about Will and me. Knew I'd moved to Blue Eye to be with him.

And I realized much too late that her awareness of that--my moving there to be with him--had made him more interesting in her eyes. I remember the day she and I were backstage as she waited for rehearsal to begin, and she asked me why in the world I'd ever moved to Blue Eye in the first place.

--I'd give anything to live where you moved from, she said. Southern California is my ideal place to live! Someday I'm going to go there to act or be a stylist to the stars. What did you do there? Are you an actress?

--I wrote, I said. Did script consultation for a few TV shows that had begun to slide in the ratings. Sold a couple of pilots, too, but they never got made. Poetry's my real work, though, and I can do that anywhere.

--But you don't get much money for poetry, do you?

--No, poets and playwrights rarely get rich. I'm sure Will would tell you that, I added, warming as I looked over to where he was standing as he coached the male lead. Which is why, I told her, I'm going to have to find some teaching, pronto.

--But why in the world did you ever move to a dead little place like this?

--I thought you knew why, I said.

--No. Why?

--To be with Will.

--*Will?* she said incredulously, and I could see her looking over toward him, no doubt appraising his worn jacket and tattered jeans. You moved here to be with Will?

--Well, yeah. We needed to be together. It's misery being passionately in love from half a continent away.

Her eyes--there's no other way I can say it--widened. She looked over once again to where he was standing, and I wished I hadn't said *passionately.* There was curiosity all over her face.

We get up from the couch and go for another walk by the ocean.

--It's hard to believe you're thirty-seven, he says. You look about twenty-five. Twenty-seven at most.

--Thirty-six, I say.

--What?

--I'm thirty-six.

--Well, whatever. You look even younger than you did when you left five years ago.

It's possible, I think to myself; things had become pretty tense with him toward the end—he was working all the time and his temper was always on alert. There were rumors about the late hours he spent with his secretary. Anyway, what good is it to look twenty-five or twenty-seven? Why can't I look nineteen? Maybe then things would be different. I despise myself for allowing such a thought to enter my highly evolved head. I know better, and I know it.

--I blame myself for your leaving, he says. If I'd given you the affection and support you deserved, you'd never have gone.

--That's easy for you to say, I smile. And I kiss his neck.

--Was it good with him?

--Yes.

--Were you tired of me?

--No.

--Yes you were.

--No. I was never tired of you. It's just that something happened. I lost faith in us. And then I met him. I can't describe it. But I never stopped caring about you.

--Don't tell me you didn't love him, because I won't believe you.

--I'm not telling you that.

I found out eventually that Will had told everyone who asked that he didn't know why I had moved to Blue Eye. You'd have to ask her about that, they tell me he said. How should I know why she moved here?

Which, of course, gave them all the idea that he was some kind of romantic god and I was some pathetic stalker, enamored of the man who'd written "Buffalo Gothic" and had it produced for public television. Because by that time a lot of people also knew what I'd told Tiffani Lynn. That I'd moved to Blue Eye to be with Will.

I have never felt so betrayed.

I kick off my shoes and walk toward the water. Jonathan doesn't ask where I'm going. That's one thing I like about Jonathan. He doesn't ask you about everything you do. Unlike me.

Before I reach the water I lift the hem of my dress and run, keep running till I'm in the surf, wet dress holding my body the way plastic-wrap hugs cheese. I just want to be inside all this movement, oblivious to everything outside it. Yippee, I say softly, in order to relieve the moment of any lurking drama. Yeehaw.

Life is full of signs, my mother has said, but usually we are not smart enough to respect them as we should. That, or we want something enough that we don't want to read the signs.

Like the day in the Blue Eye New World Laundromat when Will told me that he never felt he'd had his share of women. His *share.*

I nearly dropped the blouse I was folding, watched him continue his own folding as if he'd said nothing unusual. I thought we were madly in love. I reached into the basket for a washcloth to fold.

--Well, how many have you had? I asked him, not knowing what else to say.

--Oh, somewhere in the teens, he answered, looking a little startled. I didn't usually ask him about his past, and my question probably surprised us both too much for either of us to stop and question it. But upon further consideration, it seemed to me that if he'd brought it up, he was asking for it.

Then came his question, which I suppose I had coming, too.

--How many men have you been with?

I thought it was funny the way he referred to *having* women, but *being with* men.

--Three, I answered. I was embarrassed by the dearth, but what was the point in lying?

--Counting me?

--Yeah.

--And the other two were your husbands.

--Obviously, yes.

--Well, Will said after a moment, I guess that's plenty for a woman.

Now, I agreed that three was plenty for me, since Will completely satisfied me sexually, but I had to fold three towels before I could stop shaking with simple indignation--at least I was pretty sure that's what it was--that he considered three *plenty* for me, while at the same time considering somewhere in the teens to be less than his share.

--I miss clotheslines, I said then, and I think fabric softeners are so false. I turned to him amid the sounds of tumbling laundry. And, I told him, I don't know what you're talking about.

--Honey, he said, you're rambling again. And then he put his arm around me, gave me a squeeze and added, But you have a marvelous ass.

--Sure, I told him. But what about the fearless beauty of my poetry? And the innovative tension of my line-breakage?

I knew he thought I was kidding around. Still I waited to see if he would answer.

This is not the World Out There. It's something smaller, easy to disappear in, not heroic.

The flight back was rough. We had to circle Denver for thirty minutes due to turbulent weather. My connecting flight, which came into Denver from Portland and would carry me to Omaha, was an hour late.

I think it hurt Jonathan that I wouldn't sleep with him. How could I explain all the reasons? The more reasons you give for something, the more false you sound.

By the time I'd driven from Omaha to Blue Eye, a two-hour drive, I was practically hallucinating from exhaustion.

The house was, of course, exactly as I'd left it. I didn't go into the kids' rooms but I went through the rest of the house, room to room, greeting plants and furniture with a kind of quiet pleasure. I thought of all the people in the world, including myself, about whom my mother could have said, They have only themselves to blame.

I mused on that for a while, and I knew there was no one else I wanted to blame.

--Your life would go on just as always, I'd told Jonathan. Imagining he might say, What? Go on as always? How could my life go on as always once we'd made love again after all these years?

It's true neither of us would ever go back to the other now. Still, I guess I was wishing to hear him say that making love with me again would change his life somehow.

Instead he simply said, That's true.

--That's easy for you to say, I told him. You don't live a celibate life in Blue Eye, Nebraska.

--You're shivering, he said. You shouldn't have run into the ocean with all your clothes on.

--The ocean is the only thing that hasn't changed, I answered. And I thought, I'd take an ocean over a person any day. Myself included.

--I love you, I told him.

--I've always loved you, he said.

When we hit a spot of turbulence just before landing in Omaha, I happened to look around the plane at all the faces nearby. As the plane rocked and drifted, you could see it in the jaws, almost to a one, the tensing and straining to get us down past that last small expanse of sky. All those faces, like my own, straining toward earthly luck.

The Unseen

Say what you will about ghosts and the people who believe in them, but until you've lived in an attic with one, you don't know diddly about poltergeists. Poltergeist: Just the word makes you think of those '80s horror films. Pop culture has appropriated an entire realm of human existence. Of course, pop culture has appropriated *everything*, but at the moment I'm just talking about the category of human existence we think of as ghostly, if we think of it at all. People often forget that ghosts are humans. *Dead* humans, sure, non-corporeal, but humans all the same. To classify their existence as the paranormal is so reductive, gives them a bad rap going in, and causes people who might otherwise be inclined toward belief to deny that they've even considered the possibility. Especially here in America, where materiality is of the essence.

Think how unsettling that would be, if you were a ghost. And let's face it, you could be one someday.

Why is it such a leap to believe in ghosts if we can believe in electricity? You can't see it, either.

It may be easier for me to believe in them than it would be for some people since I was raised in the house of my Irish grandmother, who believes in miracles, telepathy, the spirit world, and all things paranormal. Gran is from County Cork, Ireland, and claims to have seen apparitions of several major saints, including both St. Theresas--the Little Flower and the Great St. Theresa, a.k.a. St. Theresa of Avila. Gran has a facility for apparitions and visions, and she isn't a bit shy about mentioning it--all the more so now that she's in her eighties. In the early days, this caused the rest of us--my mother, my sister Ann, and me--some social awkwardness, but it also taught us to have faith in the unseen. And we all have that in spades.

My mother, for example, became a nun the moment Ann and I were grown. And Ann is today a microbiologist, if you see what I mean. Vis à vis faith in the unseen. Just on the two of them I could rest my case. As for me, I write children's books, so I guess I didn't carry an awareness of the unseen into my vocational deliberations--but then, writers don't deliberate about being writers anyway--they just start writing one day, as if someone invisible were making them do it. We call the source of that impulse our muse, so if you think about it, I, too, move with confidence among unseen elements. I think it's obvious that all of us in the Flanagan family have been affected by my grandmother's rapport with the unseen.

I refer only to the family members I've spent time with: I can't speak for my father, Thomas Flanagan, because he *is* the unseen. He ran off with our babysitter, Gracie, when I was six and Ann was eleven, and never even came back to get his clothes. All my life since then, I've imagined him running naked through the world, voluptuous red-haired Gracie straining to keep up with him, a TV dinner in each of her freckled hands. Gracie always fixed Ann and me Swanson TV dinners when she babysat us--meatloaf for me, turkey for Ann--but we never did get our dinners the night she ran off with our dad.

Mama was taking a class at Harvard Divinity School that night, and Daddy wasn't home, so Gracie was minding us. Daddy was supposed to be at a Knights of Columbus lodge meeting, so I remember how odd it seemed when he came to get Gracie just after Mama left the house. He gave Ann and me each a dollar bill and told us to 'be good.' The only thing I recall about that night after Dad and Gracie left is my sister fixing the two of us peanut butter sandwiches for dinner while we waited for our mother to come home from her class. Anyway, the point is that I don't know what my father believes in or doesn't. I don't even know if he's still alive. When I close my eyes, I can't picture his face.

Mama moved the three of us into Gran's little house in South Boston then, the house where my father grew up. Gran was my father's mother, but she and my mom got along fine, maybe because they were united in their anger at Daddy for leaving his family. I think Gran always felt it was her duty as his mother to make that up to us somehow.

Mama never dated at all, after he left; in fact, she and Daddy never actually filed for divorce--she always said a divorce would do her no good anyway, since a Catholic couldn't remarry in the Church without an annulment, anyway. And Mama wasn't up for that because, as I heard her telling Gran once, an annulment effectively erased a marriage as if it had never existed at all--and that would render her children 'spiritual bastards.'

Four months after I graduated from high school, Mama left us to enter a convent in Northern Wisconsin. I was seventeen, and Ann was twenty-two and married by then. Mama handed each of us a holy card with the Blessed Mother on it, said, "Bless you, my darlings," and that was the last we ever saw of her. She belongs to a cloistered order of nuns called The Sisters of Everlasting Good Will. They spend each day praying for and loving all mankind, though they refuse to speak to it. That was nearly fifteen years ago, and since the nuns of Mama's order don't make phone calls, receive visitors, go home for visits, use e-mail, or write letters, I guess you could say my mother, too, has become the unseen.

Ann is married to a plumber, Patrick Byrne. A microbiologist married to a plumber may seem a bit of a mismatch, but they've been crazy in love since high school, and anyway, when you think of it, the two professions do have certain things in common. Microorganisms abound in Patrick's work, for example. Also, he, like Ann, spends his time investigating what lies beneath the visible surface of things. Ann says I always strain to find connections between any two things, no matter how unrelated they may actually be.

"You look for connections everywhere," she tells me, "because you feel so unconnected in your life."

She is referring to the fact that although I'm thirty-three I've never married. I've been engaged four times, so I guess that has kept me distracted. Ann says the problem is more that I don't want to risk being left, so I leave every man before he can leave me. It's a problem I'm going to have to deal with eventually, she says, or I'll grow old alone.

I don't see this as a problem. Gran's alone, and she's okay--and anyway, as I see it, I have plenty of family already. Ann's kids are great--Nan and Dan. (I tried to convince her not to give her kids rhyming names--it's so trivializing--but like most scientists, she doesn't have the best taste in the world.) Nan is nine and Dan is eleven. I write all my stories with them in mind--in fact, that was how I got into children's fantasy literature in the first place--telling Nan and Dan stories when I babysat them. (Ann has never felt comfortable with non-related babysitters, for obvious historical reasons).

Every Sunday we all converge on Gran's little house in Southie with covered dishes--Ann and Patrick, Nan and Dan, and me. Gran doesn't cook anymore, except for her specialty-- apple cobbler with an alarmingly hefty crust, which is her weekly contribution to our Sunday dinners. It's great to go back each week to the house we grew up in--it gives our lives continuity. Lots of people don't have continuity these days, which is too bad since it's an important part of making sense of your life. Once you've lost continuity, you can't ever get it back—it's a lot like virginity in that sense, though of much more intrinsic value in the big picture.

The only thing I don't care for about these family dinners is that every single Sunday, at some point, someone brings up my unmarried state.

"You'll have to get married pretty soon," Gran told me last Sunday, "or it'll be too late and you'll end up an old maid."

Nan and Dan tittered. I sent them a significant stare and they stopped immediately. I didn't know exactly how to respond to Gran at first--I don't like to be irritable with her because she's so old, but this kind of talk bugs me no end. As anyone who knows Gran could have predicted, though, she started talking again before I could speak anyway, and saved me the effort of a reply. One of the benefits of being part of the Flanagan family is that you don't have to talk too much if you don't want to. Just wait a beat and someone else will jump in.

"You're thirty-three, " Gran told me, raising a brow. "That's exactly how old Christ was when he was crucified, you know."

"So...unless I get married soon, I'll be crucified?" I asked her.

"Don't be sassy," she said, "I was just making a point. Would you care for some more ham?"

But I wasn't letting go, now that I'd got hold of this.

"Are you saying Jesus was crucified because he was single, Gran? He was strung up by the militant marriage lobby?"

A hush fell over the table. Ann nudged me. Even I knew I'd gone too close to sacrilege for Gran's taste. The Flanagans are not fond of sacrilege. Or anyway, most of them aren't.

"No...*Kate,*" Gran answered slowly and with a deliberateness that suggested she was steamed, "I'm not saying Jesus was crucified because He was single. I'm simply saying that apparently God considered thirty-three years an adequate period of time for His Only Begotten Son to Complete His Work in the World. I'm saying that thirty-three is evidently Old Enough to Know What You Want."

Gran often speaks in capital letters for emphasis. You can hear them.

"Maybe I want to live alone all my life," I said.

"Oh *no,*" Gran countered, "You don't want *that.* Marriage is the Natural State. Mary and Joseph gave us that example For a Reason."

There was no point in mentioning to Gran that she herself had remained single in the nearly three decades since Grandpa Seamus died; no point at all, because she still considered herself married to him and often spoke to him fondly or caustically, as circumstances and his post-death behavior warranted. Before I could answer, Dan piped up.

"I thought Mary was actually married to God," he said, stabbing a piece of ham with a fork and popping it into his mouth.

"Yeah," said Nan, delicately separating the two halves of her dinner role and sniffing it before taking one tiny bite and then another and another. Nan is a nibbler.

"God was, like, the biological father of Mary's baby," Dan added. "Right?"

Ann looked alarmed.

"Right," she said hastily, "Mary was married to Joseph, but they were not intimate. They were chaste."

"Who was chasing them?" Nan asked.

"Maybe God was chasing them," Dan told Nan, "because she was supposed to be married to Him, but then she went off with Joseph and lived in a stable."

"Oh, my God," Ann said, glaring at me for some reason. "This is unbelievable! Nan and Dan, you are speaking disrespectfully of the Blessed Virgin. Gran, please explain to them about St. Joseph."

Nan, Dan, Ann, Gran, I thought idly. Whatever. I just listened.

"Well," Gran said, "the Church refers to Joseph as Mary's Most Chaste Spouse."

"What's a spouse?" Nan asked.

"A husband," Patrick said. "Like I'm your mother's spouse. Though *we're* not all that chaste." He winked at Ann and she turned away.

I'd forgotten Patrick was there. He doesn't talk much, and when he does, you often realize he had the right idea before.

"So the Blessed Mother was married to two men?" Nan asked.

"No!" Ann said, now glaring at Patrick. "She was not married to St. Joseph in the way that I am married to your father. She was more..."

"Just living with him?" Dan asked helpfully.

"What's a virgin?" Nan asked.

"I will not have this talk at my table," Gran said, setting her fork down with a big clank.

This was not a good subject for the Flanagan family to have drifted into. In all my life, I have never heard my grandmother allude in any positive way to sex, nor have I heard her speak of it with any specificity, except for the time when I was sixteen and overheard her telling Ann that there was "no good reason" for a man to see a woman "in the altogether" even after marriage. Sometimes I think Gran has no idea that I'm not still a virgin at thirty-three. For years, whenever I had sex, I had to struggle not to imagine her disapproving steel-gray eyes on me, which caused a problem in my intimate relationships: I couldn't come. Could not come to save my life. My most recent boyfriend, Tony Gilardi, was the first man who ever brought me to climax, and the first time it happened it was only because he distracted me from the thought of Gran's eyes by force of some persistent cunnilingus accompanied by song (he sang a rousing version of "It's Now or Never" right into my vagina, and Tony has quite a vibrato).

Actually, though, he didn't have much success in that department once I was onto his tricks. I tend to resist fulfillment with a vengeance. It's too much like the end of something. The denouement.

Anyway, I knew the dinner table conversation had taken a bad turn for Gran today, and I felt somehow responsible.

"I'm moving to Ohio for the winter," I said, directing my news around the table in general, hoping to save the situation by changing the subject. It worked.

"Ohio!" Gran said. "Whatever for?"

"I've been awarded the post of Thurber Writer-in-Residence at Ohio State, and I'll get to live in the house James Thurber lived in as a boy."

"Now why would you want to do that?" Gran asked. "He was such a peculiar little man."

"How will you get there?" Ann asked at the same time. "If you fly, you won't have your car. You'll want a car in Ohio."

"Right," I said, "so I'm driving there."

"Alone?" she asked. Ann knew I'd never taken a road trip alone in my life, and in fact had only learned to drive three years earlier, so that I could take a teaching position at Concord Academy, which is almost half an hour outside Boston.

"Well, no, Tony is going to share the driving with me, and then he's flying home the next morning."

"I thought you broke up with Tony," Ann said.

"Well, yeah. But we'd already bought his ticket and he wants to do it, so I said okay."

"He's a prince of a fellow," Ann said.

"A good man for an Italian," Gran agreed.

The deal was that I would spend one academic quarter--ten weeks--living in the attic apartment of James Thurber's boyhood home, and while I was there I would teach one class in creative writing at Ohio State. The rest of the time I could work on my own writing. This seemed a good opportunity to really get into the children's novel I'd started, away from the demands of fulltime teaching. And what could be a better setting for a writer than James Thurber's attic?

"What about your job?" Ann asked.

"I've taken the semester off," I said. "I'm leaving the day after New Year's."

"But that's next month," Ann said, "and you're only telling us now?"

"They say the house is haunted," I told Nan and Dan, pretending not to hear Ann.

Actually, although I've always accepted the possibility that ghosts might inhabit some dimension of worldly existence, I'd never had occasion to commune with one and, frankly, I didn't really believe the story of the ghost at Thurber House, though it was providing me a good subject changer. I figured it was just hype--a way of attracting tourists. That I was wrong--so utterly wrong--will be more to the point later.

"A ghost! Wow! You'll be living with a ghost? That's way cool," Dan said.

"No, it's way scary," Nan said. "I don't want you to go, Aunt Kate. The ghost might kill you! Ghosts are mean."

"That is a common misperception about ghosts," Gran was saying, but no one else seemed to hear her because Ann was talking at the same time.

"What will you do if the ghost is real?" Ann asked me. "You'd better be thinking of that!"

This was a microbiologist talking, mind you--a woman of science. Before I could answer, Patrick stepped in with one of his macho solutions.

"Exorcise him!" my brother-in-law said as he passed the ham platter around Gran's table. He gestured with the serving fork. "Just walk into that attic," he said, "and make the sign of the cross and say *I exorcise thee in the name of the Father, the Son, and the Holy Ghost.*" He made the sign of the cross with the fork as he spoke, a slice of ham on its tines.

Gran looked mad. But she's not wild about Patrick anyway.

"It's a ghost, Patrick, not the devil," I said. "If it even exists."

I refrained from making a point about exorcising a ghost *with* a ghost, a Holy Ghost. Humiliating Patrick isn't as much fun as humiliating my sister. It must be a blood thing.

I looked at Gran then. "What do you think my approach should be if there's really a ghost there?" I asked her.

"Just be a lady," she said without hesitation. "And keep your modesty. Where's that bowl of cheese potatoes?" (She pronounced "potatoes" *buh-day-duhs*--her Irish brogue.)

I knew she was upset that I was leaving. I'd never left before--I'd even attended Boston University just to stay close to her. I felt a bulge of grief at the thought of leaving my crochety old Gran. I looked down at my plate, to avoid her seeing my eyes.

If I'd thought that was all Gran had to say on the subject of ghosts, I was wrong. After someone passed her the scalloped buhdayduhs and she'd piled some on her plate, she looked back up at me.

"If you're smart," she said, "you'll remember that he can be your ally. You'll enlist his help if you need it, instead of turning him into the enemy." (Here she glared at Patrick again.) "A ghost can be fine company," she added pointedly, "if you don't turn him into The Devil Himself."

Patrick just grinned. He knows Gran feels he married Ann when she was too young to make an informed decision, and Gran has often called him a cradle robber although he and Ann are exactly the same age. She's still convinced the marriage won't last, even after they've been married eighteen years.

"I've never even seen a ghost," Dan said in a self-pitying tone, leveling an accusing look at his parents. "I never get to do anything," he added, and then he turned to me." Can I come and stay with you in the attic for a few weeks, Kate?"

"*Aunt* Kate, Danny," Ann said, "and your aunt is going off so she can be alone to write. Anyway, you've got school, young man."

My sister often sounds exactly like June Cleaver to me--it's as if she's stuck in a Nick-at-Night time warp, and has settled on role models from old TV shows, in the absence of an incarnate mother to emulate.

"We never have any fun," Dan said, and Nan nodded her head in vigorous assent. I loved these two moppets. How was I going to bear being away from them for three months?

✳

I arrived in Columbus, Ohio with Tony on a Friday evening. Mary McAteer, the public relations director of Thurber House, had stayed on after closing time to greet me. She and I met downstairs in the Thurber House bookstore while Tony carried my bags and boxes upstairs to the attic apartment, which would turn out to be a pleasant and roomy space with a nice bedroom and a separate study for me to write in.

Mary asked polite questions about our drive to Ohio, and then she gave me a map of Columbus, some pamphlets that listed cultural events, and a complete list of restaurants in the area. She also gave me some papers to fill out for Ohio State University, where I would begin teaching in a few days, and she showed me how to set the security system after hours, when the bookstore was closed.

I was just thinking we'd covered everything when she said in the most normal and cheery voice, "Well then, I just have to fill you in about the bats and the ghost, and then I'll get out of your way and let you get settled."

I looked at her quickly, to ascertain whether she was kidding. It seemed she was not. This was the first moment when I knew for certain that there was officially a ghost at Thurber House, but I was temporarily distracted by the bats, which felt realer to me, somehow.

"Bats?" I said.

"Oh, you probably won't even see one," Mary told me. "They mostly stay holed up in the walls. But you might hear them moving around in there, so don't be creeped out. And if you do see one, a tennis racquet is always a good way of dealing with it."

"I didn't bring a tennis racquet," I said. (It was January, for chrissake.)

"Well, a broom works just as well," she told me.

"Will a broom work with the ghost?" I said, in a nervous attempt at humor that even to me sounded lame. "I hope it's a nice ghost," I amended.

"He actually is a very nice ghost," Mary said quite seriously. "He's sad and unsettled, but I guarantee he won't bother you. Sometimes you may become aware that he's there, though."

A sad, unsettled ghost. Living in my apartment. I was really looking forward to this particular winter.

"Here's a book that tells the story of who he is--was," Mary said. "I always give a copy of this to our resident writers so that they'll understand him. His life ended quite sadly."

Later on, up in the apartment, Tony and I unexpectedly made love in the moonlit bedroom and I wondered if the sad ghost could see us. Now he'd begun to seem real to me because he'd been officially introduced as such. He wasn't an it anymore, he was a he. It was the first time I'd slept with Tony since breaking up with him six weeks earlier, and I hadn't planned to let that happen. When Tony came, I felt the ghost's eyes on me in the way I sometimes feel Gran's eyes, and I couldn't come. I faked it, though, out of courtesy. And also because I didn't want to look like a frigid woman to the ghost.

We fell asleep and then sometime in the night I woke up to the sound of footsteps. Half asleep, I wondered what Tony was doing pacing the floors, and then I realized he was still beside me in the bed. A chill ran over my skin and I pulled the covers up over my bare shoulders. The sound of pacing footsteps was so clear that as I listened I could tell they were coming from the floor right beneath us, the second floor. I could hear them moving first in one direction and then the other, in a restless, unbroken rhythm.

"Tony," I whispered, "wake up!"

"Whaaa," he mumbled.

"Listen!"

"What? What?" He struggled awake.

"Shhh, just listen."

And the two of us sat together in the dark attic bedroom and listened.

"It's probably just the wind," he said. "Or the bats."

"It's not the wind. And it's not the fucking bats. It's footsteps, and you know it."

"Kate," he said reasonably, "if you're like this the first night you're here, you're never gonna make it for a whole winter."

When the cab came to take Tony to the airport in the morning and honked for him down on Jefferson Street, I couldn't help noticing that I was crying. I am not a crier, and Tony knew that very well, so he was both worried and encouraged.

"I should be driving you to the airport," I said tearfully as we made our way down the stairs and out to where the cab was waiting.

"That's just silly," he said. "You don't even know your way around, yet. You'd get lost."

At that, I just nodded my head and sobbed some more. I'm not sure Tony had ever seen me cry before, except with laughter.

"Baby," he said, "you don't have to stay here if you don't want to. Come back with me. We can get married and have twenty kids and you can give up writing forever and just cook and clean house and lose your identity entirely."

Actually he didn't say any of that part after Come back with me, but he might as well have. I realized I had to shape up or I'd end up married and be left alone to raise my kids when Tony ran off with the babysitter. For the first time I thought maybe Ann might be right about my reasons for breaking up with every man who'd ever loved me. I clung to Tony, and when the cabbie honked again, he looked so worried that I forced a big fake smile.

"I'm fine," I said. "I'm just not used to living with a ghost. Or bats."

He looked disappointed not to be the reason for my distress.

"I'll miss you," I said, to compensate, and I knew right then it had been a mistake to let him accompany me here, because now we seemed to be back together in some way that I'd been determined not to let us be. The cab honked again and Tony looked down at me with a grief-filled smile, and I felt embarrassed for both of us.

I walked back into the house feeling tragic and alone. And not alone. What would it be like to live with a ghost? Would he be watching me all the time without my realizing it? How would I know when he was in the room? Would he have the good sense and common decency not to come into the bathroom when I was on the can, for example? My God, that thought really unsettled me--so much so that I phoned Gran to ask her about ghostly etiquette.

"It depends," she said, "on how he was brought up. You can't speak of ghosts as if they were all the same person, you know."

That had never occurred to me--I'd always thought of ghosts as, I don't know, just ghosts. The idea that each was as distinct and individual as a corporeal human made perfect sense, of course, but it unsettled me. This meant I was going to have to adjust to the ghost as I would to a roommate. And the whole idea of coming to Columbus had been to be alone for a few months so I could work on the book I'd already signed a contract to write.

The first odd occurrence in my attic apartment came that very evening—my first night alone at Thurber House. I had stuck some family pictures into the frame of my bedroom mirror, just for company. On one side of the frame, I'd put a photo of Nan and Dan, as well as one of Gran (no, I didn't put up one of Ann—it's a challenge to feel sentimental about my annoying sister). Then, on second thought, I stuck two pictures of Tony in the other side of the frame.

I went into the kitchen then and fixed myself a quesadilla and a salad, and while I ate I attempted to work on my first lecture at the tiny dinette table. I had trouble concentrating, though, probably because my mind was in so many places at once—home, ghosts, why my love life was constantly in a state of flux. Bats.

Realizing that this wasn't going to be a good work night, I decided to cut my losses and put the lecture aside. What I needed was to spend a relaxing night in the apartment and get used to living here. I took a hot shower, trying not to think about ghostly observers, and then I went to the bedroom to get a tank top and pajama bottoms from the bureau. Immediately I noticed that both pictures of Tony were lying face-down on the top of it, but the pictures of Dan and Nan and Gran were still securely in the frame on the left side of the mirror.

Not really finding this particularly remarkable or mysterious, I simply tucked the photos of Tony back into the mirror frame, just where they'd been before. This time I even checked to be certain they were secure, and it seemed to me they were. I went back out to the living room and turned on the news, curled up on the comfortably-worn blue couch, and stayed there until after the late show was over.

When I headed back into the bedroom, the first thing I did was check to be certain Tony's photos were still in the mirror frame. They weren't. Again, they were both lying face-down on the dresser top, while the photos of Dan, Nan, and Gran were all exactly where I'd put them, on the opposite side. The frame must adhere more snugly to the mirror on the left side, I decided, and I switched the photos around so that Tony was on the left side and Dan, Nan, and Gran were on the right, and then I went to bed.

That night I had a dream that I can only describe as erotic without being sexual, if that makes any sense. In the dream, a tall, slim man with dark, wavy brown hair came into the bedroom and sat on the side of my bed. His eyes were deep-set and quite beautiful—green, with thick lashes. His brow was strong, and the force of his gaze was powerful. He was stroking my bare upper arm, and looking at me, nothing more. I wasn't scared of him at all, and oddly it seemed as if I knew him. He smiled at me and I returned his smile. I liked how lean and sinewy his hand was. I liked his smile, his eyes. There was really nothing not to like.

After a while—and I mean really quite a while, because it was clear he was in no hurry at all, unlike most men who are touching a woman in a bed—he slipped his hand under my tank top and gently stroked my breasts, all the while watching my face. The intensity of my physical response to his touch was acute; I can only describe the sensation as a shock to my skin in the way that searing pain would be a shock, only pleasurable. I held my breath as his hand moved down my ribcage, circling my navel, smoothing my belly, and then it slipped beneath the waistband of my pajama bottom, fingers moving lower and lower but never quite reaching the hoped-for destination. I'd never been touched so softly before, or so knowingly. It was as if this man could read my body and knew exactly what its response would be to each and every touch. Not just knew, but could feel my body's response, as if whatever he made me feel, he felt it, too. Though I'd never before been uninhibited in bed, at that moment there was nothing I would not have done with him, nothing. And then, just when he'd lulled me into the most malleable erotic state, he kissed the side of my face just beside my ear, and then he was gone.

When I woke in the morning I was still sexually aroused. I looked around the room for him, even though of course I realized it had all been a dream. Glancing around the bedroom, I saw that my photos of Tony had now fallen from the left side of the mirror frame and were once again lying face-down on the dresser top. The pictures of Dan, Nan, and Gran were still securely fixed in the right side of the mirror frame—the side that couldn't seem to hold onto pictures of Tony.

"Are you in here?" I said out loud, "because if you are, you're being intrusive."

Already I was not liking this ghost.

"Just, for God's sake, don't ever follow me into the bathroom," I added. "I mean it!"

I didn't put Tony's pictures back up--too much maintenance. I tucked them into my top drawer instead.

I dressed and went to school, still feeling quite urgently hot. Taught my first class in that state, and later was told by two students (a male and a female, just for the record) that it was exciting to have a teacher who was so passionate about her subject. (My subject for that day was the effaced narrator, so go figure.)

I grabbed a hamburger on the way back to Thurber House, and at the apartment I settled on the old blue couch to eat it while I watched the news. Shortly after that, I took a quick shower and then went straight to bed. It was earlier by far than I usually turn in, but honestly, all I could think of was going to sleep. This time I didn't bother with pajamas.

I guess I must've fallen asleep pretty rapidly--I don't remember tossing and turning at all. Once again, I dreamed that the tall, green-eyed man was sitting on the side of my bed and leaning in over me. This time he was idly stroking my thighs as he surveyed the landscape of my bare body with an intense, avid, oddly sad expression on his face, his fingers occasionally wandering close to but never quite touching my most intimate part. And then, just as I reached a point of such urgency that I would have gladly given up State secrets if I had any, he bent forward without warning and gently put his mouth on my belly, tracing a path downward, and then he kissed me there, one lingering, deep, and very intense kiss. That was all. Actually, that was all it took. My response was so intense it woke me—and of course there was no one in the bedroom with me. I doubted that it had been a dream, though, because I was still having aftershocks. And my covers were thrown back, as they had been in the dream.

A bit later that morning as I passed through the Thurber House bookstore and gift shop on my way out to the parking lot, the volunteer who was overseeing the store that day—an elderly lady with faintly lavender hair—looked up and smiled at me as I passed the desk.

"Kate! You probably don't remember me, but I'm Miriam Schwann--I was on the panel that selected you for this residency."

"Oh, right, Miriam," I said, "how nice to see you again!"

I didn't actually remember her at all—I'd been pretty nervous during that interview—but one of the handiest things I'd learned as a result of living with Catholicism's rigorous rules was how to avoid the sin of lying without actually telling the truth, either.

Miriam asked me how I was liking my stay, and I told her everything was lovely. Immediately I flashed back to my steamy dreams and could feel myself blushing.

"Any encounters with our ghost?" she asked perkily, and I was struck mute by her use of the word *encounters*.

"Our ghost?" I finally managed to say.

"Oh, I hope I didn't upset you—you seem a little flustered."

"Flustered?" I said, and then let out a shrill laugh that might more accurately be described as a bray.

Miriam asked me if I knew the night the ghost got in, and it took me more than a second to remember that 'The Night the Ghost Got In' was the title of one of Thurber's stories. The ghost hadn't quite gotten in yet, I reflected. Or anyway, not very far in. And only with his tongue. But there was always tomorrow. Or tonight.

"Oh yes," I said. "The ghost. Got in. Great story, one of Thurber's best."

That evening I settled in with the book about the haunted houses of Columbus, Ohio that Mary McAteer had given me. I went straight to the ghost of Thurber House, of course, and there I found the tragic story. It was during the 1880s that the man who lived in this house then, a jeweler, had received an anonymous note at his shop saying that if he came home early, he would find his wife with another man. He did go home early that day, and on the second floor of the house--the floor where Tony and I had heard the pacing footsteps on my first night here--the jeweler found his wife in bed with his closest friend. Devastated, he shot himself then and there, on the second floor of the house.

I thought of the man who had been visiting my dreams. But that was truly insane, wasn't it? I thought of his beautiful sad eyes, the gentleness and intensity of his touch.

The weeks sped by, and each night was another slow-motion adventure in painfully erotic touching of various kinds, but without the penetration that constitutes consummation. I was aroused all the time now. Never in my life had I been so unremittingly hot and preoccupied with sex. My students loved me, but I didn't feel I deserved it since I wasn't doing a great job. Half the time when I was teaching, I was thinking about the night before. Everyone in my class was getting an A.

Back in December, when Tony and I had made plans for him to drive with me to Columbus, I'd paid for a round-trip airline ticket so that he could fly home to Boston afterwards and then fly back to Columbus when I was ready to leave, so that the two of us would drive my car back together. But now it just felt false to let him do that for me when all I thought of, day and night, was another man. Yes, true, the other man was just a dream, or maybe dead, but wasn't that really the point? I was more in love with this phantom than I'd ever been with Tony, a real flesh-and-blood man. The unseen strikes again. And hadn't it always been so for me? At any rate, it didn't feel right letting Tony get his hopes up, under the circumstances.

I called him and said I didn't think it was a good idea for him to accompany me back to Boston. I needed the long drive back to process things, I said, but I'd call him when I got there. He sounded offended, maybe even a little angry, but not completely shocked--and he didn't argue. I'm sure he knew it was hopeless to try and talk me out of it.

The day after classes ended, I turned in my grades first thing in the morning and then came back to the apartment and stayed in all day packing my things and feeling inexplicably sad and full of dread. As I've said already, I'm not fond of the ends of things.

That night, my last night at Thurber House, I took a long bath in lavender oil because lavender supposedly helps you sleep. When I began to feel anticipatory tumescence, mid-bath, I decided enough was enough and got out of the tub. I dried myself quickly, resolving to end this thing myself, rather than letting circumstance overwhelm me as it often tended to do.

I put on my most ancient pair of flannel pajamas, the ones Gran had given me for Christmas sixteen years earlier when I was a junior in high school—I'm sure she would be shocked if she knew I still had them. They have puppies on them. Not ironic or stylized puppies, either—just sincere brown puppies. They're quite tatty by now, but they're my security pajamas.

I dragged my blankets into the living room and lay on the blue couch, pulling the covers up to my nose. I fell asleep quickly, almost defiantly.

Is there such a thing as a strictly tactile, no-image dream? A dream that is literally of the skin--residing within it? Because I didn't see him in my dream this time but I felt him, and feeling him without seeing him was even more powerfully intimate in some inexplicable way. I could feel his hands moving over my upper arms again, lightly caressing my breasts, and then his mouth was on my belly, as tender and knowing as ever, but with an urgency I hadn't sensed before. *Yes,* I said. *Yes.*

I couldn't say how long it all lasted because there was no sense of time in this dream at all, but when he finally put himself inside me for the first time ever, yes, I was shaken to my core, electrified, and then he rocked me, just rocked me while it seemed my body was exploding. When I woke in the scarce light at 5 AM, my puppy pajamas and blankets were on the floor and I was lying starkers on the couch, strangely serene.

As I lay there, the apartment felt very still in some way it had not been since I'd begun living there.

After I loaded the car, I came back upstairs and called Gran. I asked her if it was possible to have feelings for a ghost.

"Well, of course it is," she sputtered. "How many times do I have to tell you, Kate, they're just people like you and me."

"Yeah, that's what I thought," I said.

Her voice changed then, shaded into concern.

"What sort of feelings are you talking about, exactly?"

"Oh, you know, just regular feelings. Do...do ghosts ever travel in cars?"

"Well, no!" she said. "Why should they, when they can just fly through the air?"

"Do they ever fly great distances?"

"Now, why would they do that?" she asked. "If they're ghosts, that means they've attached themselves after death to one particular place that was important to them during their earthly lifetime. The life they lived there still feels unresolved, for some reason, so they just stay in that place until they've resolved things. And then at some point, when they're ready, they pass along into the next life."

"Oh," I said. I looked around the apartment, focused on the weak morning sunlight that was falling through the attic window and over the back of the blue couch. "Okay, Gran, see you soon," I said.

"Well, I certainly hope so," she answered in her most sensible voice.

After we hung up, I sat on the couch and tried to figure out how I felt, which I realized wasn't bad at all, really--in fact, it seemed as if maybe I was fine, pretty much. I could go home now, but I didn't know what I would find there, and that was okay, too, or seemed to be.

As I left the attic apartment for the last time, I didn't let myself turn in the doorway and look back, I just closed the door and headed down the stairs to the ground floor, then through the empty bookstore and out into the damp, foggy morning. At the door of my car I stopped, glanced up at the attic window that overlooked the parking lot. There was no figure there.

He and she were eating their last meal. Having broken off with her to return to his former fiancée, he'd asked her to go one last time to Biba, for old times' sake--and no doubt to show her that this was a civilized leave-taking, not an abandonment. He hadn't said that was why he was seeing her today, but it was something she perceived.

"The passion between us is so intense," he'd told her when he decided to end the relationship. "It's just hard to trust that anything this intense can last."

"So," she'd said, "you're ending our relationship because the sex is too good."

"Well, now, that just makes it sound silly," he'd said. "I prefer to think of it the way I just said it. This level of sexual intensity can't possibly be sustainable. I want a life that I can trust will stay the same, the way my parents' marriage has."

What could she say to that? She had no such example to follow in her own life. Her father had died when she was three, and her mother had never remarried.

"You talk about love the way a CPA discusses balance sheets and budget projections," she'd finally said.

He had suggested that the two of them might want to go to the Museum of Fine Arts after lunch today, or just walk in the Public Garden, "if you'd like to talk," he'd said. If she would like to talk. The way he worded the invitation reminded her how much he prided himself in doing the right thing. Sometimes she felt he was watching and blocking every scene between the two of them through slow, admiring cameras--but then he was the director of *Tête à Tête*, a weekly interview program on Boston Public Television, so maybe it only seemed that way to her. Still, as they were seated in their customary corner booth by their usual waiter, she felt for the first time the humiliation of knowing that today her company was the right thing, rather than the desired thing.

Desire. It had been their private language from the start.

She watched his hand now, on the wine list, and thought of all that she had permitted--invited--that hand to do, all the parts of her it had touched. She'd never been so free with a man before. Her desire for him had superseded her modesty, her inhibitions, her eight years of decorous marriage before they met. There was something about his conservative personal style in combination with his innate sexual assurance that she'd found deeply exciting, something about it that had made her want to test her limits, and his. And as the first months of their relationship went by, she'd found she had no sexual limits with him at all, so commanding was the desire.

A year ago, she'd left her marriage to be with him, and he had broken off his three-year engagement to the girl he'd begun dating in college. Since the beginning, she had abandoned herself to the pleasures of their mutual skin--and now, with their world for two being dismantled, it was hard to find anything real and compelling in her old life. Even her work seemed to have lost its delight for her; she found herself going automatically to teach her landscape architecture classes at Harvard, relying on notes and slides from last year's sessions rather than approaching the new semester with her customary inventiveness.

All of the life she'd known before him felt unfamiliar now that she was thrust back into it alone. It was as if she'd been on a long safari or a journey through the Amazon, and was emerging now to find her old landscape unrecognizable or uninhabitable. Was this an indication of the power of love or of the power of sex? How could you separate the two? If she hadn't loved him completely, she'd never have done the things she did with him. It was a fact that she hadn't been particularly adventuresome in bed before she knew him, and he'd said it was the same for him.

She remembered the first time they'd come to Biba, on a humid July night, several months after they'd begun sleeping together, experimenting with each other's capacity for pleasure. She'd waited until after they ordered dinner, had their wine in hand. And then she had revealed her secret.

"I have an egg in me," she'd whispered across the table as she raised her glass to him in a small salute.

"What?" He'd looked a little alarmed.

"An egg. I have an alabaster yoni egg inside me." She was learning to love the challenge of his personal conservatism. She'd slipped out of her right shoe then and put the toes of her foot between his thighs beneath the table and felt the instantaneousness of his response. It had been a pleasurable sort of pain trying to get through dinner after that, particularly after she added, "and tonight I'm an acrobat without a net."

"What?" He looked completely confounded.

"No knickers. I'm relying on my, well, snugness, my excellent muscle-tone, to keep the egg in." She grinned at him.

"Come over here, sit next to me," he'd said. His voice had the gravelly tone that suggested desire. He slid her table-setting to the space beside him and she rose, walking slowly around to his side of the table as he watched her. She was wearing a black silk wrap skirt that tied like a sarong on her left hip. She took her time, wanting to give him a chance to observe, and then she sat beside him.

When the waiter returned with their salads, he showed scarcely a flicker of response to the seating change.

"Pepper for you, sir?" he asked, holding a huge mill above the plate.

"Yes," her lover said as she parted her legs just enough, beneath the table, to allow his hand between her thighs.

"Ahh, thank you," he said.

"You're welcome, sir," the waiter answered. "And you, ma'am?"

"Yes," she said as she felt his hand moving closer to its objective.

"Say when, ma'am," the waiter cautioned, as the pepper deepened on her salad.

"More," she said as she felt his fingers discovering her other surprise: she had been waxed completely bare.

"My God," her lover blurted, and then covered with, "you take a lot of pepper on your salad!"

By the time the entrées arrived, he'd found the egg.

They had grappa after the meal, and then they had sex in the car in the parking garage, and later that night at a little club in Allston, where she sat on his lap, her back to him in the darkened room, and pushing herself down onto him with a slow movement that kept rhythm with the pulse of a tune the jazz ensemble was playing. "You're silky, like a trout," he whispered into her ear. She'd turned and frowned at him uncertainly, and he said, "The trout is the most beautiful animal in the world."

Today, a year later, she was wearing the black silk sarong again, though she had no egg in her and she was wearing underwear. She hadn't waxed. She'd not seen him in three weeks, since he decided to return to his ex-fiancée, which still made no sense to her. She was careful to make no reference to it--she didn't want to hear him defending again what he'd called "a lifestyle choice" or talking about the history he had with his former fiancée, how their two rather prominent Back Bay families were friends from way back, how he felt that this was the right thing. She could hear the capital letters as he said it: *Right Thing*.

Today their talk felt overly animated, artificial--a film he'd seen, a book she'd read, a gay priest he'd interviewed for Tête à Tête, her landscape classes at Harvard. But they found their eyes lingering each time their gazes met, and she felt pain and confusion at the physical response in her own skin to the presence of this man who was leaving her.

"I miss you," he said abruptly, frowning a little and then looking away from her.

She looked down, uncertain how to respond, then met his gaze again, eye to eye, and this time she didn't look away.

"It's your choice," she said.

After a silence, he replied, "It doesn't mean I don't love you. I do. And I know I'll want you all my life. I've never had this... whatever it is...with anyone else." And yet he had left her *because* of the intensity they shared, the erotic unknown they'd explored together, as if a real life shouldn't include such wildness, as if that wildness was not to be trusted, was antithetical to a serious and stable relationship.

When he'd first announced his intention to return to his old life, she had accused him of not trusting rapture. "Maybe you're right," he'd admitted. "It doesn't exactly seem like part of a stable life. And anyway, rapture is mortal, so there's always the danger of losing it."

So, he didn't trust what had required trust to achieve, and what had implied trust in the doing. Absolute trust. Nothing seemed quite real anymore.

It was just as she looked away to hide the sudden embarrassment of tears, dipping her head to meet her wine glass, that it happened. She felt a chunk of the veal stew lodge in her windpipe--something hard, perhaps the large piece of carrot she'd just seen in her spoon--but she smiled brightly at him while she tried swallowing to dislodge it and found it firmly stuck. Her first thought, which later would seem absurd, was *Oh my God, not in Biba!* To choke to death in Biba had felt louche, somehow. But it seemed she was going to die if she did nothing.

She stood abruptly, heard the clatter of silverware against china, saw him startle, and used her last available length of breath to croak, "Help me I'm choking."

And he stood too then, a look of confusion on his face. She ran toward the kitchen then, pointing at her throat, and heard his voice behind her, "She's choking! Does anyone here know the Heimlich Maneuver?"

Time became amorphous then, she couldn't gauge it. Someone stood behind her, she knew it was him, felt his arms come around her as a woman's voice to her left said, "Hard! You have to do it hard!" She couldn't see anymore, but she could hear and feel. "Don't be afraid of hurting her," the woman's voice said, "it won't help if you don't do it hard!" And his hands, clasped in front of her, crashed upward beneath her ribs once, twice, and then a searing pain and an involuntary groaning noise emerging from her own throat, the chunk dislodging, and a little food and liquid expelled onto her silk skirt, onto her own feet and the floor, and she bent forward, gasping, receiving the blessing of air after having lost hope of it, and all the while his arms around her, his arms around her.

She felt as if she were skulking back to their table then, having disgraced herself in some unspeakable fashion, disheveled and--even after the assistance of a kindly waiter with a damp cloth--soiled. But her purse was there and she had to get it. And had, suddenly, to sit down. They sat awhile. He seemed distant now, antsy to leave. He was no longer touching her. A woman at a nearby table called out to ask if she was all right. She blushed, nodded, looked down at her plate, feeling oddly ashamed, humiliated.

She couldn't bear that this was their last time together, that this was how he would remember her now.

On the way out to the car, he told her that now he was going to have to change the location of the re-engagement party he'd planned here at Biba for his recycled fiancée and both families the following week. "All the servers and kitchen crew saw you choking--someone is bound to say something to her about it, and she had no idea I would be seeing you again." She was stung that he would even think of this right now, much less mention it.

"I'm sorry," she said quietly, to make him feel guilty.

"I'm not saying it's your fault," he said briskly. "It's just unfortunate."

On the drive back to her apartment (there was no more talk of going to the MFA or the Public Garden) she could feel the object still lodged in her throat, deep down, that chunk of carrot, it was still there, only now not in her windpipe. Somewhere else, stuck.

Was it possible? she asked him. That it could still be in there, after a Heimlich?

He told her it was only a phantom sensation, a memory of the skin--a reaction to what had just happened.

"But I'm sure I feel it in there. I know it's still in me." She looked down at her lap, the damp and rumpled silk of her skirt. Moments passed, and they didn't speak.

"You saved my life," she finally said, and as the realization gained clarity she began to shake and couldn't seem to stop.

"I don't really believe that's true," he told her. "Somehow it doesn't seem possible that you would have died. Maybe it's just too scary to let myself believe it."

"It's true," she said, and found herself crying a little. "Sorry--suddenly I'm just so spooked at the thought of it."

He reached across to the passenger seat and patted her hand. Something about the way he did it felt perfunctory to her. "You'll be fine," he told her.

"But what if it's still in me? What if I choke in my sleep tonight?"

"You'll be fine," he said again. They pulled up in front of her apartment building on Cambridge Street and he switched off the engine. "I can't come up with you," he said. "I've really got to go."

"But you had the afternoon free. Please don't leave me alone right now."

"Look," he said, in a careful, reasoned tone, "this was hard on me, too. Try to understand--please? I need to go home and just be by myself for a while."

"I'm scared," she told him.

"You'll be fine." He 'd said it so often it began to sound like a mantra. He started the engine.

"I know it's still stuck in me--I can feel it there." She heard her quavery voice and despised it; said in a calmer tone, "Please stay with me for just a little while."

"I'll come up for five minutes, but that's it."

In her apartment they sat together silently on the couch. And, indeed, five minutes later he left. "You'll be fine," he told her again as he was leaving.

She waited for an hour, trying to believe that the carrot chunk she thought she felt was a phantom sensation. Then she phoned her cousin, a nurse at Scripps Mercy Hospital in San Diego, and asked if it was possible that even after the Heimlich had brought some food up, there still might be something caught in her throat. "I can feel it in there. I know I do."

"Well, sure--that happens sometimes. How do you feel otherwise?"

"My ribs and chest hurt when I breathe. It feels like I was hit by a trolley."

"You really ought to get yourself to an emergency room," her cousin said. "That's standard procedure for anyone who's gone through a Heimlich. You could have a broken rib."

And so she phoned the emergency room at Holyoke Center, and they sent the Harvard Police to get her. At Holyoke, she waited in waiting rooms for tests and x-rays, talked to a nurse in the examination room, and then to a kindly doctor with an Indian accent who told her that her airway was clear of obstructions, but that her ribs were bruised and she apparently still had a piece of something hard lodged in her food passage.

"During the Heimlich maneuver, it probably jumped from the airway to the food passage and stuck there," he said. "It isn't dangerous now, just painful, uncomfortable. If it were a coin or some object of that sort, we would have to remove it, but since it is an organic material, it will dissolve by itself eventually." He pronounced it ewentually.

"How long am I going to feel it in there?" she asked warily.

"Twenty-four hours--maybe a little longer. But I promise you it will be fine."

"Could I choke if I lie down to sleep?"

"No, that's unlikely--it only feels that way. You are bruised from the Heimlich--your ribs, your sternum--and you are shaken. It's normal to be afraid--you nearly choked to death. I promise, you will be all right." He wrote out a prescription for the pain and she found herself walking home through the gritty evening rush hour air of Cambridge. She'd been gone from her apartment for two hours. When they'd parted three hours ago, she told him she was afraid of dying--how could she have forgotten to let him know where she was for the past two hours? She felt panicky at the realization that, getting no answer when he called to check on her, he might have phoned the police, or driven over and summoned the super.

She'd left her cell phone at home in the confusion of the Harvard Police's arrival to fetch her. Now, figuring it was better not to wait a moment longer to call him, she stopped at a pay phone in front of the Harvard Coop. There was a yellow loogey on the metal shelf below the phone, but it was the only phone not in use, so she put her coins in and dialed him, trying to ignore the phlegm beneath her face. His line was busy. He was phoning her right now, she knew. She hurried past CVS pharmacy, where she'd planned to fill her prescription. She could get it later. Right now she had to get home. Dammit, dammit, she could've phoned him from a courtesy phone in one of the hospital waiting rooms if only she'd had the presence of mind. It would seem like the worst sort of game-playing to him, her dramatic disappearance just after saying she feared she might choke to death if he left her alone.

She entered the lobby of her apartment building, saw that the elevator light was on at her floor, and she felt sure he'd just gone up there and was banging on her door. Deciding she couldn't wait for the elevator to come back down to where she was, she ran up the stairs, ribs throbbing with each jolting step, and the press of something jammed like a Lilliputian fist deep in her throat. She had her keys out before she reached the door, and finding the hall outside it clear, she rushed inside and ran first to the message player on her landline. No messages. She checked her cell phone, then. No missed calls.

How was that possible?

She stood beside the phone for a minute, then dialed his number. This time it rang. He picked up on the third ring.

"What happened?" she asked him.

"Nothing," he said. "What do you mean?"

"I can't believe it. I've been at the Holyoke ER for the last two hours, and I was worried sick you'd think I was dead, but you haven't even called to check on me."

"I've been catching up some correspondence," he said mildly, "and my friend Richard called."

"It's been over three hours since you left here, and you haven't once checked to see if I was okay?"

There was a silence, and then, "What do you want from me?" he asked, a coldness in his voice she'd never heard before. She didn't know how to answer. It was odd, she thought, how this might not even be an argument if they were still a couple, because she would have had his love to see her through whatever failure she might have perceived in his response to the choking incident. She could've been more understanding then, felt more forgiving, and she might even have been able to accept his assertion that her brush with death was such a trauma to him that he couldn't stay and comfort her. How much harder it was to forgive someone who has left you--has been able to leave you--having seeing you passionate and vulnerable time and again, shameless with love.

"You saved me from choking," she said slowly, feeling her way through this. "Thank you." And she hung up the phone without waiting for an answer.

All evening she paced the apartment, occasionally putting her hand to the base of her throat where the chunk of food was lodged. It had to be the piece of carrot she'd seen in her spoon just before she choked--she could feel the hardness of it.

Somehow it helped to picture the object that was stuck in her food passage--it wasn't so scary if she could demystify it in that way. It's just a piece of carrot, she told herself, nothing more.

She tried to think about something else. Continental drift. The Queen. Stopped pacing, tried sitting still but then she was even more aware of it. She found that any sort of movement was preferable to stillness, for motion introduced an alternate sensation to her body that camouflaged the intrusive presence a little, distracted her from it. The phone rang at about nine and her heart leapt involuntarily, for which she was disgusted with herself--what difference could it possibly make now, whether or not it was him? She walked toward the bookcase where the phone stood, resolving not to let him inside her ever again, even via phone. But it was her cousin in San Diego, on break from her shift at the hospital and calling to see if she was okay. After they hung up she continued pacing the apartment, leaving the TV on for company but not watching it. Good. Fine. She had no desire to talk to him, anyway. Absolutely none.

She found her eye straying to the phone for hours after that, wary, as if it were a bomb about to go off. Or not.

Sitting up in bed later, she finally closed her eyes, closed her mind, but still she felt the lump lodged inside her.

At eleven thirty he phoned and asked how she was. His voice was kind and concerned now, even tender, but it felt too late somehow. It was as if his studio cameras were now rolling again while he re-shot a botched scene.

All night she sat straight up in bed, awake, finding the presence of the food chunk even more disturbing now that the rest of the world was asleep. She felt leery of lying flat, unable to rid herself of anxiety about choking to death in her sleep. Out of nowhere she remembered the Egg Man, a TV performer who used to fill his mouth with what seemed to be dozens of eggs on some local weekly variety show when she was a kid. One day she'd heard her mother telling her father that the Egg Man had choked to death while doing his act in Vegas.

The Egg Man--he was the sort of guy who knew how to take a chance, how to trust in the foolish and the sublime. Her eyes filled with tears for the Egg Man. He was one of a kind.

The next day was Saturday and she was glad she didn't have to teach, having slept not a minute all night. As the day progressed and normal hunger asserted itself, she found herself apprehensive of swallowing anything solid. In the afternoon she walked to CVS in the square and got some SlimFast to provide her the minimum daily requirements without the necessity of chewing. She didn't fill the prescription for pain pills, because although her ribs were quite sore, the pain in her throat and neck had come to seem a kind of protection, a warning system that would tell her if something was happening in there, something she needed to know about. Anyway, she wasn't sure she could swallow a pill just now. All evening she caught herself communing with the object trapped inside her like bitterness or desire.

What do you want from me? she heard herself say once.

On Saturday night she finally slept sitting up, three pillows propped behind her on the bed. She did not dream, but slept a hard and determined sleep, the sleep of the dead or the disaffected.

When she woke early Sunday morning, the first thing that occurred to her was that the lump seemed to be gone. She breathed slowly in, out; then swallowed. Swallowed again. After a time she moved aside the extra pillows and tried lying flat, laid her hand on her breast, then against the base of her throat, breathing all the way in, all the way out. It was definitely gone. It was. She lay and listened for something. The room was oddly still, as after an earsplitting roar. She lay back in the sheets for a long time, breathing in and then out into the stillness, not thinking of him at all, not thinking of him.

On Monday, she joked to her students about the unseemliness of choking in Biba, then later at home in her apartment she huddled in front of the TV with a chilled can of SlimFast and an afghan, watching whatever came on, including silly shows like "The Bachelor." She found that the sensation of swallowing even this innocuous liquid inspired real fear in her, and beyond that it brought a bloat of grief, which stayed. Setting down the nearly full SlimFast can, she wondered if she might have permanently lost the confidence required to swallow solid foods. Swallowing--that moment when food teeters on the rear verge of your tongue, ready to be sent into the depths of the throat--seemed to her now in retrospect a moment of great risk, a flirtation with eternity. People who can swallow without trepidation, she thought, are brave and foolish.

She considered all the times she'd swallowed his semen, something she had never truly wanted to do with any other man. The second time they'd gone to bed together, she'd taken him in her mouth for the first time and he had demurred, saying, "I don't like to come in people's mouths." The wording was so awkward and honest, so innocent, and he was so beautiful there on the sheets.

"Please let me try," she'd whispered, surprised at her own boldness, and he had. Then, when he came at last, it had been with an intensity she'd never seen, and--he told her later--an intensity he'd never felt before.

"Recently on Tête à Tête," he told her afterwards, "a guest was talking about how in English Renaissance poetry, to *die* was a synonym for reaching orgasm." And he said the French called orgasm *le petit mort.* "I think I understand that now," he'd told her then. There'd been no inhibitions between them after that, and they'd learned, as he often said, "to die together."

Now he'd left her for a woman who, he once confided, he wasn't sure ever actually climaxed during sex. And he seemed to be leaving with the new assurance of a man schooled in intimacy, a world traveler going home to show his slides--or better, to walk among the provincials he'd left behind, secure in the quiet knowledge that he'd been somewhere else.

She couldn't eat or sleep without effort, and she felt cold all the time now. She took long hot baths, trying to warm her skin and melt away the unease. She didn't watch herself in the long mirror on the bathroom door as she dried with the towel; the sight of her body made her sad.

On the small oak desk next to her bed, the alabaster egg sat, cool and smooth; evidence of another time, possibly another her. She held it in her hand one night until it grew warm and moist against her palm. Then she pressed it against her heart, where the fear was. Later, lying under blankets, she pressed it against herself between her legs, then pushed it inside as she had done to surprise him on that long-ago night at Biba. She tried to remember desire, the feeling of him inside her, the liberty of lust.

"I've got an egg in me," she whispered, but she felt nothing, and after a while she urged the egg out into her hand. From somewhere, she remembered his reply when she told him she felt the piece of carrot caught inside her: *It's just a phantom sensation, a memory of the skin.* She lay awake long after the sound of traffic had died in Harvard Square and even the car alarms had dwindled, and finally sometime in the night she fell asleep, the alabaster egg still in her grasp.

All night then she dreamed of making love with the Egg Man, of dancing on eggs with him at their wedding, swallowing eggs with him on TV, dozens and dozens of eggs, swallowing the Egg Man's love on TV, swallowing eggs and dying with him in Las Vegas, dying together again and again, their mouths and throats jammed with eggs, and never minding it a bit because they knew it was all for love, and in love's little death they would be born again and again.

When she woke, the sun was just swelling at the lower edge of the sky outside her east window, spreading thick and yellow in the gray morning light, and the egg was still in her hand, smooth and hard and real, warming to her touch.

Winter Work

On Monday morning just after the morning show, Molly Winter
turned off the sound and sat down to write her weekly letter to
her sister JoAnn. JoAnn rarely answered the letters, but Molly
continued writing them, anyway. Letter writing was one of her
two main pastimes, though it was sometimes a challenge to come
up with news for a letter.

Outside the small frame bungalow, traffic moved up and
down Fairmount Avenue in East San Diego and Molly could
hear an occasional car pulling into Jack-in-the-Box next door,
followed by the garbled bark of an amplified voice taking orders.
From time to time she glanced up at the silent, animated faces
on the screen, and then back down to the page, a feeling of peace
flooding through her.

Often when Molly was just going through her regular day, the
ordinariness of things gave her a kind of ominous feeling, a sense
of other things lurking just out of sight. She'd had this feeling all
of her remembered life, and it was more than just anxiety, it was
a presentiment of impending doom. In recent months the feeling
had become stronger than ever. Of course, you had only to turn
on the TV news to see why, but Molly knew that was only a part
of it.

All manner of awful things had been happening for years,
of course--addicts grabbing your purse on the sidewalk, people
coming into a McDonald's and shooting everyone in sight for no
good reason. You didn't have to be a bad person for bad things to
happen to you, Molly knew that, but lately it just seemed as if the
world was all pushed out of shape and nothing in it made sense
anymore.

Each time a more confounding evil presented itself, Molly
wondered if this could be the eventuality she'd been expecting for
so long, and if at last by its arrival she'd been delivered. But then
the feeling would come back to her and she couldn't shake it, the
sense that the Ultimate Catastrophe still lay ahead of her, just out
of sight. It seemed to Molly that she just kept moving toward it,
whatever it was, in spite of her own wariness, because she did not
know what else to do.

This was an unpleasant train of thought. Molly forced herself to focus on her letter:

Dear JoAnn,

How are you? Things are about the same here, though God knows I'm not complaining. What with all the tragedy in our world, we should thank our lucky stars when we have an ordinary day. Walter had to go to work early this morning because Home Depot is having their end-of-the-year inventory. I know he'll be tired when he comes home tonight, so I'm planning to make him a special supper--fresh fish caught by our neighbor, Fred Budke.

How are you and Tom, JoAnn. Fine I hope. And the kids. Sometimes when I think of it I can't believe Jenny and Mark are all grown up and married and have little ones of their own. It must be thrilling to have grandchildren. I'll bet they come to see you for Sunday dinners. Lucky you, I often wish Walter and I had been able to have children but somehow they just never came along. It was probably for the best, though, because Walter needs a lot of quiet and order so that he can think. He has a lot of thinking to do because of his job, though honestly I don't see that the thinking has done him all that much good.

Molly erased this last comment. Lately she noticed in herself a temptation to criticize Walter--she needed to work on that. It was lucky she used an erasable pen for her letter writing. She reread the letter now without the uncalled-for remark about Walter's thinking. It was pretty dull, but what else was there to write about? She couldn't write to JoAnn about her other pastime--really, it was more properly called an avocation--the scrapbooks.

Over 500 finished scrapbooks now filled the closet in the spare bedroom, representing Molly's work over the last 25 years. Molly considered her scrapbooks a documentation of our times that would be valuable someday (though she would never consider selling them). Before JoAnn and Tom and the kids left San Diego for New Hampshire, JoAnn had often sniped at Molly about the stacks of magazines that multiplied yearly on the floor of the spare bedroom, awaiting Molly's scissors. No, her sister wouldn't enjoy a letter that made mention of the scrapbooks. JoAnn never cared to hear about anything she didn't approve of. It had only been in the last few years that Molly had felt she could mention Walter.

When she'd begun dating him at the age of eighteen, she'd thought JoAnn should be glad for her. JoAnn, two years younger and very pretty, had many boyfriends, whereas Molly had always been shy and not too popular. But JoAnn had hated Walter from the start, claiming that Molly was "embarrassing the family by dating that goose-stepping ninny." She was referring to the admittedly unfortunate fact that once or twice Walter had worn his ROTC uniform to a family function.

And then to think that JoAnn, a girl with such an aversion to the military, had ended up marrying a sailor! Even now the act struck Molly as the grossest hypocrisy, though Tom had been discharged from the Navy later that same year and had taken a job driving a truck. Now Tom owned a Beacons Moving franchise in Concord, New Hampshire and JoAnn tended to put on airs. Molly wanted to write something in her letter that would impress JoAnn, but she couldn't think of a single thing that might do that. She forged ahead.

My neighbor, Mrs. Budke, the wife of the man who caught the fish, has cancer, but I don't know her that well. As far as I'm aware she doesn't smoke, but her husband does, and they say Secondhand Smoke is hazardous to your health. I hope Tom and you have managed to quit smoking, JoAnn. And I wish Walter would quit, or at least do it outdoors, but he says a man's home is his Castle. I don't know who would keep his Castle clean if I were to get cancer. Maybe he should think of that the next time he lights up.

There she went again with the barbed remarks about Walter. She was about to erase this one, too, and then, in the interest of good health she let it stay. She ended her letter to JoAnn with a wish for a brighter new year, and then signed it "Your sister Molly."

Then she erased the "Your sister" part. JoAnn knew who Molly was, for Heaven's sake.

On the TV screen now there was a news bulletin. Molly didn't bother to turn on the sound, but she could see an airport scene and a man being taken away in handcuffs and leg chains. The man was dark-skinned and had a beard; he was wearing a sweatshirt and jeans, and he had a blank look on his face, but very pretty eyes. All the terrorists had beautiful eyes, Molly had noticed, but you wouldn't want to say a thing like that out loud these days, for fear of seeming unpatriotic.

Molly folded her letter to JoAnn and slid it into a green envelope left over from this year's Christmas cards. Then she put an old Elvis commemorative stamp on it and laid it lightly against her tongue like Communion, its glue reminiscent of those sacred wafers, dry and stale. Molly hadn't been to Communion--or even to Mass--in years, but she would never forget that taste, nor would she forget all those morning masses in the somber light of Our Lady of Angels when she was a child, walking back down the aisle from the Communion rail in her navy blue jumper and saddle shoes, the Body of Christ stuck to her tongue or teeth, fear of the Lord in her heart as she tried to dissolve it with spit because chewing was forbidden.

Church had made Molly increasingly uneasy with the years, in large part because she couldn't understand why God had not seen fit to give her any children, when all the pews around her were bulging with big families. Being singled out that way had made her feel *watched* whenever she was in God's House. Watched and judged. In all her years of marriage to Walter, she'd never once committed the sin of using birth control, and she had never stopped hoping for a baby until she went through The Change and had to face the fact that all hope was gone. It was only then, when she knew her fate was sealed, that she had stopped going to Mass. If God saw her as such a potentially undesirable mother, then she didn't see why she should worship Him. She did still believe He existed, but she wasn't going back for visits anymore. He probably wouldn't miss her anyway, and going would only encourage Him. Why should she contribute to His sense of self-importance, under the circumstances?

Sometimes Molly still missed going to Sunday Mass at Our Lady. Maybe what she missed was that sense of doing the officially ordained Right Thing, the feeling she'd once had of pleasing the Lord and being in His embrace. Since she'd stopped going, she'd felt unaccompanied in some way she couldn't explain. Molly pressed a three-cent bluebird stamp onto the green envelope beside the Elvis to equal the current postage rate and then took the envelope to the TV tray beside the front door and laid it on her stack of letters to mail.

Out the front window she could see the Pentecostal church across the street emptying onto the sidewalk, people of all ages and races. Holy Rollers, Walter called them, and she often wondered if it was true that they did that--rolled. She envied them a little, if they did. She wasn't sure she would ever dare to roll, even here at home, much less in front of others in a church. Maybe in her younger, more carefree days she could have done so. Of course, even if she still went to church, Catholics do not roll. And Walter--well, Walter would not roll under any circumstances. He was just not the type. She watched one of the Pentecostal women getting into a blue car parked in front of the house. The woman's dress was rumpled and she had a happy look on her face. Probably the rolling was at the root of that.

All of a sudden Molly found herself experiencing uncomfortable thoughts about sexual intercourse—why, she did not know. She tried not to think about intercourse too often, because it reminded her of things better left alone--a hasty image of Walter hovering above her in the dark bedroom, his silhouette outlined by the bluish light of the TV, the sound of him chuffing as he slapped his body against hers, *chuff, chuff, chuff*. Sometimes in their early years, on the morning after an intercourse, Walter had referred to himself as "Wild Man Walter," which she had found unsettling. But they had cable now, so Walter was less interested in the intercourse.

She turned toward the dining room anticipating the pleasure she'd deferred all morning. She hadn't been alone to work since last Friday, because Walter was home over the weekend and he didn't care for her scrapbook work.

Now she sat and studied the stack of newspapers on the table before her. The Saturday, Sunday, and Monday San Diego Union-Tribune. Wiping her hands on her pant legs, she took stock. There were the comic sections to clip, then any animal photos she could find--also, all medical or health articles and all weather. Right away, she found a column by Dr. Neal Heath on kidney stones. In the same section of the paper as Dr. Heath's column there was an article on the Heimlich maneuver, used to save someone who was choking. Molly read it carefully. It was important to know these things.

Next, she turned to the comics page. Garfield was funny today. She decided against today's Better Half because it was about the wife's cooking again, and that kind of humor was cruel, not funny. Molly had all of Rex Morgan, M.D. for the last nine years, and Apartment 3G for the last five. Those girls in 3G were always getting into the strangest situations, especially Magee, who was just too beautiful for her own good.

Molly wondered what it would be like to be too beautiful for your own good. Once, in eleventh grade Home Ec, when the girls were supposed to list their own best features for a section on sewing and style, Molly had turned to the girl next to her and asked uncertainly, "What should I put?" She could still remember how the girl, Giselle, had stared at her for a long time and then, as if searching for the answer to a difficult quiz question, had asked, "Um, maybe your eyes?...well...no...jeez, I don't know."

As Molly turned from the comics page, she paused to read the obituaries opposite. It occurred to her that she should read the death notices more regularly--after all, she'd lived in San Diego all her life, so she might know someone. Abrams, Beane, Downey, Frances, Hanes, Realto, Sanchez, Storey, Wok, Zimmerman. Zimmerman! She knew a Zimmerman. This dead Zimmerman was ZIMMERMAN John, husband of Rose. Molly knew a Mabel Zimmerman. It could be a relative. Poor Mabel, if it was. She said a quick prayer for Mabel if it was. If it isn't, she finished, just take this prayer and use it wherever it's needed. Molly tried to recycle everything, more from a thrift standpoint than because she was ecology minded.

She supposed she got her thrift from Walter. He was very careful with a dollar. He insisted on paying all the bills himself each month, even though Molly had more time than he did and had often told him she would be pleased to do it. He also insisted on doing the grocery shopping, bringing home 24-paks of toilet paper and five-pound jars of mayonnaise. He'd say, "Look--I saved on the mayo and got a nice big jar for nails in the bargain." She supposed Walter was what Oprah called "a control freak."

Walter was very clean, too. Thrifty and tidy, that was Walter Winter. Last week he'd come home with a giant bottle of Listerine, giving Molly discomfiting memories of their wedding night, when just before they went all the way for the first time, Walter had poured them each a tiny goblet of a gold liquid and set hers on the bed stand beside her, then raised his glass to her in a small toast. Awash in the uncustomary ambience of romance, she'd gulped hers before realizing what it was, and as she choked and spat the mouthwash out, he'd explained, "It's good hygiene." All through the years, he'd continued to pour them each a swig of Listerine before the marital act, but after that first night he'd just used bathroom-size Dixie cups, which made Molly reflect on how quickly romance slips away.

She wondered if he'd brought home all that Listerine last week in hope of reviving the romance in their life. She frowned, trying not to contemplate that possibility before it became absolutely necessary.

Occasionally over the years Molly had wondered what sexual intercourse might be like with someone other than Walter. It occurred to her that maybe she could have had babies with a different man--after all, the doctors had told her years ago that she had no medical condition preventing conception, so she couldn't help suspecting that the problem lay with Walter. Sometimes she imagined herself married to another husband, large and ordinary looking, maybe a little soft around the middle, but with a warm, cheerful face. In the family portraits she envisioned, there were several small children gathered round them, beaming like their father, while Molly herself smiled quietly and maternally at her brood. She knew such thoughts were unbecoming and possibly even morally wrong.

Her eyes lingered now on a newspaper photo of Julio Iglesias, the handsome Latin singer. She'd once seen a man she'd been certain was Julio strolling around the San Diego Zoo with a young woman who might have been his daughter, though Molly suspected not. Molly had trailed along behind the two of them just to see if the actual nature of their relationship might be revealed by their body language. Then, just as they came to the chimpanzee enclosures, Julio stopped to watch two chimps mating and Molly heard him shout a crude "Hooooo-eee!"

She'd lost a lot of respect for Julio as a result of that, but now whenever she saw a picture of him, her thoughts seemed to turn to sexual intercourse. She was not proud of this, but there it was.

Molly worked for an hour more and then it was time to prepare Walter's lunch. He always came home at noon because the cost of a meal out was an insult to a man's intelligence. She arranged the clippings in tidy stacks, according to category. She could put everything away while the food was heating, and be done before he got home. She noted that Medical was really thick today, with Animal Pictures second. As she passed her stacks of work along the table on the way to the kitchen, she pressed her hand lightly on each stack in turn, like a blessing, clicking her tongue against the roof of her mouth once for each stack.

She remembered how, when she was a girl, the Bishop would occasionally come to the parish for a visit and bless the children as they knelt at the Communion rail, laying his hand atop each head in turn and mumbling unintelligible words. The children were expected to kiss the Bishop's ring, a massive gold ring with some sort of religious insignia laid over mother of pearl. Molly remembered the first time she'd kissed the Bishop's ring. Even now, she could recall the shock of her young lips against his large, hairy knuckle.

To this day, that was the closest Molly had ever physically come to any man except Walter, but she supposed Bishops were not to be looked upon as men, in the fullest sense of the word. Bishops were never allowed to have sexual intercourse, alone or with others. Neither were regular priests. Or nuns. You had to wonder why God didn't want those closest to Him to have the intercourse. Molly suspected it was because He was a jealous God, which made her wonder if perhaps God had known how very much she would have loved her babies, and if that fact alone had been enough to put Him against the idea. But to compete for her love with tiny babies--that was just sick! Not that she was calling God sick, but there it was.

Molly startled when she heard the front door open and close. Walter! She'd forgotten that he would be home early for lunch today! She was just getting ready to heat up two slices of last night's meat loaf in the left side of the pan, and the leftover potatoes and carrots--which she'd mashed into a hash the way Walter liked them--on the right.

Her newspaper work was still all over the table, and some of the scraps were on the floor. She pretended not to see Walter, but felt her left brow twitching as she pressed the potatoes down with the backside of the spatula and then turned the meat. She slid her eyes sideways: he was standing in the dining room gazing down at her clippings.

"Jesus," she heard him saying. She hoped he wouldn't look under the table and see the scraps. He came into the kitchen then, and stood next to where she was working at the stove. "What's the deal with you, anyway?" he asked, "I mean, are you only happy when you're making a gigantic mess?" Before she could think of an appropriate answer, he went on. "You wouldn't believe what a miserable morning I've had! First, I put up with all kinds of shit and shenanigans at work and then I have to come home to that mess all over the table where I thought I was going to eat my lunch."

She wanted to point out to him that he didn't really have to come home for lunch, but then she saw him turn toward the dining room to survey her morning's work again, his hands turned backwards on his skinny hips. Walter was a tiny, dapper man with a thin moustache and a bulbous nose. Molly had always tried to look around his nose to the real Walter.

"Come in here a sec, okay?" he said, leading the way back to the dining table like a tour guide about to show her something she didn't know about herself. She didn't want to go, but she saw herself following him just the same. "I just want you to explain this to me, okay? What is the point of all this?"

She would have answered, except she suspected he wasn't really asking. And sure enough, he went on. "Are you just trying to drive me nuts here, or do you think I like to eat my lunch on a stack of newspapers?"

"I guess I'd forget my head if it wasn't glued on," she began, trying to demonstrate to him the humor in the situation. "How could I forget you were coming home early today!" She could smell the potatoes scorching. She hurried back to the kitchen and began prying them loose from the skillet.

"This is where I sit," she heard Walter saying to the table. Even from here in the kitchen, Molly could see the Shriners ring on his hand glinting in the bright noon window light as he swept her piles of clippings from the table. She watched as most of them fell to the floor, where they landed among the scraps and latticework remains of the newspapers.

She couldn't help rushing back to the dining room, but once there she was hesitant to pick her clippings up in front of Walter, who was looking directly at her just then, something he rarely did. And although through the years Molly had often wished he would meet her gaze, right now she found it alarming. It made her think about that Oprah show last week on the subject of Husbands Who Beat Their Wives.

Walter never beat her, she knew that.

"I'm trying to be calm," he said. "I'm a reasonable person, okay? You can hear that in my voice. Right?" He waited till she nodded her head and then he went on. "I'm telling you, you're gonna have to find a neater hobby, something like knitting, because I can't take this anymore. This is IT for the scraps, okay? The scraps are OVER."

Molly stared at the heap on the floor. Nearly all her morning's work. Again, she stifled an urge to drop to her knees and scramble around retrieving it.

She glanced at Walter's nose, then looked away, trying to remember his good points. Instead she remembered Bloomquist's Bakery a few years ago. When she'd noticed a help Wanted sign in Bloomquist's window just down the street, she'd decided it was time to find a job of her own out in the world. And since Walter had been talking a lot about money problems, it seemed a perfect way of showing him that she was a good helpmeet and a significant person in her own right. On her first day at work, Walter had marched over to Bloomquist's at noon to tell Mr. B. that Walter Winter's wife did not need this penny-ante job, because Walter Winter could bring home the bacon himself. (Even at home, Walter often spoke of himself by name, which Molly thought unnecessary since she knew quite well who he was.) The whole time Walter was carrying on at Bloomquist's Bakery, she had cowered behind the doughnut counter with powdered sugar on her hands, the knowledge settling immutably upon her that her career in retail was over before it had begun.

She looked again at the clippings on the floor, and then she walked to the kitchen to fill Walter's plate.

She carried the pale green porcelain dish of meatloaf and vegetables into the dining room. Walter was already seated in his place at the head of the gray formica table that had once been his mother's. Molly had always hated this table, though she knew you did not look a gift horse in the mouth. She returned to the kitchen for the reheated coffee. Three days' worth of newspaper clippings--it would be a chore to put them all back in order. When she walked back with the coffee pot and the mug that said "Walter" she noticed that Walter's foot was on the pile of clippings and newspaper refuse, tapping as he chewed, which was taking its toll on the clippings.

Molly sat in her place and watched Walter eat, waiting for him to tell her about his morning. Her eye kept sliding to his black leather shoe on the stack of clippings. That shoe had been Uncle Ivan's before he died. Ivan was an uncle on her side of the family. He wouldn't have appreciated what Walter was doing with that shoe right now. Walter hadn't looked up from his plate yet, but that was normal--usually he ate the first three-quarters of his meal quickly, without conversation, briskly nodding his head with each bite like a little dog. Molly had thought this was cute, years ago.

Without looking up from his food, Walter began talking.

"That brownnose Wiley Green was at it again this morning."

"Really?" She wished she'd left the question mark out of her voice so she wouldn't sound more interested than she was. Which was not at all. Her eye slid back to Uncle Ivan's shoe.

"All morning he was buttering up Mr. Grossman something awful. I'll never know how Grossman falls for that crap." Molly noticed how Walter's nose grew red when he talked and ate at the same time. Sometimes his nose reminded her of his private part, but she tried not to dwell on it. "You just watch now," Walter went on, "I'll get passed up again and Mr. Brownnose will be the new assistant manager of Home Depot."

"Oh no," she said automatically, for this was a familiar story by now.

"And all because," he looked up now and pointed to his tie, "all because Walter Winter doesn't kowtow to anyone." He lit a filtered Barclay cigarette, took in a steep breath, then blew out a billow of mentholated smoke. Molly held her breath to avoid inhaling secondhand smoke.

Walter stood up and ground the Barclay into his plate. Both of his feet were now on her clippings. The article about the rabid buffalo in North Dakota was stuck to the heel of Walter's shoe. It flapped as he walked to the front door, but Walter didn't seem to notice.

"Remember," he said, "when I get home tonight, I want that mess gone."

Molly had supposed, when she married him, that he would never be mean to her the way Daddy had been to Mother, because Walter was such a tiny man. But there seemed to be something about being a man that made it possible to be mean if you really wanted to, no matter what size you were.

She stared at the buffalo picture stuck to Walter's shoe.

"Well, off to slay the dragon," he said. He always said that as he left for work. She supposed it made him feel useful.

When he had gone down the front walk and out onto the sidewalk, the clipping still clinging to his shoe, Molly let the slat of the blind drop back into place and started toward the dining room to clean up her mess.

Then she found herself heading back to the window and lifting the slat again to peer out. Cars were collecting in the Pentecostal parking lot across the street and all along the curb, too, and the people emerging from the cars seemed to be hurrying, eager to partake of whatever awaited them inside the church. The rolling, she suspected. And it wasn't even a Sunday. She saw a handsome black couple talking with a heavyset blond woman and her two children. They were laughing as they headed up the steps into the church. A blue van pulled into the handicapped space then, and a ponytailed man got out and opened the door on the other side to assist an older woman in a red coat. Molly watched them walking up the steps together, the man holding the woman's elbow, until the double doors closed behind them.

She returned to the dining room to see if she could salvage any of her work.

The kidney stone article, sadly, was ruined--as were twelve other medical and health articles and seven animal photos. A picture of an ostrich in a derby hat had survived, as had the article on the Heimlich Maneuver and all the weather reports, as well as a few comics. Molly's heart froze when she saw that Rex Morgan, M.D., was a total loss for all three days. This was a crucial part of the ongoing Rex Morgan story: Rex had been struck down by a hit-and-run motorist and left lying like a dog in the street. How could she ever hope to fill such a gap in her scrapbook? Nine years down the drain.

She glued the ostrich picture into her green Nature scrapbook, the weather reports into the blue one, and the Heimlich article into her brown Health scrapbook. Of the cartoons, only one Garfield, two Better Half, a Far Side, and all three Peanuts reruns had survived. She pasted them into her yellow Humor scrapbook.

After she'd cleaned up the rest of the mess and washed Walter's lunch dishes, Molly made herself a cup of tea and a sandwich. As she ate, she mused that she really should write to Helen in Santa Fe. Helen, Molly's older sister, was a career woman who worked at an important job in an arts council office in New Mexico. Helen had never married, but she lived with a very nice woman named Sonya, who was a sculptor. Redhaired Sonya was a little bit mannish looking, but Molly believed the right wardrobe would make all the difference in the world, though far be it from her to interfere. Sometimes Molly thought Helen liked women almost as much as she liked men. Maybe more. Helen rarely answered Molly's letters, but Molly suspected she liked getting letters from her younger sister.

She finished her sandwich and made a second cup of tea, using the same tea bag. After she'd rinsed off her plate she carried the cup of tea back into the dining room and sat at the table with her letter writing supplies.

Dear Helen,

Today Walter came home early for lunch. I fixed him some leftover meat loaf with some potato and carrot hash. He enjoyed it very much.

Walter is probably going to get passed up for promotion again because he won't kowtow. Young Wiley Green will. Is Walter mad.

How is your work going? Mine is keeping me busier than ever, especially the Health. How is Sonya? Has she been making a lot of sculptures? I can't imagine having such a talent as that. Sonya has really been blessed. And so have you, Helen, to have such an important position In The Arts.

Walter has been wearing the Florsheim shoes you passed along when Uncle Ivan died and he enjoys them very much. It was very nice of you and Sonya to take Uncle Ivan in when Aunt Ruth died. He and Walter never got along too well, or I would have invited him to stay with us since we do have the spare bedroom and you're so cramped. Actually it was meant to be a nursery, but as you know we never had occasion to use it for that. Walter and I use it for storing our work instead.

Molly erased the part about the nursery. Then she erased the "and you're so cramped" part of the earlier sentence, in case it might offend Helen and Sonya, who took great pride in their little adobe house, which had been decorated in the Southwestern Style by Ali MacGraw herself, who lived nearby.

For dinner tonight I'm fixing Walter some fish that our neighbor, Mr. Budke, caught. He gave it to us because his wife has cancer and there was no one to clean and cook it. I don't know where the cancer is but she never comes outside anymore. You can see what I mean about the Health. Animals and weather are also big these days.

Happy New Year!

Love, Molly

Helen was the only person to whom Molly ever mentioned her work. It was important to have someone to talk to about your work--Molly had more than one health article on that very subject to back her up. Helen had given Molly a hand-tooled black leather scrapbook for Christmas. It was the first time anyone had recognized Molly's work. Although Helen had never actually mentioned it, Molly felt certain that her sister knew it was real work, not just a hobby.

And now Walter said she must quit.

She looked at the black scrapbook. The cover was real leather, with little Aztec designs embossed all around the border, and a big Aztec sun in the middle. A very special book. She had been trying to decide what she should use it for. Now she knew.

Molly went to the trash and shuffled through the discarded newspapers until she found the obituary column that listed poor Mr. Zimmerman. The top of it was a little wrinkled but the bottom, where Mr. Zimmerman was, was in perfect shape. Carefully she cut out ZIMMERMAN John, husband of Rose. Probably related to Mabel Zimmerman whom Molly knew personally. She pasted it on the first page of the leather scrapbook. Beneath it, on the manila paper, she printed: POSSIBLE RELATIVE OF MABEL ZIMMERMAN.

Then her eye fell on a Florsheim shoe advertisement in the paper. There was a shiny black wingtip shoe that looked exactly like Uncle Ivan's former shoe. She cut around it and then looked at it in the palm of her hand, thinking how that shoe had stepped on her work. Impulsively she glued it to page 2 of the scrapbook, printing carefully above it: UNCLE IVAN.

Walter would not like to think his shoe was in one of her scrapbooks. She looked at the shoe on the page and felt pleased. She decided to store the black scrapbook under their bed, on Walter's side.

She smiled as she put the scissors and glue away. She was still smiling as she went into the spare room to see if she could find a place for her current scrapbooks in the bureau. The closet shelves were completely filled with her scrapbook archive from more than two decades, and she knew it was no longer safe to leave her unfinished scrapbooks out where Walter might see them and become irritated. Maybe if all Walter's files, receipts, and important papers would fit into the top three bureau drawers, her current scrapbooks could fit into the large drawer at the bottom. She began shifting the papers.

It was there in the bottom drawer among Walter's oldest files that Molly found it--the very thing she must have been dreading all these years whenever she'd sensed some dark event or revelation in the offing. It had fallen out of a dingy manila folder, and now she held it in her hand--the piece of paper that explained her life to her.

Molly read and re-read the yellowed paper as if upon multiple readings a different meaning might come to light. The paper was dated June 12, 1975--two months before their marriage. It was a receipt for payment to a doctor in Hillcrest, a urologist. For a vasectomy. A vasectomy. She stood for a time in the quiet room, listening for something she didn't hear. Then she returned the paper to the folder and put it back in the bottom drawer. She shoved her scrapbooks under the guest bed instead. To think that all these years she'd blamed God. How would she ever make it up to Him? She seriously doubted that she could.

In the living room Molly turned on her morning shows and began dusting. Today was Living Room Day. Their house had six rooms--two bedrooms, a living room, a kitchen, a dining room, and a bathroom--and for years she had devoted each afternoon to cleaning a different room, with a day of rest on Sunday the Lord's Day.

During Oprah's last season on TV, Molly had worried to herself that she appeared to be getting too thin, just down to nothing; today Oprah was a guest on Molly's favorite interview show, and Molly saw that Oprah was thinner than ever. As she watched Oprah talking about her plans for the future, Molly wondered if she could possibly find Oprah's home address to send her a letter in strictest confidence, warning her not to marry Stedman, her longtime fiancé, because no amount of time could make a woman safe from a man's deceit.

The next guest was Dan Rather, who had retired from his job as CBS news anchor under a cloud of some kind, Molly couldn't remember what. For some time before his retirement, Molly had noticed that Dan seemed to be deteriorating night by night, and she'd thought it a real shame--after all, he'd been such a sweet looking young man once upon a time, and he'd bravely gone into all those war zones where he wore army jackets just like the real soldiers did. But toward the end of his run as news anchor she'd thought he looked a little crazy, and strange things seemed to keep happening to him in cabs and out on the streets, as well as in the newsroom. Even now that he'd retired and should look more rested, there seemed to be a slightly crazed look in his eye.

Molly had started a Dan Rather file in her medical scrapbook a few years ago when she'd first suspected Dan was losing his mind, and occasionally she'd had the thought that his problems might lie in the world of intercourse. She'd long believed that many people's problems could be laid at the door of intercourse. But today, watching him go on and on, she didn't care what Dan's problem was--he was only a man, like all the rest. She just felt sorry for his poor wife.

When Walter walked through the front door as Oprah was ending, there was no sign of Molly's work on the dining room table or floor. The gray dinette was cleared and wiped off. Walter seemed in unusually good spirits, and for a moment Molly thought he'd forgotten about the scrapbooks, but then as he walked past the table he said, "Good. That dust-collecting mess is gone. We'll get to the spare room this weekend and clear out all the crap that's piled up in there. I could use some more closet space for my files."

He sat on the kitchen stool next to the stove, which he rarely did anymore. Molly kept her back to him as she fried the fish. She didn't want him to see her face. She wasn't exactly sure why. He was in a talkative mood tonight, and never stopped the whole time the fish was frying. It seemed his good mood was due to the fact that Wiley Green had made.an inventory error and Walter had caught it.

"It would have cost the company $22.73, but I said to the boss, 'Not to worry, Walter Winter is on the job.' He was definitely impressed."

Molly turned to transfer the fish from skillet to plate and found her eyes drifting to Walter's nose.

"Is that so," she said, leaving the question mark off. He seemed not to notice, but that was his way.

When they were seated at the table, Molly listened as Walter began wolfing his food down in the usual manner. She didn't care for the sound, and she contemplated telling him so. She nibbled at her own fish in a desultory way.

Suddenly Walter was red-faced and motioning furiously at his mouth.

He must have a fishbone caught in his throat! Molly remembered the Heimlich maneuver she'd read about, and rising from her chair she found herself hovering there, bent forward at the waist as if to run to him and save him, but her legs didn't move. They did not move. Only Walter's hands moved, almost in slow-motion, as he put them to his own throat, his right elbow knocking over the nearly empty coffee mug that had his name on it. Molly watched a tiny pool of coffee spread beneath an edge of his plate and then, as if the weight of the very air around them were pressing her down, she found herself slipping slowly back into her chair and saw her hands resting, palms down, on the table like the hands of a chairman of the board in a movie, about to make an important announcement. But no words came. Her hands made soft circular motions on the table, as if shining its surface.

"I wrote Helen today," she finally said. "I told her about Wiley Green."

Walter was purple and tilting in his chair. It came to her that some things have a life of their own, and those things are Out of Our Hands. She felt the weight of the great inevitable come upon her at last, and it surrounded her like an embrace.

Walter's eyes were fixed on her, which was unusual. She smiled at him and their gazes merged; in that moment she felt her old love for him restored. He was a small, helpless man who feared the unknown. She saw that now. Perhaps their children would have been like him, but that was something she would never know.

"I never knew," she said to Walter. "Imagine. All these years."

On Thursday morning Molly got out her letter writing supplies and started a letter to her sister Helen:

Dear Helen,

On Monday evening Walter passed away at the dinner table after choking on a fishbone. Walter was

Molly paused here, unable to think of exactly what to say. Finally, she erased "Walter was," and after a while she started a new sentence:

The fish was given to us by our neighbor whose wife has cancer.

Then she erased that, too, thinking as always what a good thing it was that she used an erasable pen. She thought for a while longer and then continued:

Walter was enjoying the fish very much, so you'll be glad to know he left our world in good spirits.

But would Helen be glad to know that? Possibly not, Molly thought. Helen hadn't been overly fond of Walter. After a time, Molly put her letter writing supplies away, the unfinished letter crumpled in a wastebasket. She might have to find a new pastime, she thought. Letter writing no longer seemed to hold her interest.

At least she still had the scrapbooks. She sat down with the newspapers from Tuesday, Wednesday, and Thursday. In the Union-Tribune's Wednesday obituaries she found WINTER Walter R., husband of Molly. Carefully she cut it out and glued it in her black leather scrapbook on page 2, just beneath the shiny black shoe.

Then she stood, smoothed her skirt, and walked to the front door, where she hesitated for a moment before going outside.

As she crossed the street she felt her hair lifting on a breeze, and she thought, There will be time.

When she reached the bottom of the church steps, she heard singing coming from inside the building and she felt a thrill of fear run over her skin. She had never rolled before, but she would not turn away now. What else was left of the world for her?

Moving toward the music, she ascended.

Sincerely

Since the annulment, Laurel Havens had stayed in her rented room most nights and read library books and magazines or watched old movies on her iPad, a large bag of Cheetos in her lap. More and more, she was finding it hard to concentrate on her reading or even on the movies. In fact, several times lately she'd discovered herself frozen in the act of inserting a Cheeto between her lips, hand caught midair and the crispy orange tidbit resting on her lower lip as though the ribbon of film that was her life had snapped mid-scene, leaving her dangling there without the dignity of closure. For hours on hours now, she did nothing but think.

During the eight years of their marriage (which now, since the annulment, had never actually existed), Craig often told her she thought too much. When she'd asked for the annulment, Craig had offered that as proof that she thought too much.

"I'm finally through law school," he'd said. "For fuckssake, Laurel, this is what we've been waiting for! Now it's your turn to go to university full time. Why are you doing this?"

"I've thought of it for a while now," she'd told him. "I know you'll leave me eventually, now that you're out of law school and will be supporting yourself. Maybe not right away, but it will happen."

"What? What are you talking about? Haven't we both been waiting for this? I'll be an attorney now!"

"And that's exactly when men leave the women who've put them through school," she said. "We're not of the same class now. You're an attorney. I'm a sales clerk at the Harvard Coop. It's inevitable. You'll find a woman who'd be more appropriate as an attorney's wife, eventually. It won't be your fault. It's just human nature. I guess I'd rather do the leaving myself."

"Is this about your father?" Craig had said. "Because your father left your mother and you, now you think that's just what men do as a matter of course?"

"Of course not," she'd told him, but of course she was lying. Men left you. And never came back. That was what they did. She had the father to prove it.

"You think too much, Laurel," Craig had said for probably the millionth time.

If he'd thought she thought too much then, he should see her now.

Often at night while she sat in her room she could hear Andrej, a visiting scientist at Harvard who rented the room just down from hers, pacing back and forth from his room to the hall outside her room yelling into his phone in Polish for an hour or two. He always sounded angry when he called home to Warsaw, and Laurel wondered if there was something intrinsic to the language that gave that impression or if Andrej was just chronically irascible, a bully. She knew that his field was human response to sound, and she wondered if he would be interested in knowing how she responded to the sound of his voice barking interminably into the phone just outside her room. And why, she wondered, did he have to stalk around angrily while he talked? Did it take the motion of his large, unwieldy body to add heft to his anger?

Now she switched to a rock station on FM radio, keeping the volume low, and lay back on her bed. Though she preferred jazz, blues, and classical, she scrupulously gave equal time to rock, as a way of staying in touch with the Zeitgeist. Laurel felt that the day when she could no longer identify all of the groups in Billboard's Top 50 rock albums would be the day when she had slid irretrievably over the line into social obsolescence, so she'd continued listening to rock stations when the music verged into rap and hiphop, even though it left her feeling antsy and Caucasian. She'd never been crazy about being white in the first place, and now the race was actually becoming passé. But obsolescence was only one of the things she was worried about these days.

After considerable deliberation, she'd come to the conclusion that she had some kind of personality disorder: she was too reclusive, and her reclusiveness was fraught with inconsistencies. For example, she was lonely, but still she avoided people--even people she liked. During their marriage she and Craig had become somewhat isolated socially, and for all the years he was in law school it had seemed as if the world was made up of just the two of them. Since the divorce--annulment--she'd found it impossible to break out of that habit of solitude.

Artrecia Jackson, who worked with her in the credit office at the Harvard Coop, was the only person she ever confided in. Sometimes she wasn't sure why she bothered--Artrecia had no patience with Laurel's melancholy and discontent.

"What's wrong with you, Laurel, is you're stuck inside your own head. You need to get yourself outta that head sometimes and have some fun." But that was easy for Artrecia to say--she had it made. She was beautiful, witty and vivacious, had a full social life, and needed just six more credit hours to get her degree in marketing from Northeastern. And she had a big, close-knit, black family that gathered weekly to eat and play cards, or whatever it was that big families did when they gathered.

Laurel, on the other hand, had trouble letting go and having fun. She was Catholic. Lapsed, yes--but no amount of lapsing seemed to relieve her. And she had no family at all except for her mother, an old hippie who had named her after some trees. Laurel Willow Acacia Havens. If she'd at least been named after Stan Laurel, her name might've held some appeal for her. But trees...it was so 'sixties.

Laurel had kept her last name, Havens, when she married Craig. Now it seemed one more evidence that their marriage had never actually existed. Still it was a nice name, though the truth was there was no actual lineage behind it: Her mother had legally taken it on after seeing Ritchie Havens sing "Here Comes the Sun" one Sunday at a concert in Golden Gate Park, which was where Laurel was conceived. Not by Ritchie Havens, unfortunately, but by a knobby-looking white hippie who made violins and LSD in their basement apartment in Haight Ashbury and who had driven them across the country to a Woodstock reunion when Laurel was two and then left them stranded there when he met a woman who, he was "amazed" to discover, had the same mantra he had.

He came to see Laurel and her mother once after that, on his way to an ashram in India. By then, Laurel and Ash were living in the South End of Boston and her mother had awaited his return for about three years. After he left for India, Laurel's mother seemed to know that he was not coming back to make a family with them, so she changed her own first name from Mary Kathleen to Ash and refused ever to speak his name again. In a rite of grief and penitence for having erred. Screwed up. When

Laurel pressed her, Ash sometimes claimed not even to know his name now; to have "purified" herself of the memory. Ash was another of Laurel's major problems.

Ash Havens, neé Mary Kathleen O'Hara, was a reconstituted Catholic who had become fairly fanatical in middle age. Returning to the Church after all else failed, she'd had Laurel baptized at the age of ten and then enrolled her in Our Lady of Perpetual Help Elementary School. After a lifetime of love-ins, nude picnics and laid-back overnight dads in fringe and love beads, the rigor of Catholicism had come as a shock to Laurel. The only familiar thing about the Catholic Church had been the incense. Nothing else about it felt comfortable in the least. Even Laurel's name was all wrong--Catholics were supposed to be named after a saint, and here she was, named after a tree. Three trees.

Ash, who now worked as cleaning lady and cook for the priests at St. Sophia's Church, had taken vigorously to the role of missionary in her grown daughter's life. She was determined to bring Laurel back to the fold in order to secure her own place in Heaven, which seemed pretty selfish to Laurel--like when a friend gives your name to Verizon in order to get himself a special rate. But her mother was convinced that she was going to hell for her own past errors unless she made things right between her daughter and God. She'd even bought Laurel a subscription to The Southern Cross, which was how Laurel's name had got on all those Catholic mailing lists. Everywhere Laurel moved now, The Southern Cross and the mail from the missions followed her like the CIA.

Just yesterday she'd found a "Friars of Atonement" mailer in her new Cambridge post office box. It had a free holy card inside, the kind the nuns used to pass out to students who'd gotten an A on their religion exams at Our Lady of Perpetual Help Elementary. This particular holy card had Our Lady of Atonement on it, smiling grimly and holding the Baby Jesus in her blue-draped arms while angels tended in the air nearby— one angel holding a scroll of some kind, one a fish and a chalice, one a blossoming staff, and one gripping what looked to be a small nuclear warhead of some kind.

Laurel had an ever-burgeoning aversion to missionaries, and it seemed as if they were all around her in some form, beginning with her mother. Even good-natured Artrecia was always trying to convince her of what she ought to do and how she ought to be--and, as far as Laurel was concerned, any attempt to convince felt uncomfortably close to an attempt to convert.

She'd only had one date in eight months since the marriage had ended--a guy she'd met when he came in to apply for credit at the Coop--and the date had bombed. It was in the middle of this past winter that she'd gone out with Bernard, a Harvard MBA student who, during a two-hour, Dutch-treat meal of crab cakes at Casablanca in the square, had held forth about the stock market and his philosophy of "imaging for success" while Laurel made what she considered a heroic effort to seem animated and engaged in his monologue, inserting *Oh really?* and *Is that right?* every time she could get a word in. She had no paradigm for dating behavior, having married her very first boyfriend. Artrecia had advised her to ask Bernard about himself, but hadn't warned Laurel that asking might lead to two hours of non-stop monologue.

After dinner Bernard had informed Laurel that she was "a tad overly sincere," backing up his assertion with a quote he claimed was from from Andre Gide: "One cannot be sincere and at the same time seem so." He'd rattled off the quote while they stood shivering in line at the movie theater on Church Street, and then informed her that she ought to make an effort to seem less "uber-earnest" in order to add power and weight to her persona. "It's partly a style thing anyway," he said, "I mean, that kind of sincerity is pretty much *démodé* these days."

"I guess I'd believe you," she'd answered coldly as they shuffled into the movie theater with the rest of the crowd, "if you weren't so earnest about it."

That was the last word they'd spoken until after the movie, when she'd shaken his hand briskly and left him standing outside the theater after pronouncing, "I had a really, really great time tonight, Bernard. Sincerely."

The following Monday at work, Artrecia had told her that the way the evening ended wasn't really Laurel's fault. "How could you know that he was just the wrong kind of guy?"

"Maybe it was just me," Laurel had replied, "maybe I don't know how to pick them." She had waited for Artrecia to reassure her that the very idea was silly, but then noticed that Artrecia had a thoughtful look on her face, as if considering the possibility that it was so.

Now it was spring in Harvard Square. On Friday afternoon Laurel walked out the back door of the Coop and up the alley, exiting onto Brattle. All along the street she passed musicians, knots of students clustered around them on the sidewalk. As much as she loved the square, it had always made her feel like an outsider. It seemed as if nearly everyone in Cambridge had some relationship, past or present, to Harvard. Everyone but Laurel and, possibly, the panhandlers. Laurel's only relationship to Harvard, aside from her job as a credit clerk at the Coop and her disappeared marriage to a Harvard Law graduate, was that she often cut through the Yard on her way home to the room she rented from Cissy Bremerton, the widow of a famous Harvard scientist.

Laurel had never graduated from any college, though she figured she had probably completed enough units over the years to make her a first semester junior. She and Craig had always planned that when he finished law school and passed the bar it would be her turn to go to school full time. She'd worked at the Coop all during their marriage, taking night classes at U-Mass--mostly psych courses--whenever they could afford it. She was interested in what made people do the things they do, and not do the things they don't do. She supposed her mother was the inspiration for her interest in psychology. Ash was a walking textbook of syndromes and symptoms, twitches, tics, and breaks, problems of the sort that Laurel read about in the books she regularly checked out of the school library and the Boston Public Library.

At Nini's corner newsstand, she stopped to buy today's Globe and the Boston Phoenix, along with a copy of People Magazine and the tabloid Star--her secret vice. She had a longing to know the inside stories of other people's lives. She could imagine what Artrecia would say if she knew about People and Star: Why don't you get a life, Girl, and stop living in someone else's? That was easy for her to say, with her big family and her new boyfriend--a handsome dentist with offices in Newton and Cambridge. Laurel put her People and Star between the Globe and the Phoenix, just in case she should run into anyone she knew, making a more socially acceptable paper sandwich, with trashy tabloids as the hidden meat. It was 5:10 on Friday afternoon, and she had no plans. The weekend already seemed interminable, and she'd just got off work ten minutes ago.

"So long, pretty girl," Sam called as she walked away, and she flashed him an embarrassed grin. Old men always thought young women were pretty, even when they were just regular looking like she was. Once Sam had unexpectedly kissed her on the cheek and told her that if he were about sixty years younger he might just ask her to marry him. He'd been kidding, of course, but she'd been feeling so lonely that day that she'd actually turned the idea over in her imagination. Sam was about 80 and had rheumy eyes, but nonetheless she tried to picture having sex with him. The idea turned out to be disturbing, and not in a good way.

Lately Laurel found herself imagining everyone in the act of sex--Sam, Artrecia, customers in the Coop--even Cissy, her septuagenarian landlady. She refused to consider herself nosy--she simply found it interesting to guess about people. She told herself that was perfectly in line with her interest in human behavior.

Maybe she was just hard up for sex since becoming single again. She hadn't had sex since Craig.

"Maybe you were right about us," he'd said when she called him one day, feeling a tinge of regret about having left him. "Maybe it really was time for both of us to grow up and accept who we are and where we came from."

That was easy for him to say. For him, that meant joining his father's law firm and buying a townhouse near his parents' four story brownstone on Marlborough Street.

She supposed that, for her, accepting who she was would mean buying incense, love beads, and a copy of "Sergeant Pepper's Lonely Heart's Club Band."

Shortly after the annulment was filed, when they were moving personal items from their Harvard Housing apartment, Laurel had told Craig that, after thinking it through, she felt he owed her something for having supported him all through school. Artrecia had given her the idea, and on reflection, she knew Artrecia was actually right, as a matter of principle.

Craig had replied that it was, after all, his parents who'd paid his actual Harvard tuition, and that if he hadn't been married to her, he wouldn't have needed anyone working to pay for things like rent and clothes and food.

"I would have just lived at home with my parents till graduation," he'd said reasonably.   Craig was always so mild and logical that often Laurel couldn't be sure he wasn't right, even when she disagreed with him. He had a way of sounding so calmly certain. She'd found herself thinking, as they stood there together in their emptied living room, that he was going to be a pretty good lawyer.

Artrecia had been extremely pissed on Laurel's behalf when she heard about this conversation, and she'd described the situation to her father, who offered Laurel the money to retain a lawyer and "fight for what's yours." At first Laurel had been so thrilled with this show of fatherly protectiveness--it didn't matter whose father it was--that she'd gratefully accepted Mr. Jackson's offer. Then she allowed herself to imagine how the whole thing would feel--suing Craig. Her husband. Ex-husband. Never-married-to-her-at-all husband, since the annulment. Did she have the heart to go through the ugliness, the recriminations? Did she really want to borrow money to pay for it?

And then she'd thought of her mother, how so often her romantic liaisons seemed to end with hard feelings...and of all the times Ash had gotten payday loans just to get by when things were tough--how sometimes bill collectors had actually come to their house to collect. She knew she could never go through with a lawsuit--it would feel as if she were falling into her mother's patterns. She decided she would try to finish school on her own--or not at all.

Around the corner in front of the Harvard Coop, a guy was standing on his head and playing the guitar. A hand-scrawled sign next to his expressionless purple face read, Please help me--I need money to return to Portland. Last week this same man had stood on his head all day Saturday and all day Sunday, playing somewhat listlessly while passersby threw money into his guitar case. At first glance, Laurel had misread Portland as Poland and his plea had seemed particularly poignant. Now, on closer inspection, she wondered how much money a person needed just to return to Portland. Still, she tossed three quarters into the guitar case, avoiding his eyes. "Thanks," he croaked.

As she crossed Mass Ave, she saw a poster on a pole; it said

Adult Children of Heterosexuals

a queer new hard-edged cabaret band, now playing nightly at

Someone had torn off the bottom of the poster, so she couldn't see where they were playing nightly. But it didn't matter, since she went nowhere at night these days.

Laurel cut across Harvard Yard and exited on Kirkland Street. She really should have stopped while she was in the square and bought some kind of take-out for her evening meal. She had one large room at Cissy's with a hotplate and a toaster oven hidden next to the bureau in her closet, along with a cache of non-perishables such as Cheetos, peanut butter, bottled water, and a lifetime supply of Top Rahmen. Cissy did not like her roomers keeping food in their quarters, and since she allowed them limited kitchen privileges she felt they had no excuse for doing so. But Laurel felt a painful shyness overcome her each time she descended the stairs from her room to the kitchen. She didn't really know the other roomers (Cissy delicately called them "houseguests"), and it seemed as if on the rare morning or evening when she did risk going down there, inevitably one of the other roomers would be in the kitchen fixing a snack or washing clothes in the adjoining laundry space, which necessitated an awkward getting-acquainted conversation, even if all Laurel had wanted was to grab a quick glass of the milk that Cissy allowed her to keep in an assigned corner of the fridge.

She was halfway up Irving Avenue now and a fine rain was beginning to fall. It had rained a lot this week, and no doubt this was the beginning of another spring downpour. She could smell hyacinth blooming as she passed a neighbor's yard, and she looked up into their windows. Though it was barely dusk it was gray out and the upstairs rooms were lit, which inspired in her an inarticulate yearning.

The houses of others, seen from the outside, were a constant source of wistful gloom and irritation for Laurel when she walked past them. These people's lives appeared so seamlessly wrought—she felt certain they were the sorts of lives where everyone inside the house after dinner is writing a letter to the New York Times or fitting a model ship into a bottle or recording their family tree in the back of the Holy Bible. It kind of made her hate them all. She pressed her magazines close to her chest and walked up the steep, crumbly front steps of Cissy's house.

The rain was falling in earnest now and she hurriedly took out her key, first stashing the stack of newspapers and magazines under her jacket to keep them dry. That was when she discovered that Cissy had locked the glass storm door, making it impossible to get to the front door lock with her key. This was the third time in a month Cissy had done this, and Laurel knew that the elegant old woman was trying to tell her something. She'd already made clear to Laurel in an impromptu conversation in the kitchen one evening last week that she preferred renting her rooms to visiting scientists, "because of the hours they keep"-- leaving first thing in the morning and often not returning until nine or ten at night.

After ringing the doorbell and knocking loudly to no avail, Laurel walked around the house in the rain, knowing that she would not find Cissy outside in this weather but not sure what else to do. She got as far as the back fence and found the gate locked, then started around the front again, ringing the bell as she passed it, just in the case. She was getting hopelessly drenched and was starting to feel darts of panic in her belly. Cissy had to be inside if the storm door was latched. Maybe she was dead. Maybe she'd been murdered. She couldn't possibly be alive inside the house and simply not answer the door while one of her roomers stood outside in the pouring rain. Could she? It was possible, Laurel conceded. It was certain Cissy wasn't thrilled to have her at home so much.

But Laurel felt she had nowhere to go most of the time, and anyway she didn't like walking around alone after dark. It was too expensive to use cabs or even Ubers more than occasionally, and no public transport went as far as Cissy's house, which was at the end of Bryant Street, near where Bryant met Francis Avenue and Francis ended in a cul de sac. She could have biked into the square and then locked her bike somewhere, but after having two bikes stolen in the square so far--their locked chains cut in two—she'd soured on the idea of springing for another bike.

Laurel guessed that Cissy probably did regret having rented the room to her. She was currently the only female roomer in the old woman's house, and the other three "guests" were all distinguished visiting scientists from foreign countries--two of them--Andrej and a French microbiologist named Serge--were at Harvard, and Rueven--an Israeli who was studying genetic variation in insect feeding behavior--was at Northeastern. Cissy's late husband had been the fairly well-known author of a college textbook on insect feeding behavior, which Cissy said was what had brought Rueven to her door--he had come to the U.S. to follow in Dr. Bremerton's footsteps.

Aside from being around too much to suit her landlady, Laurel knew she wasn't up to Cissy's snob standards anyway, being just an office clerk at the Coop. She'd got Cissy's address from a Harvard rental file and she guessed she'd just happened by at the right time, a few days after one of the old woman's roomers had left unexpectedly, mid-semester, to return to Italy. It wasn't likely anyone else would have taken the room before the next term began, and so Cissy had let her move in.

From Laurel's point of view, it had seemed an okay deal--quiet, close enough to work and all the action in the square, situated in a pretty neighborhood, and it was cheap--the cheapest place she'd found in high-dollar Cambridge. She'd been used to the rent she had paid in Harvard housing with Craig, and she hadn't realized how much harder it would be to pay rent on a regular apartment out of her modest salary from the Coop. But what had appealed to her most of all about living in Cissy's house was that after eight years in a marriage that was suddenly non-existent, it consoled her to think of living in a house with other people rather than alone in some apartment. But she had to admit, now that she was actually living in a house with other people, she avoided them like the plague.

Laurel banged on the door again now, and the motion of her body shifted the stack of newspapers and magazines, which caused them to slip from beneath her jacket and fall into a puddle on the porch. Just then, a pale and wrinkled woman came out of the tiny apartment at the side of Cissy's house. Laurel often forgot that the apartment was even there, though Cissy had mentioned that there was a tenant living in the little place at the side. So far, she'd only seen her a few times from a distance, usually early in the mornings when the woman took her yappy little dog out for a walk. She was also some sort of scientist--a former Bunting Science Fellow at Radcliffe who had been working on the same book for the twenty years since her fellowship ended. Cissy had spoken of this condescendingly, her implication being that the woman would never finish the book, that she was a has-been who never had been.

"Oohoo," the woman called, walking toward Laurel and waving hello in the rain, her head and shoulders covered by what looked like a red-and-white checked vinyl tablecloth. Laurel hastily stooped and picked up the wet magazines, stashing the sleazy Star out of sight. "Oohoo," the neighbor called again, "do you need to get into the house? I heard you knocking out here." The woman tromped toward Laurel, the rainwet grass squishing audibly as she approached. It was a vinyl tablecloth.

"Well, yeah, I--the storm door is locked, so I can't use my key." If this woman had heard her from a room at the far side of the house, surely Cissy would've heard her too. Unless she was dead.

"Just come in through my apartment," the woman said, her stick-like legs striding ahead in the wet grass. Laurel followed obediently. The minute they entered the musty-smelling rooms, a yapping ball of fur hurled itself against Laurel's legs, its teeth grazing her right calf. "Now just calm down, Honeybunch," the woman said, scooping up the mutt and bringing his face close to her own and saying in a sing-song chant, "Are you a little scamp? Are you? Are you? Huh? Are you a scamp?"

Laurel was checking her calf through snagged tights with her fingertips to see if the skin was broken, and wondering if Honeybunch had had his rabies vaccination. "He's had his shots," the apparently telepathic woman said as she fluffed the growling doggie's neck. The apartment was pathetic--wallpaper torn and stained, floor covered with old linoleum that was bulging in some places, missing in others, and a bucket catching a leak near the front door. Laurel thought of Cissy's gracious rooms, which were visited once each week by a cleaning crew.

"Here we are," the woman said as she unlocked a door that led from her apartment to the rest of Cissy's house. She turned and extended her hand to shake Laurel's. "I'm Marilyn Shaghorn." She smiled then, and it seemed an unaccustomed act. Her teeth were brown, her eyes uncertain. Laurel took the woman's hand, shook it gently, feeling the small, fine bones, the cool integument of skin around them. She wondered if she would end up like Marilyn someday, alone in a deteriorating apartment, a nasty little mutt by her side.

"I'm Laurel Havens," she said. "Thanks a lot for coming to my rescue."

She stepped into her landlady's kitchen, where almost immediately she noticed that Cissy was indeed home, sitting at an elegantly set glass top table in the greenhouse-style breakfast room just off the kitchen, eating dinner alone. Cissy had to have heard her knocking and ringing the doorbell! Laurel knew her landlady had normal hearing--she had seen her respond to the doorbell on several occasions when they were talking in the kitchen, even while the noisy dishwasher was running. Oh, she'd heard Laurel, all right, and she had to hear her now as Laurel stepped into the tiled kitchen and the heavy door swung shut with a thump behind her, but Cissy never looked up. She simply continued eating, her perfectly coiffed head bowed over a great-smelling pasta dish. Laurel's stomach growled. She looked around the kitchen, saw evidence of dinner preparation--salad scraps, extra virgin olive oil, mushroom pieces, a sliced baguette, a garlic crusher, a bottle of cooking sauterne, the squeezed quarters of a lemon.

She was pissed. Way too pissed to speak. She walked quietly through the kitchen and up the stairs to her room, the aroma of Cissy's dinner tormenting her all the way. She closed the door of her room and set the wet newspapers and magazines down. She looked around, suddenly hating the mismatched rugs and lifeless curtains. Everything downstairs had a worn-around-the-edges sort of elegance: the huge red oriental rug in the living room, the green couch and paisley wingback chairs, the old mahogany grand piano with its ancient sheet music and songbooks stacked on the seat, and at the far end of the room the crimson velvet Harvard captain's chair with Cissy's husband's name and the date of his retirement engraved on a brass plate affixed to the carved mahogany back. Watercolors on the walls. And books. Walls and walls of books. Things didn't match so well, but still everything was beautiful in a shabby sort of way, like Cissy herself. Cissy's own bedroom across the wide square landing from Laurel's was also filled with lovely antiques, including a four-poster mahogany bed with an ivory satin quilted coverlet.

In the rooms Cissy's "guests" rented, it was a different story: on Laurel's bedroom floor a faded blue chenille bathroom rug next to the bed clashed with an orange and brown geometric area rug with a side section that had come loose and often strayed across the discolored oak floor, tripping you if you weren't vigilant. The bed was covered with a pink floral spread and the torn window shades had aged to a dark yellow-brown beneath pale blue nylon curtains. The bedside lamp, a ceramic woman's figure in a Grecian mode, had a frayed electrical cord, its wires exposed and brittle-looking.

Even above the mothball odor of her room, Laurel could still smell Cissy's dinner.

She walked to her closet, opened the bottom drawer of the bureau, got out a small loaf of bread and a jar of peanut butter, stared at them, returned them to the drawer. Then she sat on the side of her bed, which sank dangerously. She stood back up, stared at her closed door. She could go downstairs if she wanted--all the guests had Cissy's permission to use the living room whenever they wished, though as far as Laurel knew, no one ever did. At the moment, she was sure that the other roomers weren't even here, having the sense to come home at ten p.m. and leave Cissy to revel quietly in the peace and solitude of her house.

Laurel turned on her iPad and clicked onto regional news. A local reporter was interviewing a pale, redhaired man dressed in flowing garb and identified in the chyron at the bottom of the screen as some sort of maharishi. The reporter was asking him where he was from.

"I yam from everywhere," the freckled maharishi said in a whiny voice. "Not from only one place on the earth."

She stared a minute, then turned it off, looked around. She felt trapped, shut up in this room like an errant child--one who had come home too early and had to be punished. She looked at the door again, then at the closet. No way was she staying in tonight with a peanut butter sandwich.

She dialed Artrecia's number. Artrecia had a car. They could go out to dinner and a movie. Laurel hated phoning people, and rarely did so. Artrecia would be surprised to get a call from her.

The phone rang and rang, and then the message came on and Laurel remembered that Artrecia and her boyfriend were going to a concert. She hung up before the message had finished. Had she really thought Artrecia would be home on a Friday evening?

Then, as if hypnotized, she saw her finger punching her mother's number into her phone. It was only then that Laurel realized how desperate she was.

She listened as her mother's phone rang, and had nearly given up when Ash answered. As always, Laurel was surprised at the silky, musical tone of her mother's voice. It didn't match the way she lived--cats everywhere, overflowing ashtrays, dirty dishes in the sink, bedroom slippers on the kitchen floor.

"Mother?"

"Laurel! What a surprise!" Ash sounded genuinely pleased to hear her daughter at the other end of the line. It made Laurel feel a little guilty.

"Yeah, well, I just..." Now that she had her mother here, she didn't know what to say to her. How could she tell Ash what was wrong tonight and still insist that she was doing fine on her own? Ever since the divorce--annulment—Laurel's mother had been pressuring her to move back. These days Ash rented one floor of a triple-decker in Somerville and it was pretty nice. She kept mentioning the spare room she had with a half-bath and its own separate exit to the street, but Laurel could not imagine moving in with Ash. After less than an hour with her, Laurel always had a headache, no matter what the occasion.

She heard Cissy rinsing her dinner dishes downstairs in the kitchen, and her anger rose anew. She plunged ahead. "I was wondering if you'd like to go out for a bite of dinner." Since you have a car and I have to get out of here.

"Well, I'd love to...but I..." Her mother was obviously torn-- she apparently had plans but felt stumped because it was so rare that Laurel made any overture at all. Again, Laurel felt a twinge of guilt, even as she was mentally coaching, *Cancel it, cancel it.*

"...It's just," her mother was saying in a tone of genuine confusion, "I have the cats tonight."

The cats. Oh God, the cats. Ash Havens was a charter member of a small group of cat lovers called "Petpals" who went around Boston trapping feral inner-city cats, taking them to be neutered, courtesy of a trust fund set up years ago by some Back Bay dowager. They cared for the felines till they healed, at which time they released them again to specified feral cat colonies around the inner city of Boston, where Petpals would then deliver dry cat food once a day. The group was divided into Feeders and Trappers, alternating duties monthly. Ash was a Trapper this month. There was nothing Laurel could imagine to be less pleasant than going along with her mother on a cat-trapping spree. No fucking way she was doing that.

"Can I go with you?" she asked her mother. "I could help."

And that was how she wound up bouncing around the city in Ash's rattletrap VW on a Friday night, two full cat-traps on the backseat and one on her lap. The rain had stopped, and the evening was mild. There was a lot of hissing and yowling going on in the VW, but Ash was talking nonstop and didn't seem to notice. She was telling her daughter about a man she'd met--one of the Petpals--who had offered her a foot massage one night as they drove back together from a feeding expedition at a cat colony near the Boston Public Library.

"A foot massage! And this is a guy you barely knew?"

"Right," her mother said.

"What did you say?" Laurel couldn't imagine letting a near-stranger touch her feet.

"Well, I told him I thought maybe it wasn't a very good idea."

"Good for you," Laurel said. "He's probably a foot fetishist, some kind of creep."

"Oh, I don't think so," Ash said. "It's just that I don't really want to get involved right now. Sam and I only broke up a month ago, and I'm trying to be more careful with my heart." Careful with her heart. Her mother's heart was a regional lending library, and *had* been for all of Laurel's life. Not that her mother was promiscuous, exactly--now that she'd returned to the Church, she had to be "truly in love" before sleeping with a man, unlike the old days when "a vibe" was reason enough. It was just that Ash fell *truly in love* pretty often. Twice in the eight months since Craig and Laurel had been apart. Ash was still slim and very pretty in a hippie-ish way. She wore her long, gray-streaked auburn hair in a braid down her back, and her wardrobe had not changed much over Laurel's lifetime. Laurel had been distressed to discover, on her last sashay through Urban Outfitters in the square, that her mother's tie-dye, gypsy look was coming back into style. Did this mean that Laurel would now be faced with the choice of either dressing like her mother or becoming a fashion throwback (also like her mother)? No matter what Laurel did, it seemed she was doomed to end up like Ash.

And that was the very last thing in the world she wanted. She'd spent years working at not being her mother. Everything she did, said, and wore was in reaction against her mother.

Even her marriage to Craig had been, in a sense. His family was everything she'd always imagined--two parents, a beautiful home, a sense of generation following generation to fulfill the bright promise of the family name. Tradition. Continuity. Stability. And she supposed her own background had seemed romantic to him in the opposite way. Certainly it had horrified his parents--that she knew.

Yesterday in the Globe she'd seen the announcement of Craig's engagement to Alison Goode. Alison had been a member of Craig's study group all through law school. Alison Goode had a nose job and came from the right kind of family. Artrecia wondered aloud if Craig and Alisonmight have been involved for years, but Laurel didn't believe that, and she couldn't bear to think of such a possibility. It made it seem as if nothing in the world was real.

Anyway, she reminded herself, since the annulment she had asked for, their marriage wasn't real. Technically, it had never existed.

Laurel vowed to show everyone. She imagined herself in the future--a prominent Newton psychiatrist upon whose couch Craig's future wife Alison would lie and bawl her eyes out when he'd left her because he couldn't stop thinking about Laurel.

"Maybe it was the nose-job," Laurel would tell Alison sympathetically, "...but of course, that button-nosed look was in in those days! How could you have *known?*"

"How could I have *known,*" Alison would echo, her voice rising to a wail on the last word. Lauren would hand Alison a Kleenex with which to dab at her petite, artificial proboscis.

The Pinto lurched to a stop in front of Ash's place, and Laurel realized that she and her mother had driven in silence for a while. This didn't happen often. She looked at her mother's profile, wondering if something was on Ash's mind. It was always hard to tell.

They carried the cats into her mother's third of a large and murky garage, the three sections divided with chicken wire from floor to ceiling. The air was heavy with a smell of dust, cat pee, and the axle grease of long-departed autos.

"Are we going to take them out of their cages?" Laurel asked warily, eyeing a large and mad-at-the-world Siamese in the trap nearest her. The cat sneered at her each time their eyes met, and then emitted a sound like a tire expelling air. In the cage Ash was just setting down, a calico female had huddled out of their sight, intermittently sending out a bone-chilling moan.

"Oh no," Ash said, "they'd get loose and then I'd never get them back. I've got to take them to the vet's first thing in the morning."

"On a Saturday?"

"Well, Dr. Eisenmann saves the first and third Saturday morning of each month for our feral kitties. Does it for free. Pro bono. She's an animal lover like us." Ash was sitting back on her heels, murmuring words of comfort to a small orange shorthaired kitten that was mewling pathetically against the gridwork cage door. Looking down onto the top of her mother's head, Laurel noticed threads of gray shooting through Ash's hair and felt a frisson of something—fear? Grief? Someday her mother would get old and die, and then Laurel would have no one. Ash--Mary Kathleen—had been the only child of parents who had died in a freeway pileup on the night of their daughter's high school graduation, so there were no maternal grandparents in the picture. And it went without saying that there was no "father's side" to fall back on.

She looked at her mother again, picturing Ash at eighty in a rest home, hunched in a wheelchair in a long fluorescent-lit corridor, wearing the same tie-dye tee shirt, fringe jacket, and India-print gauze skirt she had on tonight with tights and red cowboy boots. Laurel couldn't see any way around the fact that life was a stomachache and bound to get worse.

Ash had let the small orange kitty out onto her lap, and was sitting back on the oily concrete, petting its bony back while it nuzzled her.

"Look at this one, will you?" her mother marveled. "It's so sweet! Not afraid of me at all. See?--it just wants to be cuddled." Ash held the kitten up and inspected its privates from the rear. "It's a girl," she said, sounding like a proud mama on a birthing bed. "You know, I think she might still be too young for spaying. It's hard to tell, she's so underfed. She could just be small."

"What'll you do with her if she can't be spayed yet?"

"I'll take her in with the other two in the morning, to be looked at and get her rabies and feline leukemia shots, and I'll

just have to see then what Dr. Eisenmann says. I'd hate to let her
go back out there unspayed, but I guess I might have to."

"Back where we got her?" They'd found these three in the
Public Garden.

"Well, there's a colony close by, just down from the State
House."

"She'll be pregnant before you could ever find her again."
Laurel had taken up the kitten and was stroking her scrawny
head. "She's got a purr like a locomotive."

Ash looked perplexed. "Well, we Petpals never bring feral
cats into our homes to mix with our own domestic ones--no
telling what they might have. Feline luke is rampant around the
city right now. Anyway, she'd have to be quarantined somewhere
for fourteen days."

It was a cinch Laurel couldn't bring the kitten home to her
room in Cissy's house, where even Cheetos were contraband.
She settled back against the chicken wire and nestled the bony
kitten against her. "She's so tame."

"Yeah, probably part of a litter some family abandoned in
the park. It happens all the time." Ash reached out to pet the
kitten. "It's sad--she's obviously used to people."

The orange kitten had curled itself around Laurel's arm in
an unlikely and uncomfortable-looking position, and seemed to
be falling asleep.

"I bet she hadn't been out there too long when we found her,"
Laurel said. She sniffed the cat's head. It had a not-unpleasant
damp fur smell.

"Could be," Ash agreed, filling all of the cage-door feeders
with dry food and water.

"She looks like a Cheeto."

"That would be a great name for her," Ash laughed, taking
the cat from Laurel and returning her to the cage. Ash looked
into the cage again then, pressing her nose to the grid, and said,
"Wouldn't it, Cheeto! Huh? 'ould 'ou like dat name? Hmmm?"
Ash rose to her feet and looked at Laurel, a slightly uneasy
expression on her face. "Come on inside, and I'll fix us a cup of
tea. There's something I've been wanting to talk to you about."

Laurel followed her mother out of the garage and into the house, an inevitable foreboding in her stomach. She couldn't remember any of Ash's announcements ever coming to any good. And her stomach growled audibly when Ash poured them each a cup of apricot tea and intoned, over the rising curls of steam from the two cups, "As Gary Snyder says, you never find anything until you're not looking for it...."

Later, back home in her room at Cissy's house, Laurel had all night to stay awake and think of what her mother had told her. She had found Laurel's father. In Boston. She'd seen an ad in the Globe with his picture in it and recognized him right away. He was going to be in town just this weekend, and then he would be continuing on with his tour of the United States. That was the part that required deep thought: Laurel's father was a holy man. A cult-leader in sandals and a sheet. An Irish-German man who had tken the name Soon Moon Soon. *The Reverend* Soon Moon Soon. After all her efforts to avoid the company of missionaries and reformers, her father was making a living as one.

But all of her life Laurel had wished for a father. All of her life she had yearned for continuity--and though she liked the name Havens well enough, she'd often dreamed of finding her real father and learning his last name, shedding her own ersatz last name and replacing it with a real one, a name that spoke volumes about her own personal history, her family heritage. So what could a made-up name like Soon tell her? Or was it Moon Soon? Moon Spoon June. All it told her was that there were flaky genes on both sides of her family. Her heritage was Sublime and Eternal Goofiness.

All night she wandered in and out of a dark and empty sleep. Once, she heard Andrej barking into his phone in Polish, and then she heard Cissy talking to Andrej in the hall. She felt sure she heard them walking across the hall together to Cissy's bedroom, but maybe it was just a dream. Sometime past three the rain started up again, battering the windows while thunder boomed in the distance. She thought of Marilyn Shaghorn curled up in bed with her nasty little Honeybunch, a dented bucket catching the rain's codified taps by the front door. She imagined Cissy across the hall, nude, in a convoluted pose with Andrej on the four-poster, ululating while Andrej took note of his own response to her wails. She imagined her father, the maharishi--

blurred, grainy and black-and-white in real life as he had been in the ad her mother showed her tonight—but in her dreams now, everything around him was in color. He was polishing a pink Rolls Royce while pink young women lay prostrate around it, a pearly pink temple rising in the background.

On Saturday morning Laurel got up at six with what would have been a hangover if she'd had anything to drink the night before. She paced her room, munched a few Cheetos and drank some Calistoga water, then showered and dressed in her Levis and an old orange sweatshirt that reminded her of the little orange cat that would have to be let out onto the streets soon, one way or another. Cheeto. She went to the phone in the hall and called her mother. Ash answered on the second ring, sounding as if she'd been asleep.

"Can I go with you?"

"Who is this?"

"This is Laurel, your daughter." She was insulted that her mother hadn't recognized her voice.

"Laurel?"

"Yes, your daughter."

"I know you're my daughter, I just don't know…"

"Why I'm calling so early? Well, I want to go with you to the vet's. When are you leaving?"

"About seven. What time is it?"

"Six fifteen."

"Oh, Jesus, I'm going to be late. I've gotta go."

"Swing by and get me first."

"Swing by? I live in Somerville, remember? The vet's in Framingham."

"Please? I'm feeling all weird."

That was, apparently, language her mother could understand.

"Okay," Ash said. "But if I'm gonna do that, I've really gotta rush. Bye."

This time Laurel held the cage with the orange kitten in it, her fingers nuzzling the bony head through the cage door as Ash drove furiously up Storrow Drive over the Charles River and exited onto the Mass Pike, squinting over her own cigarette smoke and sipping coffee from a red plastic mug that said PETPALS on the side.

"Is this about your father?" she asked Laurel at one point.

"Yeah, I guess."

"Well, look, I'm sorry if what I told you freaked you out. Maybe I shouldn't have said anything."

"No! It would've been really wrong not to tell me. But now everything's, well, just different."

"I know what you mean. Me, too."

"You? How?" After all, he wasn't Ash's father. Just a hippie she used to sleep with in a room with a blacklight and psychedelic posters.

"I don't know. It just feels strange to realize he's right here after all this time. And to see that he's some sort of religious leader." Religious leader. That was a kind way of putting it. In the photo, his left hand was raised to the supplicant masses and his right hand was pointed toward his heart the way Jesus Christ's hand was on paintings she'd seen in church as a kid, and there was a ring on his right index finger with a stone on it the size of a school bus. Ash squashed her cigarette in the open ashtray. "After all, we did have a kid together."

"Are you going to go and see him?"

"Hell, no. Why would I want to do that? He never bothered to look me--and *you*--up, did he?"

"Maybe he could never find us after you changed your name from Mary Kathleen to Ash." This was something Laurel had worried about for years--and it was also how she'd always explained away her father's failure to communicate with her--but she'd never dared to mention the whole idea for fear of upsetting her mother.

"He knew about that."

"What?"

"The name thing."

"He did? How could he know?"

"He knew because I wrote and told him. He always knew where we were."

"You wrote him? How did you get his address?"

"He gave it to me when he left for India. An ashram here that forwarded mail to their missionaries there."

"How do you know he ever got your letters?"

"I know," Ash said.

"Why? Did he ever write you back?"

"Twice." Ash was uncharacteristically terse.

"Did he ever write to me?" Laurel pictured Ash in a witch's hat and cape, destroying daily letters to her from her devoted father.

"Do you really want to know this stuff?"

"Yeah."

"Okay, then..." Ash stared straight ahead. "No. He never wrote to you, never called, never came looking for you. He said to wish you peace. He said that once, in his second--last--letter to me. That was all. To wish you peace."

"To wish me peace?" That was news to Laurel. Her mother had never told her any of this. She'd always thought that when he left, he'd as good as dropped off the earth. Now she turned the words over and over in her mind, as if in the turning she would find some hidden message, a legacy of some kind. "What were his exact words?"

"What?"

"When he wished me peace."

"I don't remember. He just said he wished you peace."

"Well...how long did you write him?"

"Just for a year or so. He was a lousy correspondent and I finally just quit. But the point is, he's always known my name, and I've always been listed in the Boston phone book, so why should I want to go and see him?"

"Well, I have to."

"What?"

"I have to."

"The man abandoned you, Laurel. I worked as a maid to support you by myself for your whole life. He never contributed one penny toward your upbringing. And now you want to go and get chummy with him. That's just rich." It was strange to hear her mother use a word like *upbringing*. That wasn't a word that came to mind when Laurel revisited her childhood.

"We don't even have a real *name*," Laurel suddenly burst out. "I guess I always hoped he'd come back and give me a real name."

"You call Soon Moon Soon a real name? And anyway, what do you mean we don't have a real name," Ash said indignantly. "It was good enough for Ritchie Havens--it's a goddamned real name, okay?" Her hand shook as she lit a new cigarette, which she immediately sucked on with vehemence, horking the smoke out in a huge billow around the steering wheel. Laurel thought better of telling her mother that all this secondhand smoke couldn't be good for the cats.

"Our name has no real history to it," she told her mother. "You made it up. It doesn't go back anywhere." She thought of Alison Goode, certain that *her* family name went all the way to Plymouth Rock. Then she looked at her mother and saw the hurt on her face. "I mean, it's a *nice* name, Ma--but, you know, it's not a *real* name. And I think something like that makes a person's life different from the lives of all the people who have real names."

"Well, isn't that *special*," her mother said bitterly. "I guess I'm just one big failure without a leg to stand on."

"That's not how I meant it," Laurel said, but then there didn't seem to be anything more to say. Laurel wished for the first time that she was a smoker, too—at the moment it would have given her something to do as the awkward silence seemed to expand the physical space between them. She rubbed the knotty little orange head of Cheeto through the bars of the cage door, sneaking a look at Ash, whose jaw line was set in a way she'd never seen. *Well*, she thought, *I've done it now.*

For the rest of the morning Ash was tense and unchatty. Dr. Eisenmann--a plump woman with her hair in one long braid like Ash's--said that all three of the cats could be neutered, and that Ash could pick them up on Monday. Ash drove Laurel back to Bryant Street and dropped her off with a clipped, "Don't forget where you come from, okay?"

150

"I never have," Laurel answered as she got out onto the sidewalk in front of Cissy's house.

She read her mother's bumper stickers as the Pinto made its way up to the end of Bryant. There were five of them: *Dominus Vobiscum*, said one, and Laurel remembered from her Sunday missal that it was Latin for *The Lord be with you.* Near that was a yellow sticker informing other drivers that "Jesus Died For Our Sins." On the other side of the bumper was a bright blue "I am a Deadhead" sticker, a red "Shit Happens," and a "Jerry Garcia was the Messiah," in Olde English script. Laurel turned toward Cissy's house, her life flashing before her eyes.

It was a long walk from the Copley T-stop to the address on Tremont Street and it didn't do Laurel's short and wispy hairstyle any good. She wanted to look her best today. She looked up at the sign in front of the tall, square brick building, which was formerly a warehouse of some sort. The sign said NOW RENTING for ALL OCCASIONS, and beneath that were listed upcoming activities: a flea market on the third Saturday of each month, Bingo on Tuesday and Thursday evenings at 7, someone's wedding reception next Saturday--that was hard to imagine, in a place like this--and a salsa dance group on Friday nights. For today, Sunday, it said simply *His Holiness, The Reverend Soon Moon Soon, 3 p.m.*

She would wait for him. He would no doubt arrive a bit early, in the company of his closest disciples. God, she hoped he didn't have a Rolls Royce like in her dream--she knew lots of those maharishi types did. She would approach him quietly and with decorum, and she would announce herself to him no matter who was around. Then, after he recovered from the shock, they would just have to let things take their natural course. It wouldn't be an easy announcement for him to digest all at once, without warning. She smoothed her hair. She was wearing a dress Artrecia had passed along to her--a black cotton-knit ballerina style dress. She wished she had a white dress--it would look sort of angelic, which might appeal to a cult leader. But she looked nice in this one and it would have to do. She looked at her watch. It was two thirty. She sat on the steps at the building's front entrance to wait for him, and watched traffic move up and down Tremont.

At just about the time a few students with shaved heads began showing up--all of them dressed in white (damn!)--a caravan of white Audis pulled up along the curb, and she knew it was him. Well, at least he didn't have a Rolls entourage. Yet. Then she saw him get out. Her father. He was still the long, knobby man she vaguely remembered, but his head was shaved now, leaving only a long, pale reddish-brown braided queue at the upper back of his skull--the same color hair as her own. He was wearing all white garments and off-white Birkenstocks with yellow socks. He had a yellow ribbon woven through his braid and a spot of saffron-colored paint between his eyebrows. The students--by now about twenty of them and almost all female--rushed over to him, and Laurel found herself somewhat outmaneuvered, stuck at the rear of the crowd. She saw her father raise his hand as he had in the newspaper ad.

"Peace be to all of you," he said in a soft, nasal voice, and immediately the men and women who had accompanied him in the motorcade surrounded him, sweeping him toward the warehouse, their white robes flowing and commingling. The rest of the crowd obediently fell back, which gave Laurel a straight shot at him.

"WAIT!" she said. She only realized after the fact that it had come out sounding like a command. Her father stopped and turned to look at her. His followers did likewise, as did the student devoteés. She hurried toward him and saw his entourage close in around him as if fearing an assassination attempt. For all she knew, her reason for being there might be even worse, from his point of view. But she had to go through with it now. She'd waited too long as it was. A whole life long.

"I'm Laurel," she announced as she stepped in front of him. She could see his bony face, his freckled white skin, but there was no change of expression in his eyes, no gathering frown of dawning recognition. "Laurel," she repeated, "I'm Laurel."

"And I am the Reverend Soon Moon Soon," he said with a rote smile, placing particular emphasis on the d's of "and" and "Reverend" so that they very nearly sounded like t's, and caressing the oo's of his name as if he cherished them. Then somehow, in what seemed a split second, she found that he and his followers had swept ahead toward the entry to s the building. She stood in place for a moment, her legs twitching and shifting like M. Hulot's legs in that old French movie, "Monsieur Hulot's Holiday"—it was as if they couldn't decide whether to carry her forward or backward, to stay or to leave.

"Your daughter," she yelled at his retreating form, and then she saw that her legs had made their decision. As she began the long walk back toward the Copley T-stop, she said into the air, "I've had an annulment, Dad." She imagined throwing a rock at him, but it didn't help.

All the way back on the Green Line she read the ads above the windows, avoiding the eyes of the other passengers. She saw one ad for the Little Brothers of St. Francis, telling fallen-away Catholics to come in to see the good brothers and unburden themselves of shame. For a moment, she yearned to throw herself into the laps of the Little Brothers of St. Francis one by one, weeping and confessing everything, forgiving everyone. But then it seemed as if their laps would be little and incompetent and she wasn't up for any more rejection in one day.

Peace be to all of you, he'd said to a herd of perfect strangers, a bunch of people who weren't even his daughter.

At the Park Street station, she waited for the Red Line, leaning over to watch the tiny mice scrambling back and forth across the tracks. Suddenly she needed to talk to her mother. Fishing through her purse, she realized she'd left her cell phone charging in her room. Did she know Ash's phone number by heart? She walked over to the pay phone on the wall behind her and found herself dialing Ash, the number coming to her like a...well, like a mantra.

"Hi," she said glumly into the mouthpiece when her mother picked up.

"Laurel?"

"This is Laurel. Your daughter."

"Are you okay?"

"Yeah."

"So, what's up?"

"Do you think Dr. Eisenmann would board Cheeto till the quarantine is up?"

"I--why?"

"I dunno. I was just thinking of that room."

"What room?"

"You know, the spare one with a half-bath and its own private exit to the street."

"Oh, yeah?"

"I'm a very tidy person, you know."

"That's no problem," her mother said generously.

"I don't smoke."

"It takes all kinds."

"I'm not sure I believe in God."

"Well, different strokes. Give yourself time."

"There's a half-time job coming up at the Coop--if I took it I could go to school full time."

"Sounds like a pretty good idea."

"But I couldn't afford rent if I did that."

"That's a fair trade--I couldn't afford your tuition."

"I need that cat."

"I knew that already."

"So you think the vet would board her?"

"She said she would when I phoned her yesterday afternoon."

"Yeah?" Laurel stifled a smile, glowered at a nattily dressed man who was standing nearby, listening.

"Yep."

There was a silence. Then, "Sorry," Laurel said, "for what I said about the name thing."

"No--you shouldn't be sorry. Definitely shouldn't. I've been thinking about that all weekend and...maybe you're right." Her mother's voice sounded artificially upbeat.

"What?" Laurel's train pulled up, passengers boarded, and then it was gone, leaving Laurel alone on the platform, concentrating on her mother's voice. "What do you mean?"

"I'm thinking it might change our lives in a positive way if we went back to O'Hara. Got ourselves a real history again, like you said."

"After all this time? Are you serious?"

"Yes I'm serious. I phoned a lawyer I used to date--remember Henry Carrera?" Laurel didn't. "Well, he says he'll do the paperwork for both of us."

"No."

"What?"

"No, Ma. Havens is our name. It's what we have. It's our history."

"Not much of a history, is it? It only goes back, like, twenty-some years."

"Well, history has to start somewhere," Laurel said.

"It's just the two of us that way," Ash said dubiously.

"Yeah, I know," Laurel answered, "but that's all we have right now. So what?"

Ash laughed. She sounded relieved, like when someone decides not to exchange the clearance-priced birthday shirt you bought them, after all.

"So...are you saying things are okay with you and me just the way they are?"

"Yeah," Laurel answered hesitantly, "I think that's what it means, all right."

"Really? Sincerely?" Laurel had never heard her mother use that particular word-- *sincerely*--at least not that she could recall. Her mind wandered to André Gide. Screw him.

"Yeah," she said into the phone at last, just as another train pulled in. "Yeah, Ma. Sincerely."

--Yes, Paulie, I'm leaving you, he said bravely. It was the bravely that got me. How dare he show off that way? My pain.

Like most voluptuous pleasures, crying can ruin your looks and age you prematurely--same with sunbathing, drinking, and most really good food--which is why this time I did not cry when he told me it was over, after all these years. Four. Again.

The other three times, I cried so much that I developed semi-permanent pouches under my eyes. The third time, when I ran home to cry on my mother's shoulder, she pointed out the pouches and said, No man is worth that. My mother is serious about such things--she sells Lancome cosmetics at Saks. She sent me home with some stuff in a tube to shrink the pouches, a gel mask with an extract of seaweed in it.

If it weren't for my mother, I wouldn't even know David Gold, so in a way this could all be laid at her feet. He was her eye doctor, the one who'd done her laser surgery. She insisted I meet him before the surgery, just to see if he was okay. I thought he was nice, and my mother's advance work had convinced him that I was Georgia O'Keeffe. We had coffee later that afternoon, his idea, and he asked me about my work, said rather shyly that art was his first love, but medicine paid the bills. Said he was a sculptor. Mentioned that he was married, looked down as if in apology, then up, then down again. Why should I care? I thought. I do not look at married men. In fact, I stopped looking at him that very moment. At least so far as he could tell. Especially those eyes. Not to mention his hands, which were strong and lean.

That was five years ago, when sculpture still came second to his practice. A few months after that I ran into him at a Longo retrospective, and then the following month he turned up at my first one-woman show, *Profluence 10,* a series of large acrylics which, except for the hotcha title, I still like today.

He happened to walk in at a moment when I was hostage to a critic from *BayArt,* a guy who was undertaking to explain my work to me in a rapid nasal monotone, something about how in the 'nineties my work would have been outside the whole ballpark of art discourse, but that now its time had come. I could see David out of the corner of my eye, standing in front of Profluences 9 and 10 for a long time. I wondered what he was thinking and I cringed, which is a natural reflex for me. Suddenly all I wanted was to talk to him, but for a lot of the evening he hung back while people swarmed around, and every time I tried not to look at him I found him watching me.

Finally, when the crowd began to thin, he walked over, handed me a glass of wine, and said hello. We moved to the empty end of the gallery where he stood opposite me, shook his head and smiled.

--*You.*

--What, I said, feeling a little awkward.

--Just...*you.* It's so good, Paulie. The way the pieces gather intensity, one by one. What a shame buyers are breaking up the series.

--That's easy for you to say, I told him, though secretly I felt a little sad about it. Still, I needed the money, and the five paintings that sold that night would mean $6,250 after the gallery took their fifty percent.

--You're so talented, he said, I wish I could use color that way to make light.

I thought of all kinds of rejoinders such as *If I'm so talented, how come I still work 8 to 5 in an office?* but finally I just said, I'm awfully glad you like it. And I was.

After the opening, he drove me to see the warehouse workspace he shared with a guy who made Segal-like sculptures of ordinary people doing irritating things. That side of the place felt cavernous and eerie in the semi-dark: filled with florid middle-aged men in plaid pants and white shoes playing pocket pool, and dumpy women waiting for buses and scratching their bellies and thighs. As we walked across the pitted floor, David let me in on his big secret: he'd begun to apply the tools of his medical practice--laser beams--to his art. He showed me around his side of the place, and explained that he was making sculptures using light, shadow, time, and movement as materials. He walked me over an entire floor of jumping light to a small dark space where an eccentric laser rotated across shapes suspended from the ceiling, illuminating only the edges of things, keeping their essence in the dark. He kissed me there, just then, and once the revolving laser light illuminated his cheek through my eyelashes. We didn't kiss again, and we didn't mention the kiss. Later when I thought of it, it all seemed of a piece, the lumpy objects suspended above us, the blooming edges of things, the kiss, the darkness, the transient light. I wasn't entirely sure it had even happened as a part of what we two were together, or seemed to be, at that moment.

Sometime after that, David was invited to make a presentation at *Ars Electronika* in Florence, Italy to talk about his laser sculptures. He asked me out to dinner to celebrate. At Chez Panisse. He was thinking of quitting medicine altogether. Phyllis, he said, was not of a mind to celebrate this possible turn in his career, and had in fact gone off to the Golden Door spa for the week, to calm down. And probably to be rolfed and waxed, I thought.

While I was dressing for our dinner date, I kept thinking *Married man, Married man.* But from time to time I said aloud What's wrong with having dinner with a friend? A friend you met through your mother, for God's sake.

Still, that whole day I think I knew what was going to happen.

We came back to my place after dinner and stood first in the kitchen and then in the bedroom, staring at each other. I guess people are always nervous when they're about to sleep together for the first time, but I was more than nervous, I was immobilized. Even looking back, I can't see why I should have been such a ninny--I'm thirty-five years old now, was thirty-one then. And after all, I was married for six years, so I do know which way is up, though I haven't been with a great number of men in my life. Four. Counting David. He looked nervous, too.

After we'd been standing there a few years on the kilim rug at the foot of my bed he smiled a little, starting with the eyes, and said, Are you going to take that dress off or am I?

It was a new silk dress, size 6 though I often wear an 8, and I wasn't sure how to get it off gracefully because it had no actual zipper.

--It doesn't come off, I said.

When he came into me--this is after somehow we got the dress off me--I felt the shock of utter familiarity. He moved in me, sure and comfortably, like a husband.

Of course, he was a husband.

But that was the furthest thing from my mind. I came so hard he thought he'd hurt me and he kept asking, Are you Okay? and I couldn't stop spinning inside, spinning like a starfish, couldn't stop spinning long enough to explain that No, he hadn't hurt me a bit, I was fine thank you, but just coming right now, no problem, I'll be through in a sec.

This was his first adultery. All weekend he watched me strangely, almost gravely, touching me again and again like some surprising toy, and once, walking up Mission Street, we stopped to hug and just as our bodies pressed together in our thick coats in the San Francisco wind, I came again with a big shudder and felt my face go hot with embarrassment and desire and My God! he said, because by this time he recognized my coming as such, and I looked at him without a word, trying to keep my dignity. I've never seen anything like it, he said, and I knew right then he'd never leave me.

Which he did, yesterday. For the fourth time.

--I'm not a bad habit, I told him, I'm a person. Make up your mind.

From the beginning he was wracked with guilt, so I should have been more wary. Of course, guilt is a relative thing--it was easier for me, because I didn't have anyone in my life to lie to, so I didn't have cause to feel false in exactly the same way he did. And anyway, I never could remember that he was anyone else's. From the first time we made love, it seemed as if he were mine. It's not like I had any prior experience with married men, but once David and I had slept together he seemed irrevocably a part of me.

(*You certainly have taken to adultery like a duck to water,* my mother commented early on. The word startled me. Adultery. What could I say? I'd always thought of sex as a baptism of sorts, the confirmation of union. This wasn't something I was prepared to think about objectively.)

And though I can honestly say I didn't chase him, I can't pretend I ever resisted much either, when he came after me. And I did allow him to catch and keep me, once I started loving him. Once love happens, sex doesn't feel wrong in the least, even when it could be called adulterous by your mother. And others, if they knew about it.

What I've learned about sex is that as long as you're in love it feels like a sacrament.

(*I only hope my daughter's not turning into a tootsie,* my mother said.)

Soon after that and her adultery comment, I started asking David things. About his marriage.

--It's hard to talk about it, he said. Here I am, forty-four years old...I've got two grown kids who think their parents have got the perfect marriage.

--Have you? I asked.

--Well, we don't argue much.

--Do you talk?

--Not a lot.

--Do you love her? I asked, feeling that really it was none of my business, but still I needed to know.

--History is a very powerful thing, he answered.

That night at home alone in my bed, I lay awake for a long time picturing him asleep with her, and I thought of all the men in novels who say, *My wife doesn't understand me* or, *I haven't loved her in years.*

A week or two after that, late one afternoon at a seafood place on the wharf, I asked him again. I'd been thinking about it a lot, and it was something I had to know. So. I asked.

--Do you love her?

--We've been together since we were practically kids, Paulie. We raised two children together.

Suddenly I realized that his evasiveness on the subject hadn't been because he was trying to convince me that he didn't love his wife, the way married men in novels do when they talk to their lovers. It was the opposite. I didn't ask him again. It was too sad. I just ate my fish. We sat there picking flakes of white flesh from the fishbones on our plates, nibbling and looking out the windows onto the dark teal water. After a while, he just started talking again, out of the blue.

--I feel responsible for her, he said--I care about her. He looked at his plate, then up. I--look, Paulie, I never knew about this. I didn't know a man and a woman could be friends like this and have passion too. Now I don't know if I, if I ever did. Love her. Now that I love you. But that's not her fault, is it?

--No, I said. No, it's not.

We sat there for a long time, till the sky and the water went dark.

I would like to cry about all this, but I keep hearing my mother telling me You're thirty-five --you've only got about five good years left--keep crying and I'll give you two and a half.

But crying is such a pleasure at times like this, a sensual swim, a relinquishment of caution. What a gyp.

My lifelong best friend Tony, who died of AIDS last year, used to say there were three pleasures of the flesh that won't devastate you physically: sleeping, shitting, and sex. He called them the three S's. Not only will they not deplete your youthful vitality, he used to say, but in fact, two of the three--lovemaking and sleeping--could actually make you younger and more beautiful. Of course, some people believe that moving the bowels keeps one's skin clear, but by and large it is the one of the three that does the least for your appearance, either during or after the act. For example, many men will tell you later how beautiful you looked while asleep or during sex, but no one claims that a woman's face takes on an ethereal cast while she is planted on a toilet, concentrating. Which is not to say one doesn't become more beautiful during that act, but I don't know anyone who invites her lover to witness it and we do not tend to watch ourselves in the mirror then, either, so who knows what we look like at that moment? All we can say, really, is that it is a great pleasure which does not adversely affect one's looks.

One man who may have known more on this subject than most was Chuck Berry, who died recently and took that knowledge with him. His death notice mentioned that he had once been sued for allegedly planting video cameras in the ladies' room at his restaurant so that he could film women peeing and emptying their bowels, they all the while unaware that he would soon be finding his perverse gratification, as the suit calls it, watching their solitary moments. I happened to see that Chuck Berry bio piece just after the fateful phone call when I was trying not to hate David, so I guess I transferred all my anger to Chuck. Posthumously. For taking advantage of unsuspecting women.

It's not something I like to mention, but when David broke the news this time, I was sitting on the toilet. I had just experienced one of the three sensual pleasures that will not age you, and had the phone propped between my cheek and my shoulder while I reached for the toilet paper. To say the least I was dismayed by the timing, caught there astride porcelain while his words stumbled over the wire and ended with his halting explanation of how he'd feared he wouldn't stick to his resolve if he told me face to face.

In retrospect, I'm disgusted with myself for the fleeting relief I felt that he couldn't see me right then, on the can; that he would not carry that last image of me away into his future. Why should I care how he remembers me? And anyway, why deny him the full range of my beauty?

Since I couldn't cry, eat, or drink--and since sleep and sex seemed beyond reach--I did what any thinking person would do. I turned on the TV. To submerge my grief. It was a cold night, the bedroom clock was stuttering, and I thought maybe I heard my upstairs neighbor, Fidel, trying to break through my bedroom window. Fidel has been arrested six times for breaking and entering--and burglarizing--and then let go, pending trial. I've read it in the paper. They printed our address. So far he's been smart enough to break and enter in the good parts of the city where no one knows him.

I would like to move from this neighborhood--maybe even out of the Mission entirely, like to that nice apartment my friend Sue is vacating on Chenery Street--it's a calm, clean neighborhood, and I already know the couple in the other side of the house, but the rent is way higher there, and anyway it costs a certain amount just to move. I'm a little short on money right now. I used the last of my savings to go to Italy with David. He offered to pay, but I didn't want to be a tootsie.

Besides, I had a pretty fair amount saved up from works I'd sold. And I was between jobs and living on those savings by then, too, having just quit a job as secretary to three liver transplant specialists. I felt that organs were seeping into my art.

It got so that everything I painted was a deep puce, a wet-looking red or brain gray. An artist has to think of those things, even if it hurts the pocketbook. And I know it was right to quit, because since that time my work has taken a real turn and I've begun what I think may be the best stuff I've ever done: figurative oils, all showing the same woman in a series of violet rooms.

I realize that it was a little reckless to spend my savings on travel when I was out of work, but it seemed as if everything was telling me to go. For one thing, he asked me. David had never invited me along on one of his trips before--he was always too worried that he'd feel guilty once we got there, and that would ruin everything. Also, since I was between jobs it was the first time in ages I was actually free to go away. And besides all that, I wanted to be with him, really wanted it.

Anyway, David invited me along, saying he needed me with him and would have to adjust to being in love sometime. He had to present a paper in Florence about how technology has changed art. Maybe someday I'll be invited to speak on the impact of organ transplants on art.

We found a room in the Pensione Annalena, which had been converted from a sixteenth century convent. It was evening when we arrived, and the owner, Signora Calderoni, thought for a while before allowing that she could give us a room. She had no vacancies, she said at first, but then she seemed to sense our disappointment and she said maybe she had one room, not fancy. We followed her wide hips through wide and narrow tiled halls and saw sculptures everywhere we walked, all clearly the work of one artist. Later we heard that she was the widow of a sculptor, and it was his work all over the place, nude studies of women in bronze and marble, all of them with sizeable asses and a smile somewhere between shy and sly. Signora Calderoni led us to a small cluttered bedroom, and wished us *buona notte.* She had a knowing look on her face as she turned to leave, and when she stopped at the door and looked back at us for a moment, I recognized that smile. Then she walked out, closing the door softly behind her.

"We're here," David said then, and he looked so funny—proud in a way, as if he'd overcome a lot of anxieties to get us there. And of course I knew he had.

For the first time it seemed we were a real couple, with a place of our own.

Of course, it wasn't our own--even beyond being a rented room in a pensione in Florence, Italy, it was no ordinary room for rent--it was clear that our room must belong to the widow's son, because it was full of someone's clothes and personal things, and the walls were covered with Communist posters.

I carried my overnight bag into a tiny dark bathroom with an uneven tile floor and harsh, raspberry-colored toilet paper. The shower was a primitively rigged affair over wooden slats--I wondered if hundreds of years ago the nuns had used a basin and a pitcher in this same little space. I stood beneath the puny stream of lukewarm water and let it drench my hair, run over my face, soak into all of me. I could hear it drumming the wood beneath me, and when I opened my eyes I watched the water disappear between the slats around my feet. *It's me here,* I thought. I dried myself hurriedly, suddenly eager, aware of David waiting in bed for me.

At first I felt shy making love there, thinking of the widow, of her revolutionary son, thinking of the nuns long ago saying their evening office in the lavender air, but then sudden purple lightning in the night sky through the window above our bed, his mouth so gentle and wet on me, the smell of the old quilt beneath us like the smell of my Grandma Irma's old trunk of mildewy dresses kept in the garage for dress-up all through my childhood, that cool cool smell of history, that breath of past and future, and all the while his tongue pushing in and the iron bed creaking sweetly, rain thrumming the window glass, somewhere a woman's voice calling.

The next day while we waited for the travel agent to reconfirm our flight to Rome our names came up on the screen, and that's when I saw it: *Phyllis Gold.* Just beneath my name. His name, my name, her name. He'd apparently been unsure until the last just which of us he'd be taking along. I looked up at him in some confusion and then saw tears in his eyes and I'm sorry, he said, I just feel so false.

He started feeling terribly guilty then--I think just seeing her name there on the screen had a powerful effect on him. The funny part is, I was actually glad to see he felt that way--I'd even be worried, I guess, if he hadn't. But still I felt sad, alone, left out, suddenly. Even after we got to Rome the mood persisted in both of us.

On at least one occasion James Joyce persuaded Nora Barnacle to defecate for his erotic diversion. And though I can't relate to that at all, anyone would have to allow that maybe Nora's face was transformed before her husband's eyes during the act, but it's too late now to ask him and I sincerely doubt that his heirs would know or say. Anyway, come to think of it, I believe that he was stationed at her rear the whole time, watching, and she wore clean white bloomers, which according to his letters was the point. Pulled down around her thighs. So let's forget the face theory. Obviously we still have no witnesses, at least none who are likely to come forward.

I will always wish I'd been in a bubble bath or on a mountain when we broke up, so at least I could have a beautiful mental picture of that moment to keep with me. In lieu of him, whom I cannot keep with me. Because he is a married man who loves me but feels too guilty to tell his wife the truth after all those years. Twenty one. As opposed to these years. Four.

--I feel responsible for her, he told me. She was so young when I married her.

--So were you, I reminded him. I didn't mention the fact that she never did support his decision to quit medicine and pursue his art. I didn't mention that she spends the money from that laser art faster than the speed of light. The fact is, that's not the point. The point is, well, I don't know what the point is. But that's not it. I'm pretty sure of that.

--The doubleness really gets to me, he said, and yet I don't seem to have the courage to leave her. I'm afraid of hurting her, afraid of what my kids will think, afraid of going through all that pain.

--Why did you pursue me, then? I asked him, and then I couldn't seem to stop asking him. Do you think I wanted to love you? Why did you make me love you? What's the deal with you? Why'd you come after me, anyway?

--I couldn't help it, Paulie, once we'd talked to each other for an hour. I already loved you by then. You can believe it or not. I couldn't help it. Now the worst part is I know I'll never be happy without you--now that I know what it is to have you.

--Then why be without me?

--I can't take the falseness, he said, can't tell Phyllis the truth.

There seemed to be nothing left for me to say at that point.

My mother has seen Phyllis in Saks having her face done at the Chanel make-up counter lots of times.

--She's very beautiful, my mother says. My mother is a pain.

--What will I do without you to talk to? he asked me just before he hung up. As if this weren't all his own idea. That's what gets me sometimes, the way he creates his own drama and then revels in it as if it had been visited upon him. I didn't know how to reply to him, so I just said someone was at my door. He offered to wait while I got it, but I knew that he was just wondering if it was another man, so I thanked him, signed off, and let him stew.

Last night, CNN replayed the Chuck Berry bio segment. Angry as I was with him for the alleged camera in the toilet, I had to admire his talent as I watched the clips of him singing and duckwalking. I wondered if many of the viewers could only think of Chuck watching those poor squatting women on film, a bottle of Cristal chilling in a bucket beside him, a sweet leer on his face.

At about midnight, my mother called to say --Hey Paulie, I just remembered the cutest thing--when you were little you came to me one day in the kitchen and said Mama I know what adultery is--it's when little kids try to act too grown up.

I'm sure she was just checking in to see if I was okay.

She'd already called me earlier to see if I wanted to accompany her to bingo tonight. My mother drives all the way across town each week for Ladies' Bingo Nite at the Mission Dolores. My Jewish mother. When I declined to go along, she said --For God's sake, Paulie, you're still young, you've got your whole life ahead of you.

--And? I said.

--And so you should be having fun. Come to bingo with me, it's a ball.

I could picture it, and somehow I didn't think I'd feel all that young, my whole life ahead of me and all that, with a bunch of old Catholic women and one bossy old Jewish one, pressing numbers on bingo boards while ice skating music blared over the sound system.

--Sorry, Ma, I have to wash my hair, I told her, knowing full well that my mother didn't just fall off the turnip truck.

--If all those boys didn't believe that excuse when you were in high school, she said mildly, why should you expect your mother to believe it now?

--I don't, I said.

Funny thing about the Chuck segment on CNN: I was all prepared to hate him for the toilet thing, and then they played an intereview with Chuck in which he was asked who he would cast as himself in a movie of his life.

Chuck had answered without pause or hesitation:

--Oh they'd have to go and dig up Burton, 'cause no one else could play me as good as Richard could.

The Chuck Berry Story starring Richard Burton. The late Richard Burton. How could I hate him after that?

My father was a Welshman, like Burton was. He died eight years ago, but my mother never dates. She has a gay friend about her age at Saks--James--who takes her anywhere a man is required. James is a saint. The rest of the time she goes out with the other cosmetics ladies or just stays home. Except for bingo. I asked her once if she'd missed having a man in her life since Daddy died, and she rolled her eyes and said --Your father was plenty for one life, thank you very much.

It was hard to tell if that was her highest compliment or her worst insult. I didn't feel up to pursuing it at the time. Still don't.

Chuck Berry was about a million years old when he died, but he could still do the splits onstage while playing his guitar. And he was so good looking, had the most beautiful skin. It's hard to say exactly when youth is over.

Maybe someone should have asled Chuck about the faces. He may have been the only man in America who knew.

I woke up in a low mood this morning. Didn't even try to paint today, first day in years I can remember not painting. It's been an uphill struggle all these months anyway, trying to get out from under the weight of those organs. Now my heart is broken and I can't cry. Who needs this aggravation?

I watched every single thing on CNN tonight, starting with Anderson Cooper. He said woof. I couldn't believe that Anderson Cooper, an anchor on a national network news show, would say woof, but he did. It was his intro to a story about wolves in the timberland of the United States:

--We've been conditioned to regard the woof as our natural enemy, he said. At least four times in that segment he said woof.

--Timberwoof, he said.

--Little boy who cried woof.

--Wooves.

It just goes to show, you can go to any heights in life if only you want something badly enough.

David called to say that he is trying not to call me.

Mother was at Ladies' Bingo Nite, so I didn't hear from her.

After Anderson Cooper, I watched everything else on cable news, in search of more inspiration, until the shows began to repeat themselves. But nothing came up to Anderson saying woof. That, I'd have to say, was the high point of my day. It was a ray of hope.

Maybe in a couple of days it would be okay to call David and let him know that I, too, am trying not to call. But, no. I guess not. Because all that would be, really, is just me trying to find out what's going to happen to us.

I've been thinking what a shame it was that no one had thought to ask Chuck Berry about the faces while he was still alive.

But maybe it would have been wrong to know, to see those women's secret faces angelic, enlivened by the thrill of impending certainty that shivers up their sphincters, the clarity of that one moment of delivery.

Even then.

Especially then.

After all, there are some things we may not be meant to know right now on the earth. Maybe it's better simply to wonder.

Obbligato

This morning I thought I saw Oksana Petrovna down by
the water running, naked and stocky, over cliff rocks and onto
gray sand. The woman moved like Oksana--graceless, but with
a sturdy beauty animated by vitality. But it couldn't have been
Oksana. Of course I knew it couldn't.

It must be nearing Easter. Yesterday I got a card from
Mother with a rabbit on it, holding a basket with three stale
jellybeans glued to it. "From Mother" was all that was written in
her careful, girlish hand. As usual, there was no message from
my father. I really hadn't expected that there would be. Nor
would I have welcomed it.

The rug Oksana wove for me--it's a rich persimmon color--
lies on the floor like something once alive. Not that it has faded-
-it's as bright as ever--but it seems inert without the possibility
of her presence to animate it. When I look around, I realize it's
the only real spot of color in this house, except for a few bits of
pottery and a couple of prints from Aunt Kate's estate. Really,
when I think of it, it's also the only soft thing here.

For the last few months, I've been sleeping on it. I never
saw Oksana's loom, but she described it for me once, its simple
lines and sturdy construction, the heavy, smooth wood--though
I can't remember if she said what kind of wood it was made of.
Just that it was dark wood, I think. And that it was the only thing
she took with her wherever she moved.

That's the way I've always felt about my piano. The one
thing I'd want to have with me, wherever I lived.

Oksana's loom, my piano.

But now I'd take the rug along as well.

I doubt I'll ever move now, though. I like the grayness of
this place. Ocean, sand, and rocks, all gray. Grey sky, gray mist
at evening, fog each morning. Someday I'll be gray with all of it.
Grey woman, come soon.

What I really want to tell you about is what happened to
Oksana Petrovna.

It's hard to begin. The scent of the lavender tea I just poured myself is overtaking the room. Aunt Kate asked for lavender tea on her deathbed and then died before it had steeped. I served Oksana lavender tea the day she brought me the rug. Now that I think of it, I haven't had a cup of lavender tea since that last day here in this room with Oksana. Maybe it's the perfect ritual, then--reacquainting myself with this tea while I find the words that will start the story.

My name is Beth Jacobsen. I live alone here. You might not like me much by the time I've finished telling you what happened. It seems as if I should say that I'm sorry if you don't, but I guess my greatest failing is that I don't much care what anyone thinks of me. Or if they think of me at all. I'd kind of rather no one did. Once it was different, of course--all I lived for was to please someone else. I guess that's how I ended up this way.

I first saw Oksana nearly two months after I moved to Cantamar. I was sitting on a big flat rock one evening, just up from the water. I saw her running naked through the waves toward the shore. She was not a graceful person. She was short-legged, and her movements were almost comically awkward even from a distance. But she had a kind of abandon I envied vaguely.

When she saw me on the rock she ran up toward me, her heavy breasts bouncing and her thick black hair swishing back and forth just above her shoulders. A hair length I've never liked: not long not short. Awkward and choppy, an unfinished thing; I don't care for unfinished things. Her hair was blue-black. Completely straight and not shiny the way blue-black hair usually is. (Sometimes when I think of Oksana, I think of looms of long black hair woven into Oriental tapestries: strong black hair like hers. Maybe that's how her hair came to be chopped off at such an awkward length--somewhere there's a tapestry.) When she reached the rock where I sat I was struck by her eyes. They weren't large, but they were stunning in their absolute blackness, and shiny as two marbles. Deep-set and heavy-fringed, they gave her a kind of prescient look. She sat in the sand next to my rock and smiled. I wondered how a naked woman could sit in sand.

"You live up there, don't you?" she said, inclining her head to indicate the cliff behind us.

"Yes." It was the first time I'd heard my own voice in many days, and it was like hearing the voice of a stranger.

"I've seen you a few times from a distance, but you always looked like you were writing something, so I didn't bother you. We live about a kilometer down from you." She didn't say who we meant, but one kilometer wasn't far enough. Dreariness crept into my head: There went my solitude. She wouldn't begin to understand my reasons for living here, someone like her who simply walks up to a person and starts talking. I pictured daily visits from chatty neighbors. Someone stealing my private times with the ocean. She would never understand if I told her. Which I wouldn't. If only she'd stayed one kilo down the beach.

She might've read my thoughts.

"I don't usually come all the way over here, but Dag--that's my housemate--is in one of his black moods today and I didn't want to stick around."

I waited. Any minute now she'd start in on her problems and then it would all begin. As I went into the silence that is intended to keep people at a necessary distance, an image blinked through my mind: my father's silhouette. My father, standing in the bedroom doorway while I pretended to sleep. My father bending over me. My teacher. I'd lived the first sixteen years of my life in his dream; in the years since I got free of it, I've made it a point to live in my own.

I took a hard look at the woman's profile; her features were regular, almost blunt. No delicacy to them, though they were pleasant enough. She just sat there and stared at the ocean, sighed. I was relieved. I knew that if I encouraged her in the least she would tell me just what her problem was. But I could feel that my face had closed tight as a clam and I knew that she'd seen it too.

We sat in perfect silence.

Beth, swimming, two years of age. Father, a timer in his hand. Beth, swimming at four in blue, blue water. Father, moving his hand like a symphony conductor. You've got to get the rhythm. It's the secret of real champions, you know—

rhythm! Father behind her in the pool, hard brown hands on her torso, her legs, feel the rhythm, Beth, this is how it goes, like this, feel it? Push...push...push. The smell of chlorine in her nose, smell of dread. Beth at six, at ten, eyes closed against his rhythms. Beth at eleven, fourteen, in blue water. Swimming. Swimming. Swimming.

"Do you swim?" Her voice startled me. I'd forgotten she was there.

"No."

Our eyes met and merged, absorbed my lie. I looked away, fixed my gaze on the waves.

Following Father up the walk. Mother opening the door, her face a blur. What does she do while we're practicing? Then Father's voice obscuring the thought. Mother, in her world alone with her books, keeping people away with the inwardness of her gaze. And I, alone in my world, too. That left Father, unaware that he was the only resident of his dream. Three people in one house, no common language. Meanwhile the hours, the days, filled with blue water and bounded by timers. Never softened by words. The nights an absolute darkness, a silence, his awful rhythms penetrating my dreams.

"So, you live alone?" She was still there. What persistence.

"Yes." Just then a brown pelican flew low over the water and let out a muffled cry. After that the silence just seemed to grow, but the woman showed no sign of leaving.

I remember the day that began the end of it all. The end of everything that had been my life. Aunt Kate's long fingernail tapping the china saucer.

--Beth, you don't have any social life at all. Don't you have any friends you'd like to do things with? It's unhealthy for a girl of sixteen to have no friends her own age. To be totally immersed in swimming.

--Immersed...pretty good, Aunt Kate. I didn't bother to say it. My feet were following the pattern of her oriental rug

as I paced the dining room. My father was in the hospital. His appendectomy was allowing me this respite with my aunt; my first real break from swimming since I was two.

--I've tried to talk to your father, but he just won't listen, he's like a man possessed. And your mother--well, sometimes I can't believe she's my own sister. She behaves as if she's totally helpless to say anything to him. If I were your mother I'd call the man off you right now.

I looked at her quickly, then looked away, just kept pacing the pattern of the rug.

--That's why I got you over here today. There's more to life than swimming. We've got to find you some other interests. Get you free of all that--when anything becomes your whole life, it's an obsession.

Obsession. My father's face over me in the dark, his hair reddish blonde like mine, I hated my hair. *Relax, atta girl, that's my girl, relax, relax.* Chanted, like a lesson or a mantra or a prayer. If I watched at all it was through my lashes, eyes nearly shut--his face intent, pale in the night room, gulping air like a swimmer. *Mama,* I thought but didn't cry out—I'd never called her Mama, so I didn't know who I would be calling anyway, didn't know where she was all those nights. I guess she was asleep. Sometimes afterwards he cried. I never cried. Never spoke, never made a sound. All those years. I don't even know how long--at least since I was eight. Maybe he thought I was asleep. For years I convinced myself that I was.

Aunt Kate was watching me now. I smiled a wide empty smile at her, continued pacing.

--Well, I have a surprise for you, Beth. You and I are going to the symphony tonight. She clasped her hands around one knee and rocked back just a little on her piano bench, as in delight. What do you think of that, she asked me gaily.

--It's great, I said, and I heard the flat sound in my own voice. I said it to please her, but I felt nothing.

I've always wondered whether my experience that night at the symphony would have turned out the same if the music had been something else; honestly, I have no idea. But that night they played *The Rite of Spring*, which I'd never heard before. I guess I hadn't heard much music of any kind, really. At the beginning of "l'Adoration," I felt my nerves sharpening, body tensing. I knew that something was happening inside me, but I didn't know what it was. It was in "le Sacrifice" that I discovered music could be water; deep, wildly moving water and in it I, finally, was no longer compelled to be the swimmer. Alone in that endless water, no one coaching, no one insisting, I was just me, afraid at first but riding it, riding the surface swells until finally, letting the muscles of my body go slack as I never had before, I gave in, gave myself over to the sounds and cadences of Stravinsky, slipping in deeper and deeper, letting the movement toss and rock and move me beyond my own control until at last I went limp and sank into its huge wetness, that welcome oblivion.

In bed that night I dreamed music, my dreams wild and wordless and in brilliant color.

"I don't swim either...well, just barely," she was saying. "Around here you won't meet many others like us, non-swimmers. We're an oddity."

I looked up, saw her black eyes on me. Others. Like us. We. I nearly smiled at the thought.

The next morning I'd begged Aunt Kate to take me to the ocean before she brought me home.

--Please, you've got to, I pleaded.

Aunt Kate, always happy to please me, drove us to Torrey Pines Beach in her ancient silver Mercedes. The strange, beautiful, bent trees along the cliffs didn't catch my attention today. There was something I had to find out. That was all I could think about.

Minutes after my body hit the waves I knew. I went limp and let them carry me. Everything receded while it rocked me and the salt stung my skin numb. I drifted, bobbed, totally gave myself over to the water until we merged like music. I'd never wanted anything so much. In fact, until that moment I guess I'd never been aware of really wanting anything at all.

But then suddenly I found myself fighting against my willed helplessness. Completely, it seemed, without my consent my body was churning and struggling and righting itself again, again, again. Him. Damn him for all those years of conditioning.

After that day, again and again in dreams I felt the release, the relief, of letting go. I daydreamed about it the way I guess a person might fantasize about an unattainable lover. And every night the dream consumed me. Every night until he came back.

"The only time I even try to swim is when I'm in a pool. In the waves I'm lost."

"Oh," I said.

"I never go into the ocean past my knees except when I'm upset, feeling bad about something. Then I run out there as far as my nerve will take me, and let the waves knock me around. It helps me to forget myself."

Finding a way to have the experience I craved became an obsession for me, the way my swimming had been an obsession for Father. I considered simply swimming till I was exhausted and then going under, but that would have been all wrong. I would have missed the music. For the same reason I discounted sneaking some of Mother's Valium first. I wanted to be raw and natural, my perceptions keen and undiminished by synthetics. I would not do anything to lessen the experience. I wanted simply to be myself, caught in the roar, the pull, the turmoil, and finally the gentle resolution of it all.

After the visit with Aunt Kate I seemed, even to myself, like a different person. Once my father was back on his feet and ready to resume our daily routine at the pool, I procrastinated about even going out the front door to his car. He'd always expected me to be ready for him when he got home from the university where he coached the swim team, but now I would be ostentatiously planted in front of the TV watching cartoons or in the kitchen eating large snacks filled with fats and carbs. I dragged myself through every practice making a great show of my reluctance, pretending not to hear him when he barked orders. Before the year was over I knew he'd begun to realize that he couldn't make a championship swimmer out of me if I didn't want it. Finally he suggested a hiatus from practice--a classic case of burnout, he said. It would pass.

Nights, in my room, he went from coaxing to a kind of cold, mute determination. I never opened my eyes.

Soon I was spending all my hours at the piano--a seventeenth birthday gift from Aunt Kate, given six months in advance of the fact, along with a huge assortment of classical recordings. I guess she'd have got me a piano teacher, but she must have realized that I'd had enough instruction already in my life.

Occasionally I made a secret visit to the ocean, an encounter that always ended as the first had, in frustration.

The night my father finally announced that he'd decided to give up on my training--long after we both knew it to be inevitable--I smiled gratefully. His face turned cold, a look of hatred and betrayal that immediately and almost imperceptibly shaded into absence. There was no yelling, never a raised voice. He simply stopped acknowledging my presence.

I began to sleep better, although occasionally something would rouse me and I'd see his silhouette in the doorway or near my bed. Always my body went rigid as rock and I feigned sleep, but he never came closer. The visits had stopped.

High school graduation, starting college, a job filing books in the school library--all of that was on the outside of my reality, a thin integument, a shell over the meat. Only my music courses held my interest at all.

The only person I ever really talked to was Aunt Kate. My mother had gone further than ever into her books, and Father was rarely at home now. I heard Mother telling Aunt Kate that he'd found another swimming protégé. At school I discouraged people from making friends with me, though I have to be honest--no one really tried that hard. No one knew what was really on my mind. My trips to the ocean were secret, frequent, and futile.

When I was twenty, Aunt Kate died of ovarian cancer. She was only fifty-four. I knew then that I was alone. After the initial panic, it was almost a relief to have no one left to care about. No one with expectations of me.

Nobody seemed surprised that she'd left everything to me--after all, she had no husband or children of her own, and I was her favorite niece. Actually, I was her only niece. But I knew that there was more to it than that. Not long before her death she told me that she felt responsible for my estrangement from my father. She told me that he'd gone to see her several times that first year and chastised her bitterly for having diverted me from my "goals." He begged her to tell me I was making a terrible mistake in turning away from swimming. She refused. The piano gift had formalized her refusal. Now I understood why she'd given it to me so long before my birthday.

All I could think of after Aunt Kate's death was getting away from my parents' home, from my old life. And though the inheritance hadn't left me truly wealthy, it seemed a lot to me because it meant my freedom. I figured I had enough money now to buy a house and, if I was careful and lived simply, to live on the interest from the balance of my inheritance. I dreamed of a place of my own. Near an ocean, of course. It could be any ocean, I decided.

For several months I tried to find the right house, the right setting. My trysts with the ocean became ritual; water ballet. I quit my job at the library, left school, spent all my time searching. Houses were so expensive in Southern California and property taxes so high in most beach communities that there wouldn't be enough principal left to generate interest payments I could live on. I realized I didn't have as much money as I'd thought I did.

It was a sarcastic real estate woman who'd given me the idea inadvertently: "What do you want, Doll?" she asked when I complained about the prices of the houses she'd been showing me. "San Diego is a beach community--primo real estate. L.A.'s even worse. Maybe a property south of the border is what you want. It's cheapo, that's for sure--and you get what you pay for-- bad water, shitty plumbing, and highway bandits."

Within a month or so, I'd found Cantamar. Nothing fancy, but it feels real here. Not too many tourists around, not many houses, either. It's often foggy, compared to other beaches in the region, but I like that--it gives the ocean an air of mystery that feels true. The shore is brief and rocky, lined with steep cliffs, not at all prime tourist territory--it's not Malibu, that's for sure--but I wasn't planning to soak up the rays every day and hit the clubs at night. And the moment I walked into this house--it belonged to an old guy from La Jolla who wrote mystery novels--I knew that it was right for me.

"It's more of a getaway than a real residence," the man told me, assuming, I guess, that I'd just be using the place for holidays. It was a bit small and basic to live in year round, he said, and I knew that would be true for most people, but it suited me. I've never cared for large, yawning homes--I find them lonely--and this was the smallest house I'd ever seen; just one main room, along with a bathroom and a galley kitchen. The big room would be ideal for eating, sleeping, playing the piano. There's even a fireplace. Lots of windows.

And the window on the far side looks down onto the waves as they hit the rocks.

The seller brought the price down when I said I'd pay him cash for the house, and then I took over his lease on the lot it sits on, which is how a U.S. citizen has to do it here. But it's a 99-year lease with 81 years left to go. Even if it were possible to live that long, I wouldn't want to.

"It's always moving." Again this woman's talk pulled me back to the sand. She was staring out at the sea. I nodded coolly. She had no idea what the ocean was to me.

She told me about the dropped-out foreign exchange student she lived with. His name was Dag. They had two Labrador retrievers. She made rugs to sell at the local street bazaar, which attracted lots of American tourists. Once she brushed some sand from her thigh and I noted how close the color of her skin was to the color of the sand in late sunlight; a startling contrast to her black pubic hair, her dark brown nipples. I had never seen anyone naked before out in daylight, not even myself.

It began to get cold all of a sudden as the mist hurried in without warning the way it does around here in the evening. She shivered and stood to go.

I watched her as she ran along the beach toward home. When she'd run a few yards she stopped, turned, and called out, "My name is Oksana Petrovna." It was a formal pronouncement--solemn and vaguely comical. She ran on before I had a chance to tell her that my name is Beth Jacobsen. It's possible I wouldn't have told her anyway.

I didn't see Oksana again for a few weeks and I was surprised to find that I was a little disappointed when she didn't come back. After all, I didn't care to see anyone, really. I had my records, my books, my piano. I'd even been fiddling with the idea of composing, but everything I wrote sounded derivative of whatever I'd just been listening to. I found myself writing lines of poetry--or something--in my composition book, where the music should be. Then I started worrying that I might be turning into Kahlil Gibran and I threw the pages away. I stared out the window a lot. Looked at the ocean, thought how it always thwarted me. Found my eyes wandering north, in the direction Oksana would come from. If she were coming for a visit. Which apparently she wasn't.

Then one night she appeared at my door, face tense and eyes bright. The heavy mist had dampened her hair, which clung to her face and neck. She'd had an argument with Dag, she said. Could she come in?

I'd just lit a fire and was listening to Mozart's Piano Quartet in G Minor, a piece that usually gives me a sense of well-being, though it wasn't working so well tonight. The wind had been blowing the ocean around all evening and I was restless. I was sure the tide was coming in much closer to the cliffs than usual. I was glad to see Oksana.

We talked for several hours and drank Irish coffee. I was surprised to find that she knew quite a bit about music. We found a lot of things to talk about, and several times she said something that I was about to say--almost to the word. The most surprising thing, though--at least to me--was the sound of the two of us laughing in this house.

Later we slept on pillows in front of the fireplace, sharing a thick comforter. For what seemed a long time, the walls of the house shook and shivered in the wind. Then suddenly the storm died out. I stayed awake most of the night listening to the ocean. It was strange having someone so near. As Oksana slept soundly beside me I felt her solid presence in the dark. I could see her black hair mingling on the pillow with my pale hair. I found myself trying to match my breaths to the rhythm of hers. The sound of the ocean had softened; I heard it, regular, hypnotic, behind our twin breaths.

Once Oksana tossed free of the comforter and when I covered her again I let my hand rest on her far shoulder, my arm across her bare breasts. It was startling to me, her skin, skin other than my own. I wasn't used to such intimate contact. I closed my mind when an image of Father came into my head. Closed my eyes, but I left my arm across Oksana, my hand on her shoulder.

I must have dozed then because suddenly I was wide awake: Oksana's hand was on my breast--I was, for a second, embarrassed at how small my breasts were, compared with hers--but then her moist mouth was against my skin, her tongue circling my nipple softly, quickly, as if she were both eager and shy. Her flesh was firm and smelled like herbs--sage, maybe. She turned around so that her face was low on my belly, her lips just brushing my hairs, and very gently she opened me, moved her tongue inside me, pushed in deep, I gasped as she pushed and pushed. In the near dark I saw her curly black pubic hair just in front of my face and I didn't know, wasn't sure, if I should do the same to her or even if I would know how. It seemed rude not to try, and anyway I found I wanted to taste her, wanted to make her feel what she was making me feel. I moved my face toward the thick black hair between her thighs and laid my cheek against it, heard her sigh as she opened her legs just a little and I turned my mouth to the place I wanted to enter and took my first taste, heard her O and pushed in deeper, knowing suddenly all I needed to know.

A week later on a Wednesday I saw from my window that Oksana was headed along the cliffs toward my house. I had a cup of hot mint tea waiting by the time she knocked. When I opened the door I was struck by her vividness: her black hair was startling above her loose violet shift, and her cheeks and lips were rosy from walking in the Cantamar wind. She couldn't stay, she said; just wanted to ask me if I'd do her and Dag "a very big favor." They were going to travel in Dag's old van for a couple of months and couldn't take their two Labradors along. I had that nice fenced area at the side of the house--would I mind terribly...?

Of course not. What else could I say?

I watched from my window for a long time after Oksana had disappeared along the cliffs.

During the two months they were gone (two and a half, to be exact), I had no trouble with the dogs but I had a lot of trouble with myself. I couldn't seem to concentrate. Every note of music I wrote I quickly scratched out in disgust. I seemed to spend all my time staring. If I was inside the house I'd stare out at the beach where I'd first seen Oksana running. If I was down on the beach, I'd stare up at the cliffs she'd walked along to visit me. My dream of losing myself in the ocean mocked me when I thought of it now, as did the idea that I ever could have written a piano concerto. Maybe I didn't have the passion or the imagination--or the courage--to do either.

Often I thought of Oksana, of our night together in front of the fire. What I'd felt then, what I still felt, confused me. The day she left on her trip with Dag, I'd searched her face for some sign of what we'd shared that night. In the wide, insouciant planes of her face, in her small, bright eyes, I could read nothing. I could only conclude that she'd felt nothing in particular.

Days were too long--the sun seemed to hang around for hours beyond its appropriate departure time. Nights were worse. The ocean crashed louder in my ears then, and seemed to have lost its rocking rhythm. Hearing it, I couldn't sleep. Music might have covered the awful sound of it, if I'd played any--but most of the music I'd once cherished disgusted me now, seemed an affectation--who did I think I was, anyway? What did music like that have to do with me? The only recording I even attempted to play anymore was The Rite of Spring--and "l'Adoration" was all of that I could stand.

When I did manage to fall into short, fitful sleeps, I found that the nightmares about my father, which had stopped around the time I'd moved to Cantamar, were returning with a scary frequency, nightmares of him in my childhood--in my doorway, in my room, in my bed. For a long time I'd thought I was rid of those memories, but now Oksana had thawed me, let me feel again, and apparently when I opened the door to one emotion, I'd made it possible for other feelings to intrude, as well, however unwanted. Oksana was the only person I'd ever been with sexually. I didn't count my father because that wasn't voluntary. Oksana was also the only person I'd ever slept beside in a bed all night. Now that she was gone, it seemed my father had come back to torment me.

Every afternoon I'd brew myself a pot of tea and sit at the table near the window, trying to understand what had gone wrong in my life. Before I met Oksana I knew what I wanted. If she had to go away now, at least I'd hoped to use this time to come to terms with what my life had been before I knew her, to retrieve whatever part of it was still real to me. It seemed my last chance somehow. I'd only seen Oksana four times in all, yet she had found her way into my solitude and had somehow caused me to lose sight of my goals--or worse, to doubt them. I'd finally jammed my feeble attempts at a piano concerto into a kitchen drawer, and I hadn't gone into the waves for weeks except occasionally to wade. I kept track of time on the calendar, calculating when Oksana and Dag would return.

Finally, when the date was just two weeks away, Oksana called to say that she and Dag would be returning "a little later" than they'd originally planned. Two weeks later, which was a month away. I took the calendar down, put it into the drawer with the aborted concerto, and then took it out again and hung it back on the wall.

One night about a week later, a storm hit without warning. When I looked out the window I was transfixed: the waves were high and close to the foot of the cliff, fluorescent purple at the edges in the faint moonlight. I felt my insides stirring as they hadn't in a long time. I'd been listening to Stravinsky as usual, and now I even found that I could stand to listen to le Sacrifice. I turned it up loud enough to be heard from the front yard, even over the storm, and then I ventured out into the rain and stood at the edge of the cliff where the winds ripped at my robe until it blew open and the rain drenched my bare skin.

That night was the beginning of a three-week period of solitude and renewed determination. It seemed to me that I was finally coming back to the life I had planned. I found myself tinkering at the piano, noodling tunes out of it, tunes that didn't come from anywhere but inside my own head. It wasn't brilliant stuff, but it gave me some hope.

I began taking my afternoon swims again, and once more it seemed as if my moment with the sea might not be too far off. The nightmares about my father became less frequent, and although I still had occasional dreams of Oksana, I rarely thought about her during my waking hours now, except when I fed or walked the dogs. If they barked at night, I couldn't hear them over the sound of the ocean. It was actually a shock to me when, one Thursday, I saw Dag's orange van pull up beside my house.

When Oksana burst through the door, her enthusiasm followed by Dag's bored solicitude, I felt utterly intruded upon, completely turned off. I know I was rather unfriendly--not asking a single question about their trip, not bothering to assure

Oksana that the animals had been no trouble at all. Dag had an egotistical smile that irked me, and he spent most of their visit cleaning his fingernails with the car key while Oksana volunteered a rundown of their trip. I didn't see how she could stand him.

I was glad when they'd collected their dogs and gone. As they left, I noticed that her hair had grown since the day I met her--it was a nicer length now, just past her shoulders.

After they'd gone, the house was too quiet; I tried not to think of how she had glanced at me several times--quizzically, as if to ask what was wrong.

That night I ran down to the water, fully determined this time not to give in to whatever it was that always came between the ocean and me. I hadn't tried, not really tried, since before the night I slept with Oksana. And now, already, the awareness that she was back seemed to be eroding my concentration. I swam out into the rolling blackness of the Pacific, believing that it had to be now, if ever. I wanted the ocean, its immensity and power, I wanted to merge with it, and couldn't bear to go through it all again--the distraction and division she'd caused in me before. As the salt water stung my eyes and lips I swore I'd make it this time, before anything or anyone could divert me.

It ended, of course, as it always had. Afterwards, standing drenched and shivering in the dark by the water, I refused to accept the term panic for what had happened, what always happened to me at that crucial instant. It was simply, I told myself, not the right time. It must have been midnight when I dragged myself across the sand to the shallow cave I often sat in as shelter from the wind. The moon was full and yellow and standing straight overhead. The thin nightdress I'd swum out in was sticking to me now and I shivered, feeling despicable. It seemed as if my father would be waiting inside the house if I went back, so I stayed outside until I was too sleepy to think or feel.

The next day I went down to the beach again to sit in the little cave. I stared at the water. This time my clothes were clean and dry. To myself, I seemed a thing far removed from the ocean's enormity and power. Then I heard something, a thin sound in the wind, like a bird. After a minute I realized it was Oksana calling me, but I stayed where I was, hoping she wouldn't come searching me out.

When I got back to the house I found a note from her under a basket of homemade cookies. Chocolate chip. I threw out the basket, cookies and all, without reading the note. Then I went back down to the cave until the tides came in, and I thought about nothing but why I had chosen to live here at the mouth of the ocean.

That night I dreamed that Father was standing over me as I slept on the floor in front of the fireplace, just where I'd slept with Oksana. It was the first time he'd made his way into this house in my dreams--always before, the nightmares had been of my childhood bedroom. In my dream I saw him through my eyelashes while I pretended to sleep. Lowering himself, he hovered just over me, gulping air, salt water spewing from his open mouth, the briny water deepening on the floor around me where I lay. Even when I woke and realized it was all a dream I was afraid to open my eyes.

One day near Thanksgiving time (I knew the season only because that week Mother mailed me a card with a plastic turkey glued to it), Oksana came lugging a huge burlap-wrapped roll. It was about eight feet long and quite heavy. She looked exhausted when I found her at my door. She'd made me a rug, she said, as a thank you for watching Shura and Blues. It took me a minute to understand that she meant the dogs--I realized then that I never even bothered to know their names, though I'm sure she'd mentioned them more than once before. She unwrapped the burlap from around the rug--it was beautifully made, thick and vivid, the color of the blossoms on a persimmon tree. We unrolled it together and spread it over the bare floor near the fireplace. Oksana said she remembered how hard the floor had been the night she slept with me, with just my pallet beneath us. Her face seemed to convey no special meaning.

We had a cup of lavender tea then, but I guess both of us felt uncomfortable. I found that suddenly I couldn't meet her eyes. Maybe because there wasn't much there that I'd hoped to see--in her eyes--and I was afraid there might be too much in mine.

As soon as she had finished her tea, she stood to go. I was relieved. I wondered how we had possibly been so close that one night. Obviously we had nothing in common.

One afternoon--I guess it was a day or two later--I was swimming, and happened to glance back toward the cliffs once.

I saw Oksana standing near my front door, watching me. At least I'm pretty sure she was watching me. I thought of the day we met, how I'd told her I couldn't swim. Then I closed my mind and swam further out into the gray sea. When I came back up the cliff to my house later, she was gone.

It must have been nearly Christmas when I saw Oksana for the last time. I'd decided it was too cold to swim, and was standing at the top of the cliff in front of my place when I saw her running down the beach below me. Her heavy black hair was swinging across her pale shoulders and I wondered how she could run naked in such bitter cold. She still hadn't seen me when she ran into the water.

The ocean was dark and swirling, blurred at the edges by a thin mist. Just the way I'd like it to be when my time comes, I thought.

I watched her awkward movements through the water. There was a fine wind today, blowing at the ocean's foam, fanning Oksana's hair.

When I first realized that she was in trouble I started down the hewn steps of the cliff. I could reach her in about three minutes, I figured.

Then I stopped. Just stopped, transfixed. She was still far enough away that her struggle seemed like a silent film. Silent except for the ocean's accompaniment. I watched the symphony of arms and legs--white notes against the saltwater staff. I was with her, guiding her limbs, conducting the music. There was a grace in Oksana's movements, a grace she'd never possessed before. Then she bobbed, went under, surfaced once again and seemed to look up to where I was standing. The sky rose anonymous and gray above us. I thought I heard a pale, thin scream, but it might have been a seagull.

Patricia Traxler is an award-winning poet, essayist, and fiction writer. A two-time Bunting Poetry Fellow at Radcliffe, she also served as Hugo Poet at the University of Montana, Thurber Poet at Ohio State, and as visiting writer at many other universities around the U.S. Her novel, *Blood* (St. Martin's/Macmillan) was also published in Spanish, German, and Swedish translations, as well as in a UK/Ireland edition. Her poetry collection, *Naming the Fires,* received the 2019 Kansas Book Award in Poetry. Traxler's short stories have won several awards, including The Writer's Voice of New York City Award for Short Fiction, the Cecil Hackney National Short Story Award, the Georgia State University Short Story Award, and in Ireland, *The Moth Magazine's* 2019 Short Story Prize.

www.ingramcontent.com/pod-product-compliance
Lightning Source LLC
Chambersburg PA
CBHW050406190726
48284CB00007BB/2447